"Is Plato your real name?" Aggie questioned.

"Good as any! What you're named ain't got nothing to do with your powers . . . or abilities, right? I've kept Carol on a roll with the blue act, the hot one-liners, the whole bit. I've made Carol Elliott into a star," Plato announced pompously. "And when I'm finished with her . . . well, that's another matter," he cackled.

"You plan to dominate her completely?" Aggie asked.

"Ha! I have, honey." Plato said sarcastically. "I've worked on her for years. Oh, she still thinks I'm an inert schmuck, but that's the way we want it for the moment. I'll play the game, but I'm dealing. I've got her so ga-ga she thinks she's talking to herself."

"And that's what you want, isn't it?" Aggie said. "You want to drive her insane."

"Natch, babe. That's how we make the next transfer. Didn't you realize that all the nuts, the wackos the schizos, the loonies, are carriers? Yeah, man, the crazies are the transfers. They think they're hearing voices . . . but it's us. We've taken over . . . we've used them."

"This has to cease," Aggie said softly.

"No way! You can't stop us," Plato warned. "I mean, who's gonna believe you, huh? Weirdos talking to a dummy? Ya gotta be kidding. Gentlemen, get out your nets."

"Then we'll advise Carol," Jo insisted.

"And tell her what? You've been talking to me? She'll think you're creepier than you are, sis! Besides, I'll tuck in . . . I won't talk . . . I'll be a good boy and not bug her. She still thinks she controls me, and we know that's a gas. A real gas!"

KENNETH GIRARD

ALTERED EGOS

PINNACLE BOOKS NEW YORK

This is a work of fiction. All the characters and events portrayed in this book are fictional, and any resemblance to real people or incidents is purely coincidental.

ALTERED EGOS

An original Pinnacle Books edition, published for the first time anywhere.

First printing, April 1983

ISBN: 0-523-41896-5

Cover illustration by Lee MacLeod

Printed in the United States of America

PINNACLE BOOKS, INC.
1430 Broadway
New York, New York 10018

My thanks to Ed Gerber and Bruce Goodman for their advice and assistance.

—Ken Girard

ALTERED EGOS

Chapter One

Carol Elliott dug her nails into her palms. Control yourself, she muttered, and don't get hysterical. However, everything that could have possibly gone wrong was on target. The taxi to Los Angeles International Airport was caught in traffic: anxiety. A skycap dropped Plato's carrying case: carelessness. At the counter she couldn't find her ticket: confusion. And to top off the scene fog grounded her plane: frustration.

Thank God Thornton had sense enough to book her in first class; and, by chance, the seat next to her was empty—small consolation for an otherwise disastrous trip.

"Care for a cocktail, Miss Elliott?" the stewardess asked. "Martini? Isn't that your drink?"

"Thank you, *no!*" Carol replied curtly.

"All complimentary, Miss Elliott."

"When will this hunk of aluminum take off?"

"Depends on the tower, Miss Elliott."

"Right!" Carol answered. "Good thinking, honey."

The girl smiled, fluttered her lashes, smiled again, then complimentary-drinked-her-way to the other passengers. Carol berated herself for asking her anything. Idiot blonde with a mind full of spray net. What the hell does she know? C'mon, c'mon, another voice admonished, she's only doing the standard number. Carol eyed her reflection in the window.

Go ahead, tell me how wonderful you've become. How pleasant. How understanding. Oh no, babe, you can't. Miss Complimentary Drink has got it all over you. Tell me about it, babe! *Babe.* It was a Plato word. He always tossed her the punch line with *babe* as a tag. Some *babe* she had become. Carol looked away. Yeah, some babe. It was a joke. Her whole existence was a joke.

She felt the plane shudder.

"Ladies and gentlemen . . ." the captain crackled over the intercom. "We've been cleared for takeoff."

"Right," Carol muttered.

". . .our estimated arrival time at Kennedy Airport will be seven P.M. New York time."

Terrific, Carol groused. Thornton loves to stand around doing nothing: another anxiety.

She stared out the window again. The terminal crept away, and the plane swung onto the field. Settle in, babe, we're going home.

Home. Another joke. A half-furnished one-bedroom on the West Side, *but* it had a nice view (Thornton's contribution), *but* it was convenient (her contribution), *and* the doorman was straight out of Castle Dracula (Plato's contribution). Whadda ya want, babe, another set of teddy bears to clutter your life? C'mon babe, pure lines, Plato told her, you don't need all that dreck this time. Of course I don't need it, she told him. That goddamn Murray's got everything. Forget it, babe. She tried to, but couldn't. That bastard's even got my doll collection.

Even Thornton tried to sever the umbilical cord. Carol darling, it's past history. If it's history it has to be in the past, Thornton. Carol sweetheart, I never interfered. True. I never said anything when you married him. You should have, so don't lecture me now. I'm not, *but* . . . I know . . . all that counts is my future . . . my wonderful career.

They were in the air. Los Angeles, the Playboy Club, the Improv, the Q Club—the three weeks of miserable performances sped past. Take a good look, babe. She stared at the ribbons of freeway. Yeah, take a good look.

Her ghost appeared on the window. You can count on two things when you arrive: Thornton will be waiting and bastard Murray has left a message with the service. Carol stared at the seat in front of her. Suddenly, she was cold, and tucked her legs under her. Well, if you think you're cold, babe, what about me? I'm freezing my ass off in the cargo section. Next time you're taking me into the cabin. That's right, Carol babe, old Plato's sitting with the real people next time . . . if there is a next time. I don't know how we've made it this far. I mean, babe, we just messed up . . . everything was zitsville . . . and the gig at the Q Club. Bummer, babe, a true bummer.

The stewardess reappeared. "Don't forget to ring if you want anything, Miss Elliott." How about a muzzle for your face, blondie? "And Miss Elliott . . ." Yes-s-s-s. ". . . if you don't mind I'd like to chitty-chat with you for a moment. You see, I want to get into show business too." Get me out of here. "But we can talk later . . . all right?" Sure bright eyes, I'd love it. "Well, you see . . . this TV producer . . . well, he was on the last run and-d-d-d . . ." Oh Lord, don't you realize you're Miss Quick-one. ". . . well, I have to finish stewing, but we can chitty-chat all night."

Carol smiled. Unfortunately, yes, we'll have too much time. "Be right back!" Oh, how did you get into the "business"? the apparition in the window asked. Ya see, blondie, it just happened. To tell the truth it was a fluke. A mistake. A horrendous error, and I can't get out. You see, I'm not really a night-club entertainer. Oh no, I'm not a wise-cracking smart-ass with a foul-mouthed dummy.

You aren't? Surprise-surprise!

Oh no, I'm really a very nice person underneath all that glitz and smut. I'm pink, not blue.

Oh, I'm sure of that.

The hell you are. You don't know me, and don't want to know me. All you want is a contact, a hit, a fix to the next step: agent, producer, director, somebody. You don't care about me.

Oh, Miss Elliott, I just love your sense of humor . . . and that Mr. Plato is such a riot. I love him too.

Yeah, sure kid. Everybody does . . . we're a laugh riot as they say—no, said. Okay, you want to know, I'll tell you. You see, babe. Sorry, the "babe" part comes later . . . much later. I was a schoolteacher.

You were!

That's right. Third grade. A private school. Only the best, the smartest, the wealthiest. The kids were Anglos, and all the mothers had Dr. Fischer's. Nose jobs to you, babe. Anyway, to teach the little darlings to read I invented Alpha Betty, a hand puppet. Cute, the kids loved her, and learned to read too.

So you were a natural ventriloquist. Oh, how exciting. Miss Elliott, it's so exciting.

No, my father is, was a ventriloquist. He taught me the tricks of the trade. His second mistake, after having me.

Oh wow! Like out of sight! A show-biz daddy.

Right-t-t-t. Anyhow, Alpha Betty cloned Bobby Backbite, who performed in private for the teachers. However, his routine was a little different.

Giggle. Giggle. You mean a little dirty. Giggle. Giggle. Grin. Grin.

Not at first. However, old Bobby used to tell the assistant principal where to go, and various mothers what the outside world really thought of their children. Bobby was a realist, and much before his time. Poor Bob, he's long gone. I dropped his head and that's all she wrote.

And . . . go on, I love it.

Well, he never went public with his comments, and performed strictly for the teachers. However, word got out, and old Bobby got my ass in a wringer.

Giggle. Giggle.

It seems the assistant principal, Ms. Dyke, didn't appreciate some minor references to her, shall we say, sexual preferences, and . . . the rest is theatrical history. It was the first time I bombed. The following year my contract wasn't renewed, and that's it, babe.

I didn't know you were a teacher.

Neither did I, but it's all the same. The only difference between the classroom and the nightclub is the age of the audience.

And Mr. Plato? How did you *ever* think of him? I mean, he's so-o-o cute.

He thought of me. He's coarse, not cute. And if you love a stage dummy, well, babe, you're in trouble.

He just keeps me in stitches. When you were on television, I mean, it was great. He is so-o-o funny.

Right. Plato is funny, and that's why we're not on television anymore. He's so funny we can't get ourselves out of the lounge-act circuit. He's so funny we aren't able to get three minutes on a national talk show. He's really very funny, and that's why I'm going back to New York without a screen contract.

Well, I think Plato is the end.

He may be the end of me, that's for sure. You

know what it's like to be labeled as "strictly a lounge act" or "for adult audiences only"?

But you don't talk dirty. I mean, Miss Elliott . . . could I call you Carol instead?

Sure, babe. Oh boy, get me out of here.

Well, Carol, what's wrong with a little off-color joke once in a while?

"Once in a while"? Honey, I've made a career out of off-color jokes. I'm down-and-dirty, babe. I've got shoe boxes full of it. . . . I'm a walking computer of the stuff.

But you're a star.

Jesus! It was a mistake. Alpha Betty cloned Bobby Backbite, who sired Elmer, God rest his little wooden heart, who begat Plato, which attracted bastard Murray, and that's where all the trouble started.

I didn't know you had a dummy named Murray!

You got it wrong, babe. I married Murray and he made me the dummy with a dummy. It was a marriage made in heaven . . . for Murray, that is. He stopped accounting, and went into theatrical management, more specifically, shilling for me. Oh, don't worry, Thornton, he'd say, Carol's going all the way . . . her own TV series, the works. Right, I went all the way. Don't worry, Thornton, your daughter's earnings are safe. Listen, she's my wife, isn't she? Right, I was. And I did . . . Murray pushed, and shoved, and connived, and cheated, and weaseled, to make me what I am today. . . . Isn't that great?

Gosh, Carol, you're so lucky.

But it was a mistake. Look at me . . . I'm thirty-plus-plus . . . I've got a blue routine . . . I'm typed, and trapped. And I've got a partner who doesn't know when to quit. Once he gets on a roll, well, babe, watch out 'cause he's the baddest little wooden man in the West. And y'know, sometimes

I don't think I'm in control . . . imagine that, I'm still the dummy's dummy even after I got rid of bastard Murray. We can thank Thornton for that. Who knew . . . he was manipulating my fees, and running around? Who knew . . . he was running eight different sets of books and running around. There were a lot of "who knew"s and "running around"s. But that's theatrical history. I'll say one thing for Thornton: He's better late than never. Oh, don't get me wrong, I love him, but he usually saves me after the fact.

When are you going to play Vegas again?

Thanks for listening, babe, I sure needed a strong shoulder to cry on. Oh—Vegas? In a couple of months? Tomorrow night? *Whenever they call.*

It must be so exciting. Did you ever meet Sammy? And all those high rollers! I mean, gosh, I thought being a stew was glamorous, but that—

Right. It's *the* most, *the* best, it's *the the* . . . especially the two-o'clock show, when the drunks come out of the woodwork . . . or being stopped in the lobby by a group of conventioneers and asked for the latest dirty joke . . . or being told the latest dirty joke. Oh yeah, babe, it's real fun . . . and the pay's not bad either. A nice place for a lady, or young ladies, or children. I love my life—it's so glamorous, and I get treated with such respect. Alpha Betty would be so proud of her momma now.

How do you think up all those routines? I mean, I never heard some of *those* words. You are the funniest. Carol, everybody thinks you're the end.

I am the end. The end of the line . . . the last one they call, if they're stuck for a brassy broad. I mean, this platinum hair ain't for schoolteachers, and my routines ain't for the PTA or an in-depth, close-and-very-personal sequence on public television. You've got it all backwards, babe. I'm the last thing in the world you want to be . . . hey, that's funny, 'cause I'm the last thing in the world I want to be, but that's my problem, ain't it. Listen, success didn't spoil me, no way. I spoiled—and Murray certainly spoiled—my success. I really hope I'm the end . . . or near it.

Oh gosh, you are so warm. . . . I love talking to you, Carol, I mean, you're so full of understanding. Listen, we've got to chitty-chat some more. Could I see you in New York. I mean, if you're not too busy? And maybe Plato could tell me . . . well, you know . . . some of his jokes . . . those jokes?

Get me out of here.

The ghost in the window frowned at her, and she felt cold again.

Chapter Two

Carol barely acknowledged Thornton after he told her how badly she looked. Of course she was tired, the plane was two hours late, the mob scene at Kennedy wasn't a thrill, and the cab ride into Manhattan cost a fortune. All in all it was a day to forget, topping off three weeks she planned on forgetting.

However, he had put flowers in the apartment, filled the refrigerator with an assortment of foods, stacked the mail in neat piles, and in general, made it look like home. At least Thornton tried, and wanted very little in return.

"Do you want to see your messages?" he asked.

"Anything special?"

"Jack Lanzetta called on Thursday. He wants to book you into Harrah's for three weeks." Carol looked surprised. "Yes, two thousand per, accommodations, and air fare."

"What's the catch?" she asked.

"None. He heard you were a smash in Vegas and—" she laughed "—that's it, but we have to give him an answer by tomorrow." She nodded. "All the other messages are routine." He didn't want to mention the letters, at least not yet.

"I was terrible in Vegas. A new low in comedy. The whole week . . . a calamity. Two nights of mid westerners, it was like playing to the deaf . . . and then, oh God, they had tours of Orientals . . . with an interpreter. I spoke, Plato spoke, and the translator. That was wonderful. Finally, I started doing Jap jokes."

"I didn't know you had any."

"I don't. They just blurted out. Like, whadda ya call an Oriental in the woods?" Thornton shrugged. "A lumber Jap." He laughed. "They weren't amused. And whadda ya call Oriental candy?" He shrugged again. "Cracker Japs!"

Thornton roared. "Marvelous, marvelous."

"It wasn't," she said. "I felt stupid."

Thornton waved her away. "Please . . . Harry Snow said you were sensational and—" He caught himself.

"You promised me . . . you promised me."

"Carol dear, I wasn't meddling. I just wanted to find out if you were—"

She cut him off. "If I was what? Drinking my milk? Exercising? Brushing my teeth? I told you not to call and you did it anyway, didn't you?"

"It was an accident," he replied.

"Accident?"

"Yes, my fingers slipped. I was really dialing the Kendron agency on the Coast."

"Thornton, sometimes you're a pain in the ass."

"Lovely," he retorted. "I'm so glad you're home."

She patted him on the face. "Scram, fella. I want to go to sleep."

"Good enough. The rest can keep until tomorrow."

"Which means?" Carol probed.

"Nothing . . . nothing," Thornton lied.

"Is it my darling Murray again?"

"Yes, it's Murray," he answered quickly, compounding the first lie.

"What now? Is he starting another business on the community property? Or is this a new tack?"

Thornton seized on "the community property," agreed, then let Carol go into her I-hate-my-ex-husband routine.

"Can't the lawyers handle it? Why is that blood-sucking sonofabitch haunting me?"

Thornton shrugged. Be grateful for small favors, he told himself. Let her believe Murray Korn, ex-manager, ex-financial genius, and part-time husband, was the real problem.

"Jesus, he picked me clean! What does he want? The bones?" Carol demanded.

"Let's talk about this tomorrow."

"Tomorrow?" Carol whined. "Why? What haven't you told me, Thornton? Another registered letter?"

Thornton started to perspire as Carol poked at the stack of mail. "No! It's not there." A third lie. "I have it at the club."

Carol glared at him. "Terrific," she growled, then launched into a repeat of her I-hate-Murray routine. I can't keep the letters from her, he told himself. Murray? A joke. No, my dear, you have another friend. Murray? Murray's a minor annoyance compared to this— Thornton stared blankly at the three stacks of mail, and hoped he had intercepted all of the hate mail.

Hate mail? Hardly, the old man thought to himself. The letters were insane, venomous, psychotic, and unending. Thornton's hands shook each time he saw a typed envelope. The final letter, he hoped it was the final letter for that day, had taken the episode out of the "crank" category, and he had called the police.

"I'll look into it," Detective Nick Anz said.

"Damn nice of you," Thornton snapped.

Anz controlled himself. "Look, I said I would take care of the matter."

"Right," Thornton said. "I feel much better now that you're in charge of the case."

"Listen," Anz warned him, "this ain't the only case we got in New York, huh? Or the only funny mail. People get crank letters all the time."

"Not ones that threaten to cut someone's breasts off and stuff them in her mouth," Thornton seethed.

Anz nodded. "Yeah? It ain't unusual . . . and we get worse. Listen, this city . . . it ain't a city, it's a frigging zoo. We got a wide assortment of psychos running around. You should be grateful it's *only* a letter."

"A letter now! And what follows? Murder? Then you'll have a real case . . . and I'll be without a daughter."

"Please, Mr. Thornton—"

"Sir, it is not Thornton. It is Thornton Evans."

Anz apologized. Yes, he would take a special interest in the case. Yes, he would get back to Mr. Evans. He yessed Thornton out of his office so he could concentrate on other problems: a double homicide on Pell Street, and mob-style execution in the Bronx. In perspective the threatening letter to Carol Elliott ranked at the bottom. Anz slipped it into a file, and turned his attention to the daily reports, the drawers full of evidence, the usual.

Thornton raged loudly after he left the police station. He would call the mayor. He would write the governor. He wouldn't rest until he shook the foundations of the bureaucracy and brought the police department down. Yes, Thornton Evans would clean out the inefficient and find the person threatening his daughter.

* * *

"You haven't heard a word I've said," Carol told him.

"Of course I have, dear," he replied.

"Oh, Thornton, you're such a terrible liar."

"No, no," he regrouped, "I was thinking about Murray, and how we can get a restraining order . . . yes, yes, I know Judge . . . we'll put a fast halt to this . . . this harassment."

Carol shook her head. "What haven't you told me? C'mon, Thornton, more money problems? That's it, isn't it? The lawyers want the rest of their fees, right?"

He took the out, and concocted a story about the IRS "requesting" some joint returns, and the divorce attorneys making discreet, but forceful, inquiries about the last $5,000, which was almost six months overdue. Carol bought it, was properly depressed, and Thornton played the concerned father.

"I'm sorry, dear, I didn't want to lay this on you. Well, enough said."

She eased herself onto the sofa after he left. Murray, Murray, what I ever saw in you, I'll never know, she thought. You'll hound me the rest of my life. You're my original sin, and your lawyers are my karma. She looked through her messages . . . nothing exciting. Three from her commercial agents. Probably another dog-food spot. It ain't glamorous, but it pays. And God knows she could use the money. Money, that was Murray's only concern. How much. When it arrived. What he could do with it. Bastard Murray, you done me dirt. She thumbed through the rest and tossed them on the coffee table. Headache. Carol dragged herself from the sofa, rummaged through the kitchen for some aspirin. None, so she made herself a sandwich. Thornton's answer to all body pains: When in doubt, eat. She nibbled at a crust of rye bread and poked through the pile of mail. Bills: Saks, rent, the usual.

Trash mail: She was a finalist (again) in the million-dollar publishing sweepstakes, and had a recreational lot in New Hampshire reserved for her (again), and *House & Garden* wanted her to know (again) she was missing everything, yes, positively everything. Fan mail: Believe it or not she did have fans, but the stack was smaller than usual. Carol smiled, never too tired to hear from the adoring public.

"Plato, old man, it's showtime."

She lugged a rectangular leather valise to the sofa and snapped open the locks. "Wake up, babe, somebody loves us."

There he was . . . the one, the only (thank God for small favors) Plato . . . all thirty inches of cotton batting, wooden legs, fake leather shoes, and the cutest l'il paint and plaster face you ever did see. Oh yeah, that boy's a looker!

"So how's by you?" she said.

"Next time, babe, I'm sitting with the inhumans. Nearly froze my ass off in that damn cargo section," he replied.

Carol lifted him out of his case, straightened his collar, then placed him on the sofa. "Pick a gooder, babe!"

"Lemme see," he answered. "The one with the lavender envelope. It's probably a love letter . . . to me."

"Egotist," Carol said, but he was right. An Elaine Carson from Sommerville, New Jersey, thought he was "the cutest," etc., etc.

"Jesus," Plato sneered. "She must be real hard up to write somebody in my condition. Imagine the wackos out there, babe, wanting to go steady with me?"

They culled their way through the stack. Fifteen positive: "You're a riot." "Funniest act I've ever seen." "Plato, you're great." "When are you going to have your own TV show?" That was meant as a compliment, but dredged up some bad memories: Murray . . . some stuffy network execs, and Thornton's rejoinder to tone down some of the language. It became a bad scene and they lost a prime-time slot. On the other side of the ledger, the negative mail was losing heavily, and getting tossed after one sentence, which usually ran "You are one of the crudest performers I have ever seen," etc., etc. or "I never heard such filth come from a woman's mouth," etc., etc. Well, blue wasn't Carol's favorite color either, but she had to pay the rent (and Thornton's) and the lawyers. And how could she tell her detractors all that *and* she was a different person *and* she really wanted to resurrect Alpha Betty *and* dye her hair back to mousey brown.

"One more," Plato advised. "We can't hit the sack reading a downer."

"Can't," Carol told him, "too tired. My back's crumped out. Besides, my mouth's moving when you talk. Let's pack it in," she said.

"Naw, babe, clear the debris. One more. Close your eyes, and mine, and pick the most fantastic "I think you're the greatest" letter.

She did what he wanted, and it was the wrong choice.

Carol slut/bitch,

You defile the very word woman and make a mockery of all that is feminine. You are a filthy animal who should be burned from the earth, and your putrid ashes burned by the sun. Your tongue should be ripped from your mouth and burned. You are not worthy to be called woman. I will slit your breasts from your filth-laden body and stuff them in your vile mouth.

Diana the Chaste

Carol crumpled the letter into a ball and threw it against the window. Chill. Nightmare. Fear. Oh Jesus, I don't need this. "I don't need this!" Carol screamed. She wrapped her arms around her waist. "Tell ya, babe, we shoulda quit while we were ahead. Outta sight, babe, some kinda freaks out there."

Nice homecoming gift, Carol thought.

Call Thornton. No! He won't know how to handle it. *But I don't know either!* Don't come unglued, babe. Hang in there. Hey, what's the big deal? She stared at Plato. You kidding, babe? This nut's out for blood. You gotta be dippy! It's just a crank. Go eat! When in doubt, stuff your face . . . when in pain, have a sandwich . . . when afraid, have two sandwiches. *Eat, babe, eat!*

Chapter Three

Carol propped Plato into his high chair, which distracted Robb James from making "a very important point" that was "critical to their case." "*Their* case"? What a joke. They all knew damn well that Murray—yes, bastard Murray, the king of the exes—had squirreled the money away somewhere, God knows where, and Carol (and the firm of James and Stratton—of course, they would get paid first) would never see any of it. And "it" ranged in the exclusive neighborhood of $250,000. However, the suit was "solid," and they would "attach his assets." Some chance, Carol thought as she adjusted Plato's collar. No way, babe, old Murray was the baddest of them all, and didn't need mirrors to skim years of one-nighters on the second-rate circuit, and weeks of three-a-night on the lounge tour into "poor investments," which "damnit, Carol, just came up dry." Oh, Murray, I trusted you, she thought as hard-nosed attorney James went for the punch line, the sock-'em-in-the-gut finish.

". . . and after we file this counterclaim, I intend to notify the district attorney, and Mr. Korn's lawyers, that we're going for criminal proceedings!" James pronounced. *Ta-dah!*

Thornton sensed Carol's disinterest. "Yes, well, that's more like it," he said. "Well, Carol . . .?"

"Boil 'em in oil," sneered Plato. "Rack his gizzards, and string 'em to the yardarm, eh m'buckos?"

Thornton smiled through his teeth. "Cute."

"How much will all this pain cost?" she asked James.

"That depends on his attorney's response," James replied.

"Keelhaul the lily-livered rotter," Plato contributed. "And his attorney, and his attorney's attorney."

"Carol, please," Thornton begged. "Would you put our friend away, so we can finish the meeting."

"Aw shucks, I never get to have any fun," Plato sulked. Carol adjusted his collar again, then pulled the gray fedora over his eyes.

"Well, some of the fees for prior work are overdue. . . ." James reminded them. Nicely, but pointedly. And Carol knew the balance of the drill: Ring out the old bills, ring in the new. The treadmill syndrome with Murray's head at the end of the stick. Oh? She only owed them $7,500? A mere bagatelle. Why, my stars, Colonel Butler, I can raise that with one telephone call. Now, you just wait right here 'cause little old Carol's got that kind of change hidden in her music box. James was sympathetic, and he could wait, but "just a couple of grand" while he was cooling his heels would be greatly appreciated. Thornton knew it was out of the question, but promised him something, sometime, somewhere. Carol had turned them off. She stared at Plato. Well, babe, it's back on the road for us. Sorry, babe, we're in hock again and you'll have to ride cargo back to Vegas.

"Oh shit," he told her. "Steerage with the flying kennels and the discount luggage?" Yep. "You promised me." Sorry. "I hate Vegas. I hate Jack Lanzetta. I hate that damn room over the kitchen. Oh hell, you promised me." Sorry, babe, Murray's an expensive item. "You gotta rethink this, Carol babe; if it ain't him, it's the lawyers. Carol, don'tcha know the lawyers are Murray-clones. Listen to me, dump the whole thing. Pay the two dollars. Get finished."

Thornton eased James out of her dressing room. Yes, it was a damn fine plan of attack. Right, it was the only way to go. Way to go, Thornton, she thought, staring at Plato and herself in the mirror.

"Listen, Carol," Plato said, "it's only money."

"A lot of money," she told him. "And I want to nail that miserable s.o.b."

"Now, that's the real reason," he replied.

And that was the nub of the whole problem: She wanted to pay him back for all the lies; she wanted to avenge the constant trail of affairs, quick-ones, and sudden business trips. She needed lots of salve for her pride. Plato was right. She was lugging around the hurts, and the embarrassments, which were eating her up. Bastard Murray was doing a number on her emotions, and her career. She was still in a frustrating game with Murray dealing in absentia. She stared at herself in the mirror, and didn't like the reflection, but how the hell was she going to wiggle out of this one? At thirty-plus-plus with the image of a coarse lounge act draped around her—well, babe, as Plato would tell her, it's better than being buried in the suburbs with a bellyful of kids and a schmucky husband. How true. How cruel. Carol Elliott and Plato: the best in blue while black-and-blue inside.

"C'mon, babe," he told her. "Pull it together, it ain't the end of the world."

She nodded and started to put on her makeup. Makeup, she thought, it's a damn disguise.

Thornton reappeared. "Well?" he asked.

"Not now, Thornton, I've got a show to do."

He nodded. "See you out front."

"Yeah," she said dryly.

He smiled at her, felt ashamed. Poor Thornton—

his timing was always bad, and that's what had sunk his career. Straight men have to be quick on their lines, otherwise t'ain't funny, McGee. "Nice crowd," he said weakly, then beat a fast retreat. Sure, swell group, Carol groused. If you don't give 'em flesh, or filth, they're screaming for blood. Usually mine, babe. It wasn't the first time, nor would it be the last, which was the pity of it all, as Plato often reminded her. But Murray had it pegged differently: this was *the* opportunity; *the* showcase; *the* best place to be. Right, Murray, always right. A wonderful "showcase" at the Q Club East as the entr'act between—now, get this—the male go-go dancers *and* the female mud wrestlers. Oh yeah, this is where it's at. This is today. Hey man, a hundred other comediennes would give their left tit to have this spot. Murray, you have such a way of expressing yourself. Whadda ya mean? This is the new show business: sex, laughs, more sex. Hey, Carol, you want to have dignity? Recite the Constitution in front of the DAR. Listen, I'm not gonna let you stay here. Hey, you and Plato: Vegas! TV series! Maybe . . . your, well, *our* own club. We got a packed house every night. And the money! Listen, we take it while we can get it. (You sure as hell did, babe.) And I got a whole tour arranged. (Not the road, again.) Ya wanna build a national rep, you gotta travel.

"And you know he kept us on the road to keep himself in the sack, right, babe!"

Carol threw her lipstick at the mirror, and buried her head in her hands. I've got to kick him. It's killing me. I've got to let go. Murray and money. Disgust and fatigue. The noise, and the audience. The scene whipped through her mind. She felt she was drowning. And now some crazy broad was writing her letters, and threatening to snip off her boobs. It was great to be alive, there were so many wonderful people to meet.

The stage manager barged into her room. "Five minutes, huh, Carol!" he said brusquely. "And don't spare the horses, kid. Give it to 'em high-and-hard. Right?"

Get me outta here.

But they didn't.

Carol held Plato, and Plato held Carol, as they watched the madness; madness for LADIES ONLY UNTIL 10 P.M., then it was madness for everybody until 2 A.M.

Chick-a-boom, chick-a-boom, boom-boom-boom. A constant spray of green, red, and amber polkadots washed the room again and again, zapping the male go-go dancers and their adoring, ever screaming, ever rabid, all-female, all-uninhibited public. Yeah, Murray, this is the new show business.

Chick-a-boom, chick-a-boom, boom-boom-boom. Throw that pelvis, hear them yell, c'mon, fellas, they think it's swell. More screams as blond Billy limbos to the front of the stage, and gets his briefs stuffed with money. The polkadots disappear into the audience, and come up on Don, a bruiser, a brawler, and a pretty good dancer, who starts a series of poses and flexing moves in the middle of the stage. *Chick-a-boom*, scream, *chick-a-boom*, make believe he's going to do it with you, sister. Don throws his last move, and lets the groupies run their hands over his calves. A good time was had by all. Now it's Latino, yep, that's what he's billed himself as. No ego there, just plain old Latino, who's really a very nice Jewish boy with dark curly hair and Spandex briefs, purple no less, that leave nothing to the imagination. "Oh boy, give me vanilla," Carol whispers to Plato.

The *chick-a-boom*ers swell the tempo to crescendo, and rim it out. Scream on, but there ain't no more. Billy, Don, and Latino take their bows. How about a kiss, big boy? No way, you weasel-faced frump, unless you pay.

Rim shot. A drum roll to quiet the mutineers. Cool it, gals, but Thornton's no substitute for the beefcakes.

"Get off, Thornton," shouts the sweating brunette.

The hefty blonde in the pantsuit agrees.

"Bring back the boys. Bring back the boys," screams the audience. Sure, they want to see young bodies, not an aged vaudeville-comic-turned-emcee who looks like their grandfather. However, it's part of the routine: Thornton takes abuse. Thornton brings back the sleek ones for a last bow-and-grind. Squeal, squeal. Oh, Martha, I never thought it would be like this. . . .! I've been missing everything.

"Okay, hold it down," Thornton bellows. "You had your thrill for the week."

More hecklers. Thornton handles it well, and settles the herd.

Get ready, Carol, it's your turn in the ring. She straightens Plato's collar. Suck it in, babe, and *go!*

And in the not-so-distant distance: "And now direct from her sold-out Las Vegas engagement . . . from her SRO performances at the L.A. Playboy Club . . . let's give a big Q-Club welcome to the first lady of comedy and her able assistant. C'mon, let's hear for . . . *Carol Elliott* and Plato. . . .

Rim shot, and she's on . . . as usual with the usual.

"Thank you, thank you. First, I have an announcement." Carol eyes them seriously.

"Ya better not tell 'em," Plato stage-whispers. "These women are mean."

"Yeah," scream the mean women.

"They'll tear us apart."

"Yeah," comes back.

"I better tell 'em," Carol answered

Plato shook his head. "I dunno."

"Ladies, and I use that term very loosely . . ." Cheers from the loose ladies. ". . . the management informs me to inform you that Latino will not perform again this evening . . ." Groans, and hisses. ". . . you see, he's got a hangnail."

"Aw, bullshit," from the secretarial pool.

". . . and will the lady missing an inch of Revlon's Dusty Rose take it out of his Jockey shorts." Punch line! Groans, and cheers.

"Whaddid she mean? What hangnail?" Mildred whispered to Josephine.

"It's a gag."

"I didn't get it . . . I don't understand."

"Oh, Millie, you're such a fruitcake. I'll tell you later."

And that, as they say in middle-class circles, broke the ice and the party rolled. Oh yeah, vintage Carol Elliott and Plato, no stopping them now. First, the zinger feminist jokes: Let's kill the boss. Always big with the downtrodden. The act simply tumbled out of both of them: stream-of-consciousness material; insults measured with irony. The good-girl image spiked by four-letter words, and Plato there with the rejoinder. Time to pick on the audience. They loved it.

"Oh, hi there, hefto. Wheredidja get your jeans? Oh, made by Gloria Peterbilt. Smart, smart."

Carol noticed Thornton watching. He knew better. It was her standard set with gags 625 through 710 lined up at the jokemeter. Nothing new. Nothing special. The words came out of computers, one flesh, one wood. It was standard Plato: the three-sixty head turn, the collapse, the eye roll. Even Carol started to watch herself in action, and let the act and the audience take care of themselves. Carol floated out of herself, above the sweaty little tables. She had the stage Carol take over while the inner Carol, the worried Carol, could step out for a cry and just make it back for the finale. Thornton knew she was wandering, and saying, "Get me out of here."

Inner Carol hid as vintage Carol ran for the tape. I really got 'em tonight. Suddenly, she felt a chill, and the "Carol slut/bitch" letter edged into her mind. Diana the Chaste? Helluva name. You here? I bet you are, cookie! Great! I'm busting my ass, and she's measuring me with a knife. Should have told Thornton. Another twinge of fear. Cut off m'tits, huh? *Why me?* Get me outta here. Inner Carol peered into the audience. I know you're out there. I know it. Lovely, 'lovely—which bitch wants to chop 'em off? Instantly the Carols merged. *Murray!* Charming, sleazy, bastard Murray was sitting at a back table with his latest quick-one. Of all the gall! You rat! Carol pulled the act to a screeching halt, then made a fast exit to the cheers of her fans, and ex-husband. However, the pudgy blonde sitting in the middle of the bar didn't laugh, but dug her nails into her purse.

Chapter Four

Carol was in a blind fury. She swept past Thornton. She pushed Louie, the audioman, out of her way. And nearly slammed the dressing-room door off its hinges.

That two-timing bastard! *Wham!* Seven years' hard luck. They promised me he would never set foot in here again. *Crash!* It was a nice cosmetic case. Goddamnit to hell! That s.o.b. shouldn't have gotten past the bar.

"Forget it, babe," Plato told her.

She glared at him.

"All right, all right, have a spasm but—"

"But what? He's not worth it?"

Plato stared straight ahead.

"You've told me that before!" She was almost screaming. "Well, what about all the years he was conning me? And you, oh yeah, babe, *you too!* We were both his meal ticket."

Plato stared straight ahead.

"Listen, I told them not to permit him in this club ever again . . . alone or with . . . well, you saw that thing leaning all over him."

"Carol, get it out, and get finished with it."

"He's got his balls, coming in with one of his whores."

"Empty the gunnysack," he told her.

She was trying, but there were too many hurts in the bag: Skimming was one thing, but the lies and the cheating were another. Where were you? Out. What did you do? Nothing. Who did you see? Nobody, really, sweetheart, nobody. Who called? Nobody. You sure? What is this Carol, the third-degree? Sorry. I love you, Murray. Me too, kiddo, me too. *Liar! Cheat! Thief!*

"Let go, babe," Plato told her in Vegas (alone in her room), in L.A. (driving around the freeway), in Chicago (alone in her room), at home (alone in her room).

She wanted to, but—

She knew it was a nowhere trip but—

She wanted to sear the bastard out of her mind, but it was too painful, and Murray clung to her.

"Why am I talking to *you?*" she yelled at Plato.

"There ain't anybody else," he answered.

"Thornton," she told him.

"Can't go running to Daddy all the time."

"Why not?" They were face-to-face.

"Gotta grow up someday," he said.

She stared at him. "He takes care of me."

"Not always. Remember old Thornton . . . well, he ain't walking away from the Murray nonsense with exactly clean hands, is he, babe?"

She slapped him. "Dirty mind. He explained everything to me . . . he didn't want to hurt me. . . ." She could rationalize the entire incident. She told herself it was a father's prerogative. He was really protecting me, and letting Murray clean up his act.

"Carol, babe," Plato told her (in Chicago, in New York, in God-knows-where in the Midwest), "love ain't looking the other way."

"He gave Murray a second chance."

"At your expense."

"He was protecting me," she pleaded.

"So how come he took five thou?"

She slapped him again.

Why was everything turning out so complicated? The lawyers, the Miss Quick-ones, Murray spun through her mind. Why was he at the club? Who let him in? She didn't ever, *ever*, want to see him again. You're not getting it together, Carol. You're on your way to a breakdown, Carol. Spin, spin. It's a helluva long way from Alpha Betty. Spin, spin. They're after you, babe. Everybody wants to nibble a hunk out of the meal ticket. I hate the road. I hate Vegas, she whined. I'm alone. I'm always alone. Spin, spin.

She grabbed Plato from the sofa, and ran.

"Where you going, Carol?" Thornton called after her. She ran. "I want to explain . . . it was a mistake. The man on the door was—"

"You don't have to explain anything," she sobbed.

She ran, and pushed Louie out of the way again.

"It's *always* a mistake," she told Plato.

She fumbled with the car keys.

"I'm tired of being the victim," she sobbed.

She sat him in front with her. He toppled over, and she propped him against the armrest.

"I want out . . . I want out!" she said.

"Let's scrub it all, babe," he answered. "We'll chuck the act. Get out of town . . . for good."

Carol moved the car into traffic. Right! We'll dump the act. I'll dye my hair back to whatever.

"We'll start all over," he advised her. "A clean slate. A new look. No more Carol Elliott."

Right! No more blue stories in blue nightclubs.

"You'll get a job as . . .? Well, don't sweat it, babe, there are plenty of decent American jobs out there."

Right! We'll live quietly: watch TV, go to bed early, have a good breakfast, do a good day's work and—

"—and die of boredom," he told her.

She accelerated. It wasn't the answer she wanted to hear. She ran a red light.

"I won't be bored. I won't," she screamed.

The traffic blurred. Red and white tears stained her eyes. She raced through another smeared stoplight.

"I didn't want to be me," she told Plato.

"I know, babe, I know but it's too late. Sorry."

"It's not too late," she yelled.

"Sorry," he mumbled.

She slammed on the brakes. "Listen," Carol warned him, "I can walk away from this tomorrow."

"Really?" he said.

"Yes," she said. "And that means you too!"

"Let's drive, babe," he told her.

Right! She moved the car back into the traffic, and finally onto the East River Drive. The United Nations sped by, then Sutton Place. Just drive, she told herself, drive it out, and start over. Don't think about anything, just enjoy the drive.

No traffic, no lights except for the car behind her. Funny, but not funny; he's been there since I got on the drive, or was it before? Before? No, it couldn't be, listen, babe, you're letting this get out of hand. She swung off the drive at 72nd street, ditto. She slowed down, ditto. Creep, she muttered, just like me to attract another freak. She turned up Madison Avenue, ditto. Now her hands were sweating. She made a left turn on Seventy-ninth Street, and her friend continued uptown.

You're getting paranoid, she told herself.

"Let's go home," Plato told her.

Yeah, let's do it, she thought. She looked in the rearview mirror. Nothing but steam devils coming out of the street. No speeding, no tears, no paranoia. Right.

"You're getting crazy," he told her.

Carol glanced in the rearview mirror: nothing.

"Now, who's gonna be out at this hour?" Plato asked. "C'mon, babe, home, a hot shower . . . tomorrow's gonna take care of itself."

He was right.

"Ya always working yourself into a condition," he told her. "Ya know what it is?"

"What?" she answered. The light turned green, and she accelerated.

"Ego, babe, ego. You're always imagining—"

She was halfway across Fifth Avenue when the other car exploded into the passenger side. The impact sent her car spinning.

Rollercoaster. Carol lurched to the right, then left. Plato rag-dolled into the backseat. Oh, babe, hang on.

Ice storm. The tires spun crazily, and the steering wheel gyrated frantically. It was snowing glass.

Explosion. The noise was unbelievable. The metal detonating on impact. The tires shrieking as her car careened toward the sidewalk.

Hellscape. The shower of glass, and the smell of burning rubber mixed with noise, and the violence of the collision. Not now, she screamed silently.

Another explosion as her car slammed into the side of a building. The passenger side whipped into the limestone angrily. The force blew out the back window.

And then there was silence.

A long pause and Carol realized it was over. Nothing but silence. Silence and the night. Don't move, she told herself, don't move. She stared straight ahead. Fifth Avenue, the steam devils, the night: They were all there.

Then the grinding pierced her consciousness. Oh no, good God, not again. She watched the other car shift into reverse, screech, then lurch toward her.

Get me out of here.

She struggled with the door.

He's really coming at me, she thought.

Jammed, the damn door's jammed.

He's really coming at me.

Oh shit! The bastard wants to—

She squeezed her eyes closed, and gritted her teeth.

The second explosion knocked Carol into the back of her car. *RAG-DOLL TIME:* She was sprawled over the glass, and wedged between the seats.

More grinding, and squealing.

She clenched her teeth waiting for the impact.

The squealing receded, and she smelled burnt rubber.

Then silence, and the blackness washed over her.

I'm dead, she thought. Oh shit, I'm dead. She waited, still nothing. No, I'm not, because I'm still in this damn car. Don't move, don't even lift a finger. Don't worry, babe, I ain't. She heard her own breath and a warm ooze that grew cold as it trickled down her lip.

"Oh shit," the voice said.

"Whadda ya got, Harry?"

"Call the cops, Frankie. Oh shit, what a frigging mess."

"Lemme see, lemme see." Pause. "Jesus H. Christ. What a frigging mess."

"Will ya call the cops," he ordered.

"Yeah." Pause. "Harry . . ."

"Yeah, I see it. Aw shit."

"Ya think the kid's dead too?"

"Will ya call 'em?"

Silence. Blackness.

The ooze crusted on her lip. Tell them you're not dead, babe. Can't. Can't talk. I'm too cold to talk.

She sensed somebody was watching her.

"I'm not dead," she mumbled.

"What?" he answered.

"I'm cold," she said.

"Oh jeez. Listen, lady, don't move," he stuttered. "We got the cops and the ambulance coming. Don't move."

"I'm cold," Carol repeated.

"Okay, okay, I'll get ya a blanket."

Now the sirens.

Now the people.

Open the car, and "Whadda ya got, Harry?"

The red lights and the staccato of the police radio pulsated through the car.

The voices were all around her.

Just get me out of here, Carol whispered to herself. She tried to move her legs.

"Please, miss, stay in that position. We'll get you out as soon as we can."

"I'm freezing," she repeated.

More red lights, more people. "Hey, bring that blanket over here." Pause. "This is Ammed six-niner-two, we've got an injury accident at Seventy-eighth and Fifth." Pause. "Okay, folks, let's move back." Pause. The pros had taken over, and the machinery of the hospital-police complex was moving into fifth gear.

So why the hell don't they get me a blanket? Carol thought. She wiped the blood from her upper lip, and dragged herself to a sitting position.

"Hold on, lady, don't move. I mean it . . ."

Carol stared at him blankly. I bet you *do* mean it, buster. A droplet of blood hung on her upper lip. What the hell, everything's gone, the damn car's demolished. She pressed her hands against the seat, and stared at the paramedic.

"We're getting the blanket," he said.

Carol nodded. "Right," she said.

She moved her foot, and pushed part of the cushion off Plato.

"I thought that was . . . well, I mean, we thought it was a child," stammered the paramedic.

She extracted Plato from the glass and chrome. Not a scratch: His face wasn't chipped; clothes, not a tear. Wouldn't you know it, he'll walk away from this unscathed. Carol handed him to the paramedic.

"I'm getting out of this buggy," Carol said.

"I don't think—"

"Good. It's dangerous to your health," she replied. She brushed the last bits of glass out of her way, and crawled through the window. Now they had the blanket. She stared at the wreck.

"Listen, lady, you better—"

But the whole spiel tumbled away. "I'm all right," she told them.

"Naw, that's impossible, lady. I mean, nobody, but nobody, walks away from something like this—"

"Sorry, fellas, I know I'm all right."

"Naw, you got internal injuries. We gotta take you to the hospital."

"No way, you can take me home."

"Miss, you're in shock. Now, let's be reasonable."

"I'm not, I'm fine. Look . . ." Carol held Plato.

"Well, sport, how'dja like the ride?"

His head turned toward her ex-car, then back. "On a scale of one to ten. A minus-four. Where'd you get your license? Sears?"

It didn't get a laugh, and they took Carol to Bellevue, but she and Plato sat up front.

Chapter Five

Dr. Evan Stampler clicked his pen and tucked it away. "By rights you should be dead," he told Carol. "The report says the car was totaled."

"And I didn't even make the last payment," she quipped.

"Amusing," he replied. "Please lift your right arm, then lower it slowly, Miss Elliott."

"Gotta say, 'Simon says.' " He looked at her sternly. "Not funny, eh, Doc?" He didn't answer, and she complied. "Now can I can go home?" Carol asked. Stampler scanned the notes on his pad, then stared at her. "First one that looks away loses," she said.

"You know it's a miracle you're alive," he said. "You don't have a cut, a broken bone, and the neurological report came back negative."

"Well, no sense, no feeling," Carol joked. He didn't laugh. "Sorry, just trying to break the monotony."

"How fast were you traveling?" he asked.

Carol shrugged. "I dunno . . . I was just turning on Fifth . . . it couldn't have been more than twenty, maybe less."

"Did you see who was in the other car?"

"Are you kidding? Of course I didn't."

"You must have caught a glimpse of something."

"I heard it, then I smelled it," she snapped. "I told the police all of this."

"Didn't you see anything the second time?"

"Listen, Doc, I was sprawled over the seat when he came back for seconds," she answered.

"Why did you say 'he'?"

"Why are you playing detective?" she retorted.

He shrugged. "Just curious, by rights—"

She cut him off. "You said that already. Can we go home now? It's been great, but all good things— as they say."

"Your father is coming for you," Stampler said.

Carol frowned. "That's wonderful. Daddy is coming, Plato. Old Thornton, who just loves hospitals, will bring baby home." Carol shook her head. "Did you need an adult to sign the release?"

"I would prefer you to stay," he replied.

"No way, babe," Carol shot back.

"No chance of spending the night here? Food's passable." She shook her head. "Private room," Stampler suggested. Carol smiled, and mouthed no. Stampler knew it would be impossible. "Okay," he said, "wait here; I'll get the forms." Carol smiled, and batted her eyes. "But don't leave this cubicle."

"Yes, Doctor," Carol mocked. "Dr. Stampler," she said seriously, "have we ever met before?"

"That is the corniest line."

"No, I mean it," Carol replied. "I think I've seen you, or met you . . . did you ever come to the Q Club?"

Stampler looked at her. "Miss Elliott, I don't like female comediennes, especially, well, I just enjoy a different kind of humor."

It hurt, but she took, it gracefully. "Thanks, Doc, I needed that," Carol answered softly.

"Sorry," he replied.

"Yep, me too," Carol whispered after Evan Stampler left. "Hear that, Plato old sock, the doc don't like his jokes hot; well, can't win 'em all." She propped Plato against the pillows. "Comfy, babe?" Carol stared at him. "Helluva night, huh?" Suddenly she felt tired. "Hope they eased Thornton into this scene gently. My luck he'll have a heart attack." She glanced around the cubicle. "Hey, babe, what's all white and smells like a hospital?" There's gotta be a joke in here somewhere, Carol thought. "The last time I was in a hospital . . . sounds like a song. Y'know, I think I was six, maybe seven . . . a swing hit me in the jaw. It hurt, babe, and the blood . . . Poor Thornton, well, we know his views on hospitals." She looked at Plato, then the floor. "He's a-no' gonna like his babe in here." She looked at Plato, and froze.

"Hey, babe, did your eyes move?"

He didn't answer. She touched his face.

"Your eyes did move, didn't they?"

Oh, Carol, don't be a melodramatic asshole, she told herself. The frigging dummy can't move, or talk, or be anything without your hand up its ass. She looked at him again. Maybe you better spend the night in this milk factory, she thought. Goddamnit, you're getting wacky. One, his eyes did not move. Two, you're under emotional stress. And three, automobile accidents ain't fun, so just cut it out. And four, his eyes didn't move. Look at him, lifeless. You want him to move, to throw a three-sixty? If you want it, just pick him up, babe. She reached for his face, but drew her hand back.

Plato's eyes shifted to the right, then straight ahead.

"You didn't do that, babe," she told him.

"Do what?" Evan Stampler said as he stepped into the room. Carol didn't answer him. "Your father is on his way. . . ." The rest of his chatter faded into the background. You moved your eyes, you little bastard, she thought.

"He shifted his eyes," she said quietly.

Stampler cocked his head. "What?"

"Watch Plato, he'll move his eyes."

"If you control him," Stampler answered.

Carol stepped away from the bed. "No, by himself."

"Oh sure, and he dances too!"

"Watch," Carol said. *"Watch!"*

Stampler did, but Plato's eyes were fixed.

"He'll do it," Carol insisted. "Just watch." Stampler did, but nothing happened. "I'm telling you, his eyes moved . . . twice !"

They waited. Nothing. Carol shook her head. "Listen, I'm not making this up. I saw him . . . oh, what the hell. Forget it, just forget it."

"Why don't you get back on the gurney? This has been a long night and—"

"Save the bedside manner," she snapped. "And please try not to look at me like that, all right?"

"Like what?"

"Like my head's scrambled."

"I wasn't," Stampler replied. "However, you've been in quite an accident—"

"No shit," Carol interrupted.

"—and," he insisted, "you're suffering from delayed trauma." Carol looked away. "It's possible, Miss Elliott, you know?"

"I'm not staying here another five minutes, or overnight for . . . observation . . . Besides, I hear the nurses are lesbos and the beds are hard."

"Okay," Stampler said, "have it your way, but I want you to sign off on everything except your tonsils."

"My pleasure," Carol shot back. "Anything to get out of here."

"Sign these," Stampler ordered.

More scrawling, more forms, then he took the papers back "downstairs." *"Seig heil!"* Carol called after him. She avoided Plato's eyes, but the uneasiness didn't pass.

Thornton made nervous small talk with Evan Stampler while Carol scribbled her name on the "master" form. Thornton's head bobbed with the "I understand"s and the "I see"s. Carol hurried the signing process, as he was getting edgy, and irritable.

"Would you mind giving me your autograph?" the nurse asked. Carol looked at her blankly. A helluva time for that. "I just love your sense of humor, Miss Elliott." Yeah, me too, kid, Carol thought. "Y'know, some of those jokes . . . well, you're too much, just too much." The girl started to reach for Plato's face, but Carol quickly pulled him away. "I'm . . . I'm sorry," she stammered.

"That's okay, hon," Carol answered. She shoved the last of the forms toward her, dashed off *To Joyce from your Pal, Plato,* and joined Stampler and Thorton at the end of the corridor.

"Well, my dear, did you sign your life away?" Thornton quipped.

She knew he was anxious to leave. "C'mon, let's blow this joint. Take a good look."

Evan Stampler shook his head.

"Yeah, I know," Carol remarked. "I wish I could stay but . . . if anything's wrong, you'll be the first to hear from my attorney."

"Clever, very clever," he answered.

"Gotta million of 'em," Carol said.

Stampler handed her his card "Just in case."

The cab ride back to her apartment was a disaster, topped off by a curt good-bye to Thornton and a door slam.

Carol was glad to lock herself inside the apartment. She propped Plato into his chair, checked the locks on the door again, then sprawled on her bed, and rolled the comforter around her. Safe, she thought, and I'm not coming out of the cocoon . . . ever. Let 'em all go to hell 'cause I'm never leaving this room again. She glanced at the clock: 4:37.

Carol tried to sleep, but too many fears darted through her consciousness; too many questions, and no answers, and no hope of an answer. She tried to relax, but Murray popped into her thoughts. You could always count on him for annoyance. Now she felt guilty about Thornton. Of course he was only trying to help, but you couldn't let him have his moment, could you? It's always his fault, isn't it? Well, babe, he didn't ask to have you either. You can make amends tomorrow, she told herself. Carol glanced at the clock: 4:43. She watched the display face click: 4:44. Wasted another minute doing nothing, didn't you? she said to herself. Typical, 'cause your life's been a waste.

The accident edged in: the smell of the tires, the noise. Jesus, the noise. And did he really come back a second time? No, no way, that's your imagination. Oh really, check it out with the police. Suddenly, she sat up. Where's my car? Yeah, what the hell did they do with the car? She dropped back on the bed. You're worried about that? Jesus, you're lucky to be alive. "By rights you should be dead," she repeated. She looked at her hands. Nope, still here. Not even a cut; just a nosebleed. How come, babe?

And Plato. Nothing chipped, nothing torn.

I should be dead, and he should have been crushed, but we walked away from it. "Y'know, lady, it's a goddamn miracle," echoed in her brain. You better believe it, fella.

She stared at the clock: 4:47. I was covered with glass, and not a scratch. How? I was thrown into the backseat, but no bruise, or break. It's crazy, she thought.

And Plato was under the backseat, but not a flake of paint missing. It's wrong, all wrong, she said to herself.

Carol stared at the ceiling. "How the hell did I survive that crash?" she whispered.

And Plato? Yeah, what about that business in the hospital. Your eyes moved, fella, I know it. No, it's my wonderful imagination, she reasoned.

Bullshit, she thought, you looked at me.

She got out of bed, and marched into the living room. Okay, babe, let's get this straightened out.

Carol flicked on the table lamp beside Plato's chair. He was inert, arms dangling limply at his sides, head tilted slightly to the left. Carol straightened his collar, and aligned his head. Not a speck of paint gone, but he *was* covered with glass.

"Okay, m'man, give it to me straight. How'd we escape?" she asked. He was motionless, his eyes blank and unresponsive.

"C'mon, let's have it out, fella. Did you move them peepers, or old Carol's got brain damage?"

She watched him intently. The eyes didn't move.

"Okay, now we know," she told him. "Sorry about that . . . maybe in the next life you'll be the inhuman, and I'll be the dum-dum."

Plato's eyes shifted to the right, then at Carol.

"Do it—again," she said hoarsely.

He did.

She heard herself breathing, and felt her fingertips become cold. "Again," she whispered.

He moved them left, then back.

Carol wrapped her arms around her stomach. "Imagination," she said. "Maybe Stampler was right . . . maybe I should've checked in there overnight." She knelt in front of Plato. "Again," she said quietly.

He rolled his eyes.

"Oh Jesus," she whispered.

Plato stared at her. "It wasn't an accident," he said.

Carol curled into a fetal position and pulled the comforter over her. Her mind spun. I'm having a nervous breakdown. It didn't happen. It's all tumbling out. I'm ready for the farm. He didn't move his eyes. It's in my head. It's been coming for a long time. Plato didn't speak. You make him talk. You throw the three-sixty. It's an act, a trick. He can't talk. He's a dummy, a cloth-and-wood dummy. She hunched deeper into the covers trying to rationalize the moment.

One, I'm a ventriloquist.

Two, Plato is *me*.

Three, all conversations are rhetorical.

Four, it's a schtick.

Five, you better get your ass out of this bed and make sure what just happened didn't happen, and you're *not* frigging crazy.

And if it's a nervous breakdown? She didn't like the idea. Better reorder the list.

One, I'm tired. Of what? Everything, the whole scene is a hassle. So maybe you tried a number on yourself tonight? Oh c'mon! C'mon, my foot. A little subconscious death wish. Suicide? A lot of shit's been coming down lately. I didn't drive that car into the wall, she screamed at herself. Okay, you didn't, but you could have, right? No, she answered. Listen, we all want to escape . . . what would life be like without the Murrays, and the routine, and the travel, and the lawyers? I didn't ram the car!

"I am not going to have a breakdown," she yelled. "And that little bastard does not talk to me. I talked to myself . . . like always, because there's no one else to talk with . . . anywhere, anytime."

She threw the covers aside.

"Okay, Plato, we're gonna get this settled right now," she said, and marched into the living room. "I'm not going to have a nervous breakdown for you, for bastard Murray, for anybody." She shook her finger at him. ". . . And Mr. Plato, wise-ass of the world, you *did not* talk, or move your frigging eyes! *Got it*, babe?"

He looked straight ahead.

"That's better," Carol told him.

Plato's eyes shifted upward. "It wasn't an accident," he told her.

She felt a chill, then a metallic taste in her mouth. It's a bad dream, she thought. Okay, the crash, and fatigue, I'll buy that . . . okay, I'll get some help. I'm talking to myself, but that's par for the course.

"It wasn't an accident," he repeated.

Carol clamped her hands against her ears. "I don't need this," she whined. "I can't handle it."

"It wasn't an accident," he said quietly.

"You can't," she whispered. "This is all out of me . . . out of my screwed-up head . . . you're just a goddamn puppet."

Plato rolled his eyes, then stared at her. "Man . . . woman . . . man . . . woman. In the club . . . in the street."

Carol shuddered.

"I can't take much more. Why are you dumping on me? Why the hell is everybody dumping on me?"

Plato shifted his eyes straight ahead.

Carol stood in the center of the room clenching and unclenching her hands. She felt a wave of nausea, then a chill. "I'm really going crazy," she sobbed. "What the hell did I do? I hate it! *I hate it!*" she screamed. She lunged for Plato, and dug her nails into his cheeks. "You didn't talk, you filthy bastard," she yelled. Carol tore at his clothes. "I'm going to kill us," she screamed. "I hate us." She grabbed a cushion from the chair and held it to the dummy's face.

Suddenly, she stopped. "What the hell am I doing?" She rushed into the bedroom, and frantically dialed Thornton's number.

Chapter Six

"All I need is a rest," Carol said quietly. "I'm just tired, and need something to settle me down."

Evan Stampler nodded. "Your father mentioned that you had a conversation with the dummy and—"

"No. That's wrong," Carol snapped. "I always talk with Plato. It's an act. Don't you understand, it's only an act. He *didn't* talk to me, and he *didn't* move his eyes. It was fatigue . . . an hallucination. Why is everybody making such a big deal about this incident?"

"Why did you try to destroy him?" Stampler asked.

Carol looked away. "I didn't . . . I was overwrought . . . the accident . . . the accident triggered a lot of shit. A lot of people have been dumping on me. So I took it out on Plato. What the hell's the big deal?"

"Miss Elliott, I can't help you. You need counseling," he told her.

"I'm not going to a shrink," she retorted.

Evan Stampler shrugged. "And you're not getting any prescriptions from me," he countered.

"There are other doctors," Carol answered.

He motioned to the door. "Good luck."

"Good-bye," she replied and started to leave.

"This isn't going to go away," he said.

Carol turned, and stared at him. "It's none of your goddamn business. I can take care of myself. I always have."

"And look where it's got you," he said.

"You sonofabitch, who the hell are you to make a judgment?"

"Thornton told me you were hysterical, and convinced the dummy spoke *and* looked at you," he persisted.

"It's an act," she growled. "The frigging accident did something to me . . . it was all in my head. I control Plato," she told him. "I'm always in control."

"Then explain the incident!"

"There wasn't any!"

"Oh?" he answered. "Thornton said—"

Carol cut him off abruptly. "Thornton said," she mimicked. "Well, he's no great shakes himself. What does he know? Look, I got a little out of control. It was a combination of everything," she insisted.

Stampler nodded. "You like to be 'in control,' don't you?" he asked.

"Don't give me any two-bit analysis, I know myself better you do," Carol replied.

"Really?" he said. "You didn't stuff rags in the dummy's mouth? You didn't poke out his eyes?"

"Damn that Thornton," Carol whispered.

"It doesn't seem like you were able to 'control' yourself last night. Or has this happened before?"

"No," she said vehemently.

"Did he ever talk to you before?"

"I make him talk," Carol insisted.

"That isn't what you told Thornton—"

"He should shut his fat face," Carol shouted.

Stampler eyed her. "Doesn't seem you're 'in control' right now," he said.

"Watch me," she replied. "Take a good look, Dr. Stampler, 'cause it's adios-time."

Evan Stampler didn't respond.

"Well?" Carol sneered.

"Good-bye," he said calmly.

Carol's fingers tightened on the doorknob.

"Aren't you leaving?" he asked.

Carol stared at him. Get the hell out of here, she thought. Yeah, babe, split. You can work this out yourself. You don't need this putz, or Thornton, or anybody else. Just tell him off, and scram.

"I don't need you, and I don't need 'help,' " she said.

He nodded. "Thank you for not wasting my time," he answered. "Good morning, Miss Elliott."

She didn't move. "Don't talk to me like that."

"Look, I don't have the time to play games with you. You want to be 'in control' or the victor? Fine, tell me off, and take your problems to someone else."

They stared at each other. Carol released her grip on the doorknob. "I'm not buying into this," she replied.

Stampler smiled. "I didn't think you would."

"And you're not a psychiatrist," she said.

"Correct," he answered, "but some of my best friends are psychiatrists."

The half joke caught Carol off-guard. "That was one of the worst," she told him.

Stampler shrugged. "I'm better known for gallbladders than one-liners."

Carol sat on the arm of the couch. "I'm still not buying into this . . . besides, I don't have money for shrinks."

Evan Stampler knew he had to choose his words carefully. Defuse the situation, he told himself, and lead her to someone for treatment. His mind churned. Perhaps the accident caused the trauma. Of course it did, dummies don't speak independently. She's a classic schizophrenic. Nice diagnosis, Doctor, he berated himself.

"Whatever you've bottled up is seeping out. Why don't you just try to talk to someone before you have another explosion?"

"I don't have the *money* or the time," she insisted.

Stampler nodded. "Some clinics will work out a payment schedule to assist you."

It struck a raw nerve, and Carol was back on the offensive. "Another long-term payout? Like the lawyers? Like Murray? Oh yeah, he's gone but he's still here. Listen, I've got the next three years of earnings pledged all over town, and I'm not going into hock for some other asshole. I want to be finished with everybody, and then, babe, I'm taking off."

Evan Stampler looked down. Dumb, he berated himself.

"And what the hell does 'explosion' mean? You think I'm hearing voices, huh? A little schizo, right? Well, babe, the goddamn dummy *did* talk, and he scared the shit out of me. And you know what he said, huh? The accident was deliberate. That's right, someone wanted my ass dead."

Carol went for the door, opened it. "Take a fast gander . . . 'cause that's all there is," she told him, then slammed the door behind her.

Stampler toyed with his pen after she left. Well, he thought, you certainly handled that poorly. He stared at the rain clouds pushing their way toward the East Side. Perhaps the dummy did speak to her? No, it was impossible, a first-year med student could analyze this one.

Carol muttered to herself as she walked down Central Park West. Idiot doctor, she groused. Why did I ever let Thornton talk me into seeing that jerk? Thornton, Stampler, Murray, the grinding of the accident, and the hospital throbbed in her mind. Bastards, they're all bastards wanting to take a chunk out of me, she seethed. She crossed Lincoln Circle. The wind whipped up, and the air became heavy. Well, boys, she warned, you can all take a good look 'cause this lady is calling a fast halt to all of the nonsense. I'll work this out in spite of *all* of you.

"Taxi," she called. The cab made a quick stop and backed up. "Eighty-sixth and the Riverside," she told the driver.

"So, you're the boss," he said.

"Right," Carol answered, and settled back.

They were stuck in traffic near Lincoln Center. "It's the pits," the cabbie said. "Just like this town, everything snafued." He leaned on his horn. "Ya mind if we take a couple of streets down, then I cut over?"

"Go ahead," Carol said.

He forced his way out of the tie-up, took a side street, then down Columbus Avenue to avoid more clogged streets. It started to drizzle. "Aw shit," the driver said. "Figure this, huh?" Finally, they were on West End Avenue. "Well, at least we're getting there," he said.

It was raining steadily. "How long you been driving?" she asked.

"Me? Twenty years plus," he answered.

"That should qualify you for combat—" her words hung in midair as a maroon Pontiac sped past them.

"Sonofabitch," the driver snarled.

Carol felt her hands grow icy. "Go after him," she said. The driver glanced at her in his mirror. "Go, go . . . follow him," she ordered.

"Hey, he only came close."

"Do it," Carol insisted.

The driver accelerated, swerved onto a side street,

but the Pontiac had disappeared. "Now what?" he said.

"Go up Broadway," Carol told him.

"So, you're the boss," he replied.

They zigzagged up Broadway, across Seventy-fifth, then Columbus Avenue, another side street, then Amsterdam, but the car was gone.

"So, nu?" the driver asked. "What's this? The West Side Grand Prix?"

"Go up Broadway again," Carol said.

He stopped the cab. "No way, lady, I ain't spending the rest of the day chasing nothing."

"Once more. I'll pay you double."

He shook his head. "It's wet. I'm tired."

"Goddamnit!" Carol shrieked. "You'll do it until I find him!"

The cabbie pulled over, turned the flag down. "Sixteen twenty-five," he asked.

Carol stared at him icily.

"Listen, lady, get the hell out of my hack."

She didn't move.

"Hey, I told you something," he warned.

"Take me home. Eighty-sixth and Riverside," she said.

"No, ma'am, you're a frigging wacko. I want you outta this cab. Just fork over what's on the meter."

Carol's nostrils flared. She fumbled through her pocketbook, took a twenty from her purse, threw it at him, and stormed out of the taxi.

Carol hopscotched her way across the street, then huddled in a doorway of a doll shop as the rain pelted the sidewalk. Just my luck, Carol thought, stuck in the middle of nothing. She wiped her face, and slicked back her soaking hair. Damn that Thornton, she cursed, if it wasn't for his lousy idea. Carol was too entwined in her own hates, and accusations, to notice the door opening behind her.

"Oh my, you're soaked to the bone," the smallish woman said. Carol turned about quickly. "I didn't mean to frighten you, my dear."

"Sorry . . . I didn't expect anyone to be, er," Carol stammered. The woman beckoned to her. "Come in, child, you'll catch your death out there." Carol hesitated. "Come on, come on, this weather's not going to let up for Lord knows how long." She looked at the rain-slickened street. "What a horror . . . all that water, just gives me chills." She held her hand out, "Come in, come in."

Carol followed the woman inside the shop. Dolls peered at her from the two wood and glass counters at the sides of the tiny store, from the shelves lining the walls and the bridge tables pushed against the back wall. Dolls of every description: wax-faced, bisque, porcelain, Kewpies. The collection seemed endless. Carol followed the woman to the rear of the shop, then through a curtained-off area into a sewing room. Yards of velours, silks, velvets were neatly stacked on a large dining room table.

"Oh, we make our own clothes here," the woman chattered. "Devil of a time getting decent material these days." She smiled at Carol. "You like dolls, don't you, my dear."

"Yes, yes I do," Carol replied.

The woman nodded. "Thought you did. Well, you'll have the tour after you get dry." She opened another door. "Towels are in the *lavatoire*, and there's a robe somewhere. I don't really remember. No matter . . . it's in one of the closets . . . and there must be some scuffies around too."

Carol stared at the room. It was a Victorian dressing room. The woman chuckled softly. "Isn't it precious? Everything's just as we remembered." She folded her hands across her breast. "Oh dear," the woman sighed, "some of the damask isn't holding up. Well, that's our problem, isn't it?" The woman smiled at Carol. "Tidy yourself, and we'll have tea. Nothing like a nice cup of jasmine to soothe the rough edges."

Carol nodded. The woman gave a pixieish shrug and closed the door behind her. Carol peeled off her wet clothes, dried her hair, and put on a wine-colored velvet robe. She walked about the room touching the draped tables crowded with miniatures, curios, and pictures. Well, it sure beats standing in the rain, Carol thought. My God, this is an antique dealer's dream. She looked at a small silver picture frame: two girls dressed in turn-of-the-century dresses smiled at her. Where the hell are you, babe? she thought. Not in this era, that's for sure. Let's see if the 'scuffies' are in the closet. Carol slid back the door: Another surprise, it was empty, except for the slippers. Okay, she said to herself, this is it . . . showtime, and a-one, and a-two . . .

"Oh, you found everything, how superb," the woman said. "Aggie," she called. "Agnes, come meet our guest." She smiled at Carol. "Aggie loves company . . . gives her a chance to use the good silver," she whispered.

"I heard that, Jo, and it's true," came from the sewing room.

"Can't keep a thought to yourself in this house," the woman giggled.

Carol forced back a laugh as sister Agnes appeared. She was a midget. Carol fought to control herself. The first sister was small, but Agnes was even smaller. No, no, she's not a midget, she's a tiny woman. Yes, a perfectly featured woman, but extremely small. Carol stared at her. Well, say something, dummy, she told herself, you're acting like an idiot.

"The robe's beautiful," Carol blurted out.

"And it's her color too, isn't it, Aggie?"

Sister Agnes eyed Carol critically. "It would be more effective if she let her hair grow out. Never cared for yellow tresses m'self."

Carol felt self-conscious. "Yes, it does clash with my hair," she said nervously.

"Well, that could come later." The tiny woman extended her hand. "I'm Agnes Markham," she said.

The other woman's face fell. "Oh dear, I never introduced myself. Sometimes I'm so rude." She curtsied. "And I'm Josephine Markham," she said sheepishly.

Tea turned out to be coffee, and excellent coffee at that. "Well, doctor says we can't have coffee because it does, well, who knows what, so call it 'tea.' It makes doctor happy, and we don't break our routine." Carol laughed. "Everybody imagines us as two old biddies, isn't that so, Aggie? But we don't care. We have the dolls, and other amusements." They pointed to their collection. "Oh, we never sell. No, no, these are our babies." Rows of dolls stared at Carol. "And we dress each one, yes, every little lady has her own wardrobe, isn't that right, Aggie?" Carol stopped counting. Were there two hundred? Three hundred?

"I used to have a collection . . . a few dolls," Carol said weakly. "Nothing like this of course."

"I thought so," sister Aggie replied. "You looked like a doll person . . . or puppets." Carol stiffened. "Yes, yes, that's it. She's the puppet lady, Jo. I told you she'd appear." Agnes looked at Carol intently. "Yes, it's her," she said firmly.

"I . . . I do have a puppet," Carol said.

"More tea?" Josephine asked.

Agnes looked at her sternly. "Don't bother with the tea. I want to read her." She motioned Carol back to her chair. "Has anyone read you, my dear?"

"Read?" Carol answered.

"Psychic reading," sister Jo whispered.

Carol shook her head.

"Good," Agnes said as she settled herself in a chair opposite Carol. "Very good. Some of those people are charlatans. Very destructive. Try to relax, dear. Let me visualize for you." Agnes closed her eyes.

"So exciting," Josephine cooed. "When she closes her eyes . . . well, you'll see."

Oh brother, Carol said to herself, if this isn't the end. Two biddies, tea that's coffee, a time warp, and some hocus-pocus. Oh, wouldn't Thornton love this.

"Well, he might and he might not," Agnes said.

Carol blanched.

"Who's the older man?" she asked.

"What man?" Carol blurted out.

Agnes swayed back in her chair. "The one with the white hair. He's very concerned . . . no, worried about you. I think . . . yes, it's a *T* . . . a *T* name."

"Thornton, my father's name is Thornton."

"Well, he's concealing something from you." Carol folded her arms across her stomach. "Letters . . . oh yes, quite a few letters. My, my, such language. Filthy letters, filthy. Sick, disturbed person . . . has someone with the initial *D* been troublesome?"

Carol's jaw clenched. Her hands were cold.

"No need to answer," Agnes said. "There's some confusion here . . . man, woman, man, woman . . . very unsettled. The dummy . . . you have a dummy, don't you?"

"Yes," Carol said hoarsely.

"We should like to read him . . . yes, bring him here next time. He should release the problem."

Agnes Markham's eyes opened.

"How did you know I was a ventriloquist?" Carol asked.

"Oh, I didn't," Agnes answered. "I merely said you have a puppet . . . or a dummy. He's a problem child, isn't he? And you shouldn't have been that hard with Mr. T. It isn't his fault, you know. Truly, he's a good person, and loves you quite a bit." She smiled at Carol. "And do something with your colors. Yes, the hair was much more in keeping when it was chestnut."

Carol felt chilled.

Who the hell are these women? And where am I? She plastered a smile over her face.

"And try to stop profaning," Agnes told her. "It honestly isn't you, is it?"

Carol kept staring at Agnes. "How did you know about Plato, and the letter?" she asked.

"Through the reading," Agnes replied.

"Can you tell me something else? I mean, what about this person?" Carol asked.

"Which one?" Agnes answered. "Seems you're involved with a number of persons."

"What about the kook who wrote me?"

"Kook?" Agnes said. "Oh! The unbalanced one." Agnes shook her head. "You'll have to come back with your little man."

"Ah, here's Papa Noir now," Josephine announced. "Just in time to take Miss Carol home." Sister Jo waved at the taxi through the window. "Isn't he marvelous. Always on time. And your clothes must be dry by now. Come, come, get dressed. They're probably wondering where you are."

The Markham sisters wanted her out of their home. However, there were too many questions unanswered. The hows and whys clung to her.

Do you have your purse? She did. I want to ask you about this person? Next time. When will that be? Soon. How can I get in touch with you? You can't. Do you have a telephone? No.

"It's been a beautiful afternoon," Jo Markham

told her. "Aggie and I do want to keep up the relationship."

Carol felt rushed, and dazed. She wanted to ask more questions, but it was to no avail as they escorted her into the taxi.

"Make sure she gets inside safely, Papa," Jo cautioned. "Good-bye, it was wonderful to meet you." Agnes closed the door, and the cab sped off before Carol could respond.

"Whar ya go-ing," the huge black man asked.

"Eighty-sixth and Riverside," Carol said.

"Yes, ma'am," the driver replied in a deep West Indian accent. "I getchu thar right fast," he said. "Papa Noir make sure everything's sound-and-safe."

Carol glanced at him through the rearview mirror. Jesus, he's got violet eyes. Papa Noir smiled at her, and Carol looked away. Oh brother, get me out of here, she thought.

"I think the ladies will see you again," he said. "They don't have too much contact with others unless it's a special situation." He looked at her in the rearview mirror. "And you, ma'am, I can tell, are special . . . very, very special."

Chapter Seven

Papa Noir gracefully wheeled his way through the traffic and pulled into the front of Carol's apartment house.

"Well, that warn't too bad," he said in a sing-song voice. "You want me to walk you upstairs, and make sure the house is plenty safe?"

"No," Carol replied with amusement.

"Ladies Markham want no harm arrive on you."

"That's very nice," Carol replied. "How much do I owe you?" she added quickly.

Papa Noir looked at the meter. "By golly-gee, Papa forget to lower the flag. Ah well," he said, smiling, "I guess you got no tariff this day."

Carol fumbled in her bag, and handed him five dollars, but he refused.

"Sorry," he said, "can't do it. Sister Agnes wouldn't approve . . . besides, 'special' people never have to pay. You keep the green for another rainy day," he laughed.

Carol smiled weakly. "Thank you," she answered. "I . . . I think . . . well, your eyes are absolutely fantastic."

Papa Noir chuckled. "Oh yes, me peepers to others are unusual. Many, many in the family have 'em, so to Papa it no big deal." The rain drummed harder on the roof of the cab. "Oh me," he said, "it's a soaker. C'mon, I open *parapluie* and walk you to the door."

"No, no, that's okay," Carol replied.

"Well, we watch until you safe," Papa said.

Carol nodded, and dashed from the cab. When she turned around Papa Noir was gone.

"Wet enough for ya, Miss Elliott?" the doorman asked.

"Yeah, Pat," Carol replied as she walked to the mailroom.

"Hey, listen," he called after her. "I gotta package for ya. Not a big one. Not from one of de stores. I tossed it in de porter's room."

"Terrific. Suppose it's glass?" Carol quipped.

"Ah shit, yer a riot," he replied as he flipped through a ring of keys. "Hey, how's de little guy? He still tellin' all dem dirty jokes?"

Carol didn't acknowledge the crack.

"Ya ain't got no mail," he said. "Nobody's got no mail. The frigging postman ain't even come." Pat pushed aside a stack of Bloomingdale's and Saks boxes. "Now, where the hell . . . ? Aw, here it is, Miss Elliott." He handed Carol a neatly wrapped package the size of a shoebox.

"Who brought this? United Parcel?"

"Beats the shit outta me."

Carol looked at it and shrugged. "When did it arrive?"

"I dunno . . . someone left it in de hall a couple of hours ago."

Right-t-t-t! They sure didn't hire you for genius, she thought. At least it's not ticking, she told herself. You're *so* positive, babe. It's really a trip getting presents. Carol turned the package over as she waited for the elevator. Probably from Thornton. Naw. Murray's stuffed a shoebox with hundreds, and a suicide note. Naw. Papa Who? is giving me a voodoo doll with Murray's face. Naw, but it be a swell gift, she thought.

Carol hesitated as she slid the key into the lock. It all came rushing back. Holding the cushion on Plato's face. Oh jeez, I must be crazy. Tearing at his clothes, and twisting his neck, then jamming a dish towel in his mouth. Holding him in front of her, and screaming obscenities. Insanity.

Flashback. Bad scene. She's out of control.

"Thornton"—choking, sob—"I just tried to kill Plato." Silence. What the hell's he gonna say? It's sick.

Carol closed her eyes, unlocked the door, and walked in. Don't look. Turn on the lights, and act casual.

Are you *really* crazy? He's a frigging inanimate lap puppet that you made fifteen years ago, *and* dum-dum, he's actually Mr. Plato the ninth 'cause the others bit the dustbin.

Carol tossed the package on the hall table, flicked on the lamps, dropped her raincoat on a chair, and went to the refrigerator. Not too shabby. Thank God Thornton filled it. Well . . . let's see . . . how about . . . suppose I make.

Stop kidding yourself. You'll have to face him sometime. Don't wanna look. Right! You'll love the rest home. A terrific spot to swap stories with the other patients. Hey, didja hear the one about the talking puppet? Don't wanna look. What the hell's wrong with you? He didn't talk. He didn't walk, and the eyes don't have it. Sure as hell don't have violet eyes like Papa Who? Out of sight, babe. I mean, today was rollercoaster time.

Carol pressed her lips together. Okay, let's have a diet root beer, some cheese, and the Italian salami.

"Hey, Mr. Plato," she called, "it's party time."

Screw your courage to the sticking point 'cause

I'm loading a tray with goodies and coming over. One foot, two foot. Left, right, left. Don't stop. *I said don't stop!* Good, Carol, you made it. Okay, look at him. Naw. Gotta. Naw. Gotta sometime. He's the meal ticket. Don't rush me. Rush you? Jeez, you're really round-the-bend. He's a frigging inhuman . . . *Okay, okay* . . . I'll do it!

Flashback. Bad scene. The nails score his face.

Do it!

Done. I looked.

And?

Not that bad.

I told you!

I thought . . . well, I thought it was worse.

"Whaddaya jivin' about, babe? I'm all right. A little paint. A little plaster. Besides I could use a new set of threads. Some duds with glitz."

Now the tears.

"Sorry . . . sorry . . . sorry. I don't know why I did it." Plato looked straight ahead. "It's been crazy, and everything's coming down. I had to unload."

The head, scraped and chipped, remained fixed, and his eyes stared blankly at the rain pelting the picture window.

"I can't explain it," Carol sobbed.

He didn't move.

"What the hell's wrong? I can't get out of this shit . . . I get deeper and deeper. The more we work, the worse it becomes. Right, babe?"

His eyes looked straight ahead.

"I'm sorry. Okay?"

The "okay" came back in Carol's head.

"Thanks, babe. I'll make it up to you. A new wardrobe. I'll get out the sewing machine and we'll fix you up."

The "great" was also in her mind.

"And we'll soften the act . . . *and* cut down on the road trips. We'll make it."

The "right" was also internal.

Carol was relieved. The day tumbled out of her. And this guy, Stampler! I mean, he wanted me to hook into a "group." Imagine me in a circle with psychos? But that's not the best. I met two of the strangest! These little old ladies. Hey listen, Agnes . . . yep, can you believe it? Agnes was about four feet tall.

"Right on, babe. I loves them tiny gals," he quipped. Carol adjusted her hand inside his chest.

"And-d-d-d they have . . . let me tell you." She regripped the knob that turned Plato's head. "Izzat better?"

"Sure 'nough, honchild," he answered.

"These biddies have dolls! Them's what Murray stole from me, and sold. Well, babe, they ain't nothing."

"They got a Jumeau?" he asked.

"A counter full of 'em," Carol replied.

She adjusted his collar, and tried to smooth his wig. Sorry about that hair-pulling bit, she thought. The face is pretty scored too. Carol ran her fingers over a long nail wound, and bits of paint powdered Plato's lap. I'll make you another head. She held him at arm's length. A little softer this time. Maybe less stylized.

The rain splatted continuously against the window, warping their reflections. The maroon Pontiac swept across her mind. You're dippy, she told herself, that wasn't her. *Yeah?* The smell of burnt rubber, and the noise were replayed. God, I was cold. I thought I was dead cold, babe. Evan Stampler blended into Papa Who?'s violet eyes. Oh, them eyes, babe. Subliminal flashes of little Aggie, and big Jo. Pixies, babe, lovely aging Tinkerbelles.

"Hey," she blurted out, "l'il Aggie does a mind-reading bit . . . and she wants to see you!"

"Right," Plato/Carol answered. "Everybody's in show biz. Especially the little people. Cute."

"It would be fun," Carol replied. "And you're about the same size. What the hell, we've got nothing to lose . . . maybe she'll clue me into myself. I mean, I know you didn't shift them baby blues, or talk."

Plato's distortion stared at her in the picture window. Carol lifted him off her hand onto the couch. His scarred face was blank and his lips mute.

Carol, Carol, Carol . . . you're in some deep shit if the best you find is . . . sorry, babe, but flesh is better than pine, and cotton.

You see, babe, I'm really lonely.

And I'm kinda tired of all of this jive.

And I'm not getting anywhere.

And I'm so . . . damn lonely.

Don't cry, she begged herself.

I'll try.

Subliminal flashes of Murray, Thornton, the sweaty women clamoring for Latino, the empty hotel rooms in Vegas piled upon each other.

I gotta cry. Tryin' to hold on too hard.

Carol pressed her hands to her face. The wet salt trickled through her fingers and down the back of her hands.

"Sorry," she muttered. "It's a bummer."

She leaned her head against the back of the couch, and watched the rain fight the window. I'm in the same boat, guys, we'll never get through.

Carol patted Plato on the knee. "In the next life, babe, I'm coming back as a man. None of this second-fiddle junk, no sir. I'm gonna be a furrier that turns movie mogul, yes sir. Not an ounce of sense, and less emotions. I'm gonna ravage every broad I meet, then give 'em a box of fake diamonds as "a small token of m'deep appreciation, ma'am."

"Hey, *we* got a present," Carol exclaimed. "And it ain't ticking." She retrieved it from the hall table, sat Plato on her lap, and started to unwrap the package.

"Three guesses!" she said.

"A pony!" he quipped.

"Sure, fella," Carol replied, fumbling with the twine and paper.

" A dozen long-stemmed roses?" he asked.

"In a shoebox?" Carol pushed away the paper.

"Ya got me!" he answered.

"Indeed I do, Mr. Plato, and your brother tain't in this here box neither," Carol replied as she lifted the top, and fingered through the lavender tissue paper.

"We're gettin' close."

"What the hell izzat?" Plato asked.

Carol lifted the black brassiere out of the box, and held it in front of her. The cups had been cut out leaving only the straps and back band.

"You gotta be kidding!" she told Plato.

"Sure ain't an uplifting experience," he replied.

Carol held the brassiere in her fingers, and shrugged. If someone thinks it's sexy they're wrong, she thought. She dropped the bra into the box, covered it with tissue.

"Sorry, old boy, none of them long-stemmed beauties, besides it warn't me size. Oh brother, can we attract the weirdos."

She propped Plato on the end of the couch, and dialed her message service.

"Oh yeah-h-h, Miss C. Ya got a couple. Lemme see . . . oh yeah, Thornton twice. Call him at the club after seven. Mr. Lanzetta. Call him collect in Reno."

Damn!

"Mr. Korn."

Terrific!

"And . . . Mr. Robb James said you got the number. And-d-d-d-d . . . I guess . . . yeah, that's it! Nice to have you back, Miss C."

"Thank you," Carol replied softly.

"How's Mr. P?"

"Fine."

"Oh just a minute . . . here's anudder one."

Swell!

"She didn't leave no number . . . only said . . . I'm quoting now . . . 'Hope you like the present. Wear it while you can.' And it was called in by 'Diana.' "

"Oh *Jesus!*" Carol whined.

"I'm sorry, say again."

Carol slammed the receiver into the cradle.

God help me out of this nightmare, she thought. Cold. I'm cold. Her hands were trembling, and she put them under her arms. Call the police. I'm so cold. She tightened her arms against her sides. The acid taste in her mouth made her gag. Saliva oozed onto her lips. I hate this! I hate this! Carol felt the metallic-enzyme taste mix with the saliva. She gulped several times, trying to force back the nausea. Beads of perspiration hung icily on her neck. Every muscle in her body contracted, and she gasped for breath.

Instead of screaming, vomit spewed from her mouth and splattered onto the picture window. Carol tried to support herself with the arm of the couch, but her puke-slickened hands slid off and she dropped to the floor.

She lay there convulsed in tears, her hair in a

reddish beige pool of food; mucus seeped from her nose.

Across the floor was Diana's present.

One empty cup of the brassiere dangled over the side of the box.

Carol raised herself to a sitting position. She wiped the vomit from her face, but her eyes were too filled with tears to see Plato's eyes shift toward her, then the "gift."

Chapter Eight

Nick Anz reread the newest Diana letter to himself, then folded it and placed it in a plastic bag with the others. "This the last letter?" he asked Carol.

"Yes," she replied softly.

"Okay, we'll take it from here," he said.

"Just like before?" Thornton snapped. "If you had been more aggressive you might have avoided this incident."

"Mr. Thornton—"

"Mr. Evans to you," Thornton replied.

Nick Anz nodded. "All right . . . Mr. Evans, I told you a couple of weeks ago this sort of thing was common and—"

"A couple of weeks ago?" Carol remarked.

Thornton avoided Anz's stare. "Detective Anz and I . . . well, we had some talks," Thornton stammered.

"About the other letters," Anz added.

"From Diana?" Carol asked.

Thornton nodded. "Two others," he said.

"Seven," Anz corrected him.

Carol felt someone had hit her in the chest, and sat back in the chair stunned.

Nick Anz moved from behind his desk, and closed

the door to his office. "You know anyone named Diana?" he asked.

Carol shook her head. "No."

"Or Diane?"

"No," she repeated.

"Ya sure? Give yourself a moment. Someone that worked for you? Or you met on the road? Think about it. It don't even have to be with a *D*. Someone ya had trouble with, huh? Think about it, okay?"

"We've never had anything like this before," Thornton interjected. "Carol's mail has . . . well, her act doesn't go over for the DAR, and she's received a few letters in the past, but never anything that . . . that vicious."

"How about calls?" Anz questioned.

"No!" Thornton replied sharply.

"Yes!" Carol rebutted him. "In Vegas . . . no, no in Miami. Some woman wanted to have me banned, but the hotel people didn't think it was anything to worry about."

"You see, Detective, Carol and Plato sometimes are a bit raucous," Thornton explained.

"Ya don't have to tell me, Mr. *Evans*," Anz replied. "I know . . . she works blue, huh? And sometimes it goes overboard, right? I heard about the dummy."

"It's not *really* what you think," Thornton said.

"Come off it, Thornton," Carol snapped. "Yes, I work *'blue'* . . . for adults only . . . and the act is full of smut."

"Oh, Carol, it's not that bad," Thornton told her.

"What the hell's the difference?" she yelled. "Some freaky broad is trying to cut off my mams, and you're toning down the act. He knows I get up there with foul-mouth and say something more than 'oh shit.' Isn't that right, Detective?"

Carol interrupted Nick Anz before he answered.

"And why didn't you tell *me* about the letters, Thornton?"

"I . . . I didn't want to upset you."

"Worry me? You never protected me, so don't play big daddy. Let me tell you, fella, that is the biggest bunch of bullshit. Thornton the Papa? *Jesus!"*

"Hey!" Anz bellowed. "Cool it!"

Carol slammed her chair against the wall and stared into the detectives' room through the glass partition. Thornton crossed his arms and looked at his shoes.

"That's better," Anz told them. "Let's work on the problem at hand, huh?"

"Sure," Carol replied softly without turning around. "Let's play hide-and-seek with Miss Diana."

"What about the woman in Miami?"

"Never found her."

"Did she sound like our friend?" he asked.

"No. It wasn't like this. It was some old lady that didn't think young women should say 'piss' or 'shit.' "

"It was an old woman, huh?"

"I think so . . . that was two, three years ago."

"Nothing since then?" Anz asked.

"No. Nothing," Carol replied.

"Except the hit-and-run accident," Thornton said. "Or shouldn't I mention that?" he added sarcastically.

"What accident?" Anz wanted to know.

He wrote down the information and punctuated with "un-huhs" as Carol recounted the story.

"So where's yer car now?"

Thornton told him they towed it to the Lexington Avenue Garage. Anz would send one of his men to look at it.

"And you didn't see no one?"

"I told you *that,*" Carol answered.

Nick Anz thumbed through Carol's letters. Same typewriter. Same key pressure. Same salutation. Oh yeah, a real wacko, he thought.

"Anybody ever call you 'slut/bitch' before?"

"No," Carol answered. "Maybe?" she added.

"Any other 'presents'?" he asked.

"Not for me. Plato gets most of the mail, and an occasional toy . . . or a blanket. Harmless junk . . . not like that!" Carol said pointing to the brassiere.

"Yeah," Anz said dryly. He pushed the bra back into the box, and closed it. "Lemme ask you something. Who would benefit the most if you were dead?"

"The world," Carol snapped.

"Sure," he quipped. "But I'm looking for a more intimate relationship. You married? Got a kid that hates you? A manager with a heavy insurance policy? Who?"

"Murray," Thornton said quickly. Anz held out his hands. "Murray Korn," Thornton replied.

"My ex-husband," Carol explained. "He had me insured. It was an accident . . . or life policy. I dunno."

"Oh?" Anz replied. "How much?"

"Two hundred thousand," Thornton answered.

"Oh yeah?" Anz said. "And which company?"

"It's canceled. Murray paid for it out of Carol's earnings, and we let it lapse after the divorce."

"Meaning we couldn't pay the frigging premiums," Carol interjected. "My income went to the attorney."

"Where is this Murray Korn?"

"Here," Thornton told him. "He has an office in the Greybar Building. Korn Productions, Inc."

"He was a real 'production,' " Carol said dourly.

"And he was named beneficiary?" Anz asked.

"No. CARMUR Productions, I think. I . . . I really never saw the policy," Thornton told him.

"Wonderful Murray. He would still make something off me when I died," Carol remarked.

"I gather it wasn't a friendly divorce," Anz said.

"Not quite," Carol replied. "But it was fair. Fifty-fifty. He got the dolls, the cars, the bank accounts, and I got to go on the road to pay my lawyers."

"At least you're free of him," Thornton suggested.

Nick Anz shot Thornton a glance. "Really? What makes you so sure?" he said.

Carol and Thornton didn't speak to each other during the cab ride to her apartment.

"What makes you so sure?" kept echoing in Carol's mind. Impossible, she thought. It wasn't like him to try this kind of stunt. Murray? Naw. Posing as a psycho broad? Naw. He might like to "do it" with a nut. Naw, it wasn't vintage bastard Murray. However, Anz wasn't convinced, and planned to "check it out." Carol stared at the traffic. Murray? Might be! Could be? Naw. Well, babe, stranger things have happened. Plenty of husbands knock off their wives for dough . . . for a younger chick . . . for kicks. Murray? Naw?

Yeah, it was okay that Anz would "look into yer ex-husband's business."

"I hope he nails him," Carol muttered.

"Who?" Thornton asked.

"Who do you think?" she fired back.

"I doubt this has anything to do with Murray," he replied. "It's too bizarre . . . no, no, at his worst Murray would never pull a stunt like this."

"Really?" Carol snarled.

The cabbie stared at her in the rearview mirror, then looked away.

"Why didn't you tell me about the *goddamn* letters?"

"I thought . . . this was a crank, and it would go away," he insisted.

"Another piece of bad judgment."

"Carol . . . I wanted to protect you."

She slammed her hand into the seat. "Where were you when I met that bastard? Why did I get screwed out of thousands of dollars . . . when you were supposed to be taking care of business?" Thornton bit his lower lip. "What about the five grand?" He knew that was coming. "Tell me!" she snarled.

"I don't think this is the time to discuss our differences," Thornton replied.

"Why not?" Carol replied. "You gonna tell anybody, cabbie?"

He looked at Carol in the mirror, and shook his head.

"Carol, please!"

"Thornton, *why?*"

"Driver, pull over at the next corner."

"Good idea . . . when in doubt bail out," Carol sniped.

Thornton stepped out of the cab, handed the driver a ten, and walked away.

"So nu, lady? You want I should go where?"

Carol laughed. "So nu I don't know?"

"C'mon, I ain't got time fer games."

"All right, go up Broadway, and let me off at Eighty-sixth," Carol replied.

Carol's mind spun wildly as the cab lurched in and out of the afternoon traffic. Aggravation with Murray melded into Thornton's weaknesses. Call Jack Lanzetta, and take it, darted across Thornton at the police station. Nick Anz, typical cop, straight out of central casting.

Horns. Traffic. Accident. Argument. New York.

Murray wouldn't try to kill me, would he? Anz had his doubts. The bra was kinky, Carol thought.

No, it was sick. She relived the smell of vomit, and being afraid. Some crank, huh Thornton? Diana? Diane? Dee-dee? Sorry, Detective, I don't remember. She stared blankly out the window and imagined a nondescript woman running after her with a knife.

"Crazy, crazy," she muttered.

"Ain't I seen you before?" the cabbie asked.

"No," Carol replied.

"Hey, ain't you . . . er, Carol Elliott?" the driver asked as he cut past another cab, and turned up Broadway.

"Only on my bad days," she replied.

"Yeah, yeah, I knew it was you. Hey, where's Mr. Plato, huh?"

"Having a sex change."

"That's great," he answered. "I saw you on TV. What was it . . . er, couple years back? You killed me!"

"That's what it's all about. I'm a killer," Carol replied. Oh yeah, she thought, the word of the day is *murder*, and I'm the murderee. Miss Nondescript lunged at her, but missed and Carol was screaming.

"Hey, Carol . . ." the cabbie told her, "I gotta a great joke. It's like it wuz made for ya."

Oh shit. Please, not now. Can't you see she's trying to kill me. Carol closed her eyes trying to escape another attack. Miss Nondescript was laughing.

"Here's de thing," he continued, "this guy picks a whore at a bar—"

"I heard it!" Carol interrupted.

"Oh yeah? I don't think so," he replied. "What'sa matter, you too big to take some material from a cabbie?"

"No," she answered. "I don't feel like hearing any jokes, okay? It's swell. Thanks a bunch, but not right now."

"Sure," he replied sullenly. "I got the picture."

The woman with the knife faded into aggravation with the driver. What did you expect? Questions about your latest leading man? Hell no, babe, they always want to tell you the latest dirty joke. I hate it, she thought. Sorry, you're Carol Elliott and foul-mouth. The best in blue. Nick Anz questioning Murray swam in. "Look at the bra, Mr. Korn. You recognize this bra? Oh, you confess. Okay, book him." Murray the tit sniper? Naw, he's a fondler.

"Okay," the cabbie said, "we're here."

"What?"

"Eighty-sixth and Broadway," he said, and pulled down the flag on his meter. "That'll be anudder three and a quarter."

Carol handed him a five. "I'm sorry . . . about the joke. Today hasn't been my best," she said.

"Sure, sure," he replied "I guess everybody's hitting you with material. So what's the big deal, huh? At least I got to meetcha." He stuck out his hand, and Carol shook it. "You probably got enough off-color gags to last you a lifetime, right?"

Blue. Blue bra. Red spotlights. Red light. Green light. The colors pulsated continuously as Carol stepped out of the cab.

"Do you know a cab driver . . . a big, black man with violet eyes? And a West Indian accent?" she asked.

"Violet eyes on a black guy?"

Carol nodded. "He's called Papa . . .? Papa something, I don't remember."

"Ya got me . . .! You sure he had violet eyes? C'mon." He brightened up. "What's the gag?"

"I'm serious. He's got short gray hair. A big man . . . probably from Haiti, or Barbados."

The cabbie shrugged. "Sorry, but why don'tcha

call a couple of the companies. He's gotta be registered."

"Yes," Carol said slowly. "You're right." She fished another five out of her purse and handed it to him, but he declined. "Please take it," she said.

"I'd rather ya hear the joke," he answered.

Carol smiled. "Okay, lay it on me." He did, and she was sorry she had.

Of course! Right! I should've thought of that myself, Carol thought as she crossed West End Avenue. She hunched her shoulders against the wind coming off the Hudson River. Whadda ya gonna say? "Do you have in your employ . . .?" Sure, lady. Hey Charlie, wait till ya hear this one! Sorry I asked, mister. That's all right . . . ha-ha-ha . . . purple eyes, no! Ya want somebody with green hair? *Ha-ha-ha*! I'm tellin' you, Charlie, this city is full of bananas. It wasn't a good idea after all. Papa Noir, little Agnes, and doting Josephine crowded into her thoughts. Sorry you came back? she asked herself. Is this Fun City? Where else can you meet such interesting people? This is where it's at, babe. Oh yes, it's certainly here.

Carol hesitated before she went into her building. Package. Bra. Vomit. Stench. Fear. Please, God, nothing today.

"Hiya," John the day door/bodyguard said as he opened the door. "Really windy, huh, Miss Elliott?"

One foot, two foot, pass the package room, you step. Get into the elevator. Get home, get safe.

"Oh, Miss Elliott—!"

Shaking, quaking. Sorry, you lost.

"A guy wuz here to see ya, but I didn't let him upstairs." The rubber bumper thudded against his hand. The door buzzer started to whine, and she stepped back into the lobby.

"What man?" Carol asked nervously.

"A big black . . . and he got purple eyes," the

doorman told her. "That wuz some sorta creepy, huh?"

"When was he here?" Carol asked quickly.

"Ya just missed him."

"Did he leave a message?"

"Naw, he left ya a package."

Oh no, not again! Anz holding the bra, and looking at her. It's a sicko, he told her. Thornton hiding the letters. You dealing with an unbalanced mind, he told her. "Dear Carol slut/bitch . . . stuff them in your vile mouth."

"Ya all right, Miss Elliott?"

Carol fought to control herself as she followed him to the package room. Her hands were shaking as he pawed through a stack of UPS boxes, a stack of Sunday's *Times*, and then—

"It's a good-looking paper, don'tcha think?" he said and gave her a small package wrapped in lavender rice paper tied with a pink ribbon.

"And it's perfumed too," he added.

"Yes," Carol replied. "Very nice," she said nervously. "I didn't . . . I thought it was something else."

She held the present carefully as he walked her back to the elevator.

"Ya can imagine my surprise," he told her, "when he hands me this . . . yer gift. I couldn't understand him at first. Some sort of funny accent . . . and them eyes . . . jeez, I never saw anything like that. That's creepy, huh?"

"Which cab company was he with . . .?"

"I didn't see no cab. He asked fer ya, then left the box. First, I thought he wuz gonna make trouble, but somehow . . . well, ya knew this guy wasn't no . . . like the rest of them black people . . . especially with them devil eyes."

"Devil eyes?"

"Sure, that's what the coloreds call them types . . . ya know how superstitious they are."

"Was there a note? Or a letter?"

The doorman held the elevator open for her. "Naw. That's it. Nice gift. I like the smell." Carol stepped into the cab, and he let the door close her in.

"Devil eyes," she thought as she looked at the package. Well, it's better than yesterday's beauty. Carol hesitated before entering her apartment. It's all right, nobody home except us dummies. She walked in quickly and bolted the door behind her. A slight odor of vomit mixed with cleaning solution tinged the living room. She tossed her coat on a chair, and gingerly opened the present.

Carol hesitated before lifting the lid off the box. Please, dear God, not today. She tore the rose-colored seal and pushed away several layers of pink tissue paper to reveal a tiny bisque-headed doll dressed in a Victorian ball gown. It's gorgeous, Carol said to herself. The delicately shaped features of the doll were accented by perfectly coiffed hair, and two blonde sausage curls that touched her bisque shoulders.

Carol stood the doll against the package and examined her intently. Beautiful. I never owned anything like this, she thought. The ballgown was handsewn with silks, and seed pearls. Breathless, Carol muttered. It was more a small woman than a doll. Carol touched the wig with her fingertips. Real hair. Little Aggie's? Sister Jo's? Every element of the face was in proportion. It wasn't a doll, but a miniature woman waiting to come to life.

"I want you to breathe," Carol said. "You're too beautiful to be a doll."

Carol studied the detailing of the gown. It was the work of a superb couturiere.

"You're too good for me," Carol whispered.

Carol was about to place the doll back in the tissue bed, when she saw the envelope with her name written across it. The invitation was written in longhand with sweeping penmanship of a lost, gracious era.

Mistresses Agnes and Josephine Markham request the pleasure of your company for luncheon on Thursday, March the 25th, at one o'clock post meridian. Transportation will be provided, thus we further request you be in front of your residence at twelve-thirty. Please bring your little man.

"My pleasure," Carol said to herself. She put the scented note beside her beautiful lady.

"Plato, m'boy," she called, "it's time for some new duds, and another head. We're going to a party."

Chapter Nine

Chick-a-boom.

Grind it to me, baby. *Scream.* Oh jeez, Helen, I think I'm gonna faint.

Chick-a-boom. Latino's on his knees at the edge of the stage. Did you ever, Helen? *Did you ever?* Gimme a dollar. *C'mon,* gimme a dollar. Latino grinds his briefs slowly while sweaty hands stuff it with money. I touched him, Helen, *I really touched him.*

Chick-a-boom, and he prances away.

I'm gonna do it with you, boy. I want a hard one. Oh yeah, hard and sweaty. Latino throws some poses. Oh jeez, Helen, he's some piece of work. Gimme another drink. Imagine what it would be like? Giggle, giggle. Oh, Selma, he's probably a fag. *No way!* Oh yeah? *Yeah!*

Chick-a-boom.

Scream, and scream again 'cause this is where it's at, baby. Right on, sister, 'cause I won't tell if you won't tell. Gimme a high five. Hey, waitress, two more banana daiquiris! Grind it to me, Latino baby! Do it! Do it!

Nick Anz drained his Scotch, and shook his head.

"This is unbelievable," he told Thornton.

"The new entertainment," Thornton shouted above the screaming. "Women's fantasies. The dream come true."

Latino, Don, and big Billy in their finale.

"Gross," Anz remarks, and looks away.

Thornton smiles. The noise is piercing. "C'mon, we'll go backstage."

"Sure," Anz mouths. He swings off the barstool accidentally elbowing a blonde to his left. "Sorry, miss." No response, she's into the grand finale. Anz isn't even there. She stares hungrily at big Billy. Anz shrugs and follows Thornton through the Q Club to Carol's dressing room.

"Well?" Thornton asked.

"It's insanity," Anz replied.

"Hardly! Wait till you see the reaction to the mud wrestling. This is child's play."

"Disgusting. Those women out there . . . jeez!"

"I don't understand why you're shocked."

"Because . . . it's dirty. Stuffing money in those goombahs' underwear . . . it's sick. If I ever caught my old lady in one of these joints!" Anz looked at Thornton with annoyance. "How can you let your daughter work here?" he said.

"It's show business," Thornton remarked.

"Bullshit! It's perversion. A sick turn-on," Anz said quickly. "No wonder she's getting those letters! Her buddy Diana the Chaste is probably sitting out there popping her cookies right now, huh?"

"Most likely," Thornton answered.

"Your daughter's asking for it. We told her not to perform. Can't you reason with her?"

"Occasionally. However, at fifteen hundred a week she's not about to call in sick."

"And if she gets killed—?"

"Tell Carol," Thornton replied.

"How do you expect us to protect her, if she won't cooperate? Is the money that important?" Thornton nodded. "That's senseless."

"Not if you're up to your neck in debt," Thornton said. "Besides she only has another night here, then she'll go to Reno for a few weeks."

"That solves the problem?" Anz snapped.

"Maybe? Maybe not?" Carol said sharply as she walked into her dressing room holding the new Plato.

Thornton forced a smile.

"Isn't this cozy," Carol remarked as she sat Plato in his high chair at the end of her makeup table. "The victim, the concerned father, and the protector," she sniped. "And of course, the victim's faithful companion . . . Plato. Arrest any speeders today, Detective?"

"Real funny, Miss Elliott," Anz shot back.

"One of my better ones," Carol replied as she began to apply some stage makeup to her face. She stared at Anz in the mirror. "Well? What's up, doc?"

"Carol, please . . ." Thornton begged.

She glared at Thornton.

"It's not amusing," he continued.

"No kidding!"

The screams from the main room filtered through the door as the boys' set ground to a finish. *Chick-a-boom,* and wildness. "We want more! We want more!" The *thump-thump* and "a-one, and a-two" of the trio blared over the yelling.

"I better get out there," Thornton told them. "Almost time to settle the buffalo."

"Terrific," Carol replied sarcastically. "When in doubt bail out."

Thornton set his jaw, and let the remark pass. "About ten minutes, Carol," he said firmly.

"Yeah," she replied.

"See you later, Detective."

"Sure," Anz replied. "Real fine."

Carol ignored Anz as she finished applying the final touches to her makeup. The *chick-a-boom* came to a halt. The screams of delight gave way to derision as Thornton appeared. *"Get off, you old creep!"* filtered into the room.

"He takes a lot of abuse," Anz noted.

"Sometimes he deserves it," Carol replied.

"Not in your case," he said.

"All right," Carol answered quickly. "Let's not get into Thornton. He's a marvelous father," she said sarcastically. "Does that make you happy?"

"You'd make me happier if you didn't go out there the rest of the week."

Carol placed Plato on her lap.

"Cute," Anz told her as Plato's eyes moved left, then right, then straight at him.

"Cute as a button with m'new pate, and m'new threads," Plato replied.

Anz smiled. "When in doubt pull the dummy out?" he asked Carol.

"That's par for the course," Plato told him. "Ya see, when the dummy's dummy gets a teeny bit cornered she hides behind l'il ole Plato." Carol swiveled Plato's head in a three-sixty. "Gets 'em all the time."

"Am I gonna talk to you, or Carol?"

"Don'tcha like me, big boy?" Plato replied.

"Suit yourself, " Anz told her.

Plato rolled his eyes.

"Sorry about that," Carol said softly. "It's force of habit. Force of bad habit." She put Plato back into his chair and straightened his collar.

"We spoke with your ex-husband, Miss Elliott."

"Oh?" Carol replied.

"We're not finished checking him out, but from all indications he's clean. Nothing seems to indicate that he's connected with your 'friend.' "

"I didn't think Murray was behind this."

"It's not a hundred percent sure, but—"

"He's not!" Carol insisted.

"But!" Anz repeated. "What about a friend, or a close associate? Someone he was involved with?"

"And he was involved with numerous people," Carol retorted. "However, none of his quick-ones seemed that quick, or that violent."

"He stepped out regularly?"

Carol laughed. "Yes, he 'stepped out' on a regular basis. Almost every time I was on the road, or went to the ladies' room. I'm amazed darling bastard Murray isn't dead from exhaustion."

"Ya ever catch him?"

"Yep," Carol replied softly. "Twice."

"Any names?"

"Darlene . . . Charlene? She was the one named in the divorce action. The other . . . well, it's tough to recognize anyone with the sheet pulled over them."

"What did Darlene, or whomever, look like?"

"A showgirl . . . a wind-up toy. All teeth and tits. Thornton'll give you the divorce papers. Her name's in them."

"The other one?" Carol looked away, and shook her head. "Did this woman give you any problems?"

"No," Carol replied. "Never heard from her."

"Calls?"

"No."

"Letters?"

"Oh, for Christ sake!" Carol snapped. "That idiot wouldn't come after me. Why? For what reason?"

"You caught her in the act. It's reason enough," he said. "It could be her . . . or someone else."

"Someone not directly involved with Murray," Carol answered. "A stranger . . . a kook . . ." The word dissolved into the Markham sisters smiling at her. Oh, Aggie isn't with it. You bet, sister Jo, 'cause she's in the time warp. Why don't you bring your little man for a reading? Mistresses Agnes and Josephine Markham request . . .

"Miss Elliott . . .?"

. . . the pleasure of your company. Papa Noir's violet eyes, and the miniature's blonde curls whirled. It's the most beautiful doll in the world, she told sister Jo in the future. Oh, she likes it, Aggie. I told you she'd like it. Papa Noir was smiling. The little ladies think you're someone very, very special, he told her in the past. I like that 'cause no one else thinks I'm special . . . special . . . special.

"Miss Elliott?" Anz repeated.

"Yes?" Carol said quickly.

"Your ex-husband mentioned a 'Celeste Citron.' "

"Never heard of her," Carol replied.

Anz watched her closely as he threw out a few other names, but none struck a chord. There was a long line of "someones" coupled with Murray Korn. The guy's a goddamn satyr, Anz thought. He pressed another "one" at Carol, seeing if she would react. Nothing. It doesn't add up, Anz told himself. She should've raised hell five minutes ago. Cool cookie. Something spinning in this broad's head.

"Ya think any one of those women would be jealous . . . envious enough to kill you?" he asked.

"Envious of me!" Carol lashed out. "Are you crazy? Who would want to be like *me?"*

Anz was stunned by the intensity of Carol's reaction.

"I'm nothing. I'm a near-forty foul-mouthed comedy act, with no future and stuck with it! You've got to be kidding. I hate *me.* I hate this frigging little dirty puppet that's the inner *me!"*

Anz stared at her intently.

"I don't blame Murray for jumping every sweetie pie he met. I sure as hell didn't make it in the sack. I don't make it anywhere! And they think I'm special? Oh, what bullshit . . . how blind can those broads be!"

"Which 'broads'?" Anz asked.

"None of your business," Carol snapped.

"It might help us."

"I'm a disgusting act. Like all of this . . . the go-go boys, the mud wrestlers. I belong right here pulling down a grand-plus a week. I give 'em just what they want . . . smut. And *they love it!* I'm not special. Who would want to kill me? Well, after myself . . . probably anyone that's ever seen me."

Carol pulled Plato out of his chair, and opened the door to the backstage. Thornton's schtick echoed through the curtains. Carol stared at Anz. "Come on, Detective, watch us from the wings. Tonight I'm gonna really be at my best. I'm gonna kill 'em, then myself, if you don't want to do it first."

Thornton's introduction bellowed from the front of the stage. It was showtime.

The one, the only Carol Elliott and Plato stepped into the spotlight and started "the killing."

Anz recoiled at her story about the lesbian and the three sailors.

Thornton winced. It was one of her worst.

Shock! Shock! At first the not-so-lovely lovelies played it cool. So what's new at the office? Didja hear that one? Listen, Selma, Oh yeah, crude Carol and putrid Plato were slaying them in ultrablue.

Anz wanted to rush onto the stage and slap her. Barracks talk. Filth. Get off, lady, get off. No way, fella, 'cause the public loves 'em dirty. Why hell's bells, Scarlett, it's a new era . . . a new all-time low for civilization.

Thornton smiled at Anz weakly, then made a fast exit. The worst wasn't over as Carol rubbed their noses in it with the priest gag, the Polish wedding-night saga, and more. Get off, lady, Anz begged.

Carol turned her head and smiled at Anz.

"How'm I doing, fella?" she yelled.

He looked away, and she attacked the audience again. Instead of being repulsed, they responded. Instead of walking out, they encouraged her.

"She's out of control," Anz muttered.

"Who cares?" replied the stage manager, and kept chewing on his cigar. "She's got 'em laughing!"

"And now . . . for my finale!" Carol exclaimed. "My able assistant Mr. Plato and I will do our not-very-world-famous mind-reading act."

"That's if anybody out there's got one," Plato quipped.

"Are you ready, troops?" They were. "Let me concentrate."

"That's what he always tells ya. Concentrate, and don't eat apples while we're in the act," Plato said.

"No, no . . . while we're *'doing* the act,' " Carol corrected.

Plato rolled his eyes. "It sure is an 'act' when you're doing it." Three-sixty headspin. Howls.

"Cool it, pine-pecker." Howls. Plato stares at his pants, then rolls his eyes. Howls. "I want you to close your eyes. . . ."

"Ya won't touch it, will ya?"

"No . . . touch it? Talk about a bump on a log." Howls. "Close your eyes." He did. "We're gonna do some mind reading." He opens one eye, and she shuts it.

"Oh *my!* Oh *golly!*," Plato shouts. "Listen, lady, if you want to do it with me . . . you are real-ly in trouble." Plato stares at a fatty, who puts her head down. Oh, for heaven's sake, Alice, I didn't think of *that*. Giggle, giggle.

"Can we continue?" Carol asked.

"I'm closing my eyes," Plato said slowly.

"I wish it was your mouth," Carol retorted. Guffaw. Guffaw. "I need the cooperation of this large and intelligent audience," Carol requested.

Plato guffawed, and Carol slapped her hand over his mouth. Another eye roll, and a nod.

"I want all the ladies to close their eyes."

"While I unbutton their blouses," Plato added.

"Slow down hickory-humper." Carol closed her eyes and pretended to mediate.

"Whadya see?" Plato whispered.

"A bonfire with you as the feature attraction."

"Shut my mouth." He did.

"I'm going into my trance . . . I see a pair of lace bikini underpants . . ."

"Okay!" Plato screamed.

"And a black brassiere . . ."

"Yes, ma'am!" Plato said enthusiastically.

". . . a sheer black bra!" Carol added.

"Love it!" Plato panted.

"A black garter belt!"

"Whip me! Whip me!" Plato groaned.

Carol paused before throwing the punch line.

"Well?" Plato asked.

She kept her eyes shut tightly.

"We're waiting," Plato whispered.

"Someone's dressed as a woman," Carol stammered. "It's not a gag. I really mean it," she said seriously.

The audience shifted nervously. Titter, titter, smile, shrug. What a downer, Helen.

Carol stared at each table. "I saw you . . . I saw you," she said slowly.

Not a laugh in the house.

"Hey, Thornton," the stage manager called. 'C'mere, she's flipping out."

"It's not funny . . . where are you?" Carol called. She shielded her eyes from the spotlights and peered into the crowd. "Diana . . .?" she asked.

"Yes-s-s-s-s," came back in a mocking falsetto.

The audience loved it. She's a creepo, Helen.

"No. No. It's not funny," Carol said.

"Oh, yes it is-s-s-s," replied the heckler.

More howls. Carol tried to see her tormentor.

"Get her off," Anz yelled at Thornton.

"We want the mud, not the dud," begged the falsetto heckler.

"Right on," echoed the crowd. And the chant of "mud, mud, mud" grew.

"Damnit, get her out of there," Anz insisted.

"Yes . . . of course," Thornton replied, but couldn't move. Anz pushed past him, walked onto the stage, and took Carol by the arm. She immediately pulled away.

"Diana's here," she told him.

He grabbed her arm. "C'mon, Carol," Anz insisted.

She struggled, but he tightened his grip.

"She's here. . . .!" Carol screamed. "Let go of me." Carol pointed at a heavy-set blonde sitting at the bar. "You're Diana, aren't you?"

Carol tried to wrench herself free, but Anz began pulling her offstage.

"Where are you going?" Carol shrieked as the woman ran into the lobby and out of sight. Carol tore away from Anz and ran through the audience.

Jeez, Helen, this is really far-out.

"Get the frigging boys on!" yelled the manager. "Get out there, Thornton . . . goddamnit, where the hell are those fags? *Latino? Billy?*"

Chick-a-boom. Chick-a-boom.

Carol shoved a waitress aside, and ran after the blonde. Anz pawed his way through the main room.

"Carol! Come back!" he called.

"Diana? Diana?" Carol screamed. She burst through the front door, and ran into the street, but

it was deserted. "Where are you. . . . ?" Carol sobbed. "What do you want from me. . . . ?" She leaned against a parked car and began to sob hysterically.

Chick-a-boom. Chick-a-boom.

Jeez, Helen, has she got problems!

Who cares! Here comes Latino. Gimme a dollar.

Chapter Ten

To the uniformed nanny pushing her carriage toward Central Park the building appeared as one more faceless nonlandmark between Lexington and Park Avenues. How could she, or anyone else, know that the insipid facade masked another rich man's madhouse? Or that the polished brass plate to the right of the front door merely engraved RESIDENT HOME was a euphemism to ease the consciences of the donating family, or husband, or grandchildren. It was easier to say, and of course accept, that dear Harold was "resting." The middle class would impolitely refer to it as being "away." And the poor? Who cares! Ah, here comes Doctor. Do try to be civil, Lawrence, he's a friend of Morgan Benedict.

Little could the nanny imagine that her baby's tears were matched by the residents of Resident Home, and its latest guest, Miss Carol Elliott sans dummy, who occupied one of the "cheap" rooms on the fifth floor. Despite overlooking the airshaft, 509 had all the conveniences of the luxury suites facing the street: same tile flooring, same private bathroom without mirror, and same set of leather restraints. In spite of the disparity in price range Resident Home was definitely egalitarian. However, this was small consolation for Thornton Evans when Carol was subdued by a pair of "hosts" and led away.

Carol barely finished screaming, "Get me out of here!" when the effects of the injection made her eyes swirl and she toppled into a bottomless sleep.

Fragments of Murray, sister Aggie, and Plato exploded in and out of Carol's dreams. Now the noise and emcee at the Laff Club: ". . . and now directly from Vegas, Miss Carol Lane and Plato . . ." Roar! Roar! ". . . now the best in blue . . .!" *Smut. Filth. Kill her.* ". . . and here she is, the gal with the garbage . . ." *Murray, why did you do it?* "Gee, babe, can you do a third week in Reno?" *I'm tired. I want to come home.* ". . . now a special attraction. Diana the Chaste will perform a double-boob twist . . ."

"No!" Carol screamed. She tried to sit up, but the arm restraints held her against the mattress.

Carol fought wildly.

Ping. Ping. Ping. Red lights, and alarms.

"Attendants to room five-oh-nine please."

Carol turned her wrists frantically, tearing the skin. She tried to kick her legs but they were firmly strapped to the bed. She wrenched her body from side to side.

Ping. Ping. Ping.

The white nurse and the black orderly rushed the reddened queen, and sedated her again. Carol's body convulsed against the world, then sank into the bed.

When she opened her eyes several hours later the white nurse was sitting at the foot of her bed.

"Good afternoon, Miss Elliott."

Carol shut her eyes, and turned her head to the wall. It's not a dream, babe. You really did it to yourself this time. She raised her hands slightly. Gotcha trussed up like a turkey, m'gal.

"Would you like to sit up?" the nurse asked.

Carol nodded, and she was unbuckled.

"Sit up slowly, dear."

Gotta say, "Simon says." Not funny, eh, Doc!

"Would you care to freshen up?"

Carol nodded, and the nurse helped her off the bed.

"Sorry, dear, let's keep the bathroom door open. You don't mind, do you? It's a silly rule, but—"

Sure thing, nursie. Never can trust a looney in the bathroom.

Carol splashed water on her face and stared at the empty wall in front of her as she dried herself.

"No mirror?"

The nurse smiled. "Not yet," she replied.

"I'm still dangerous?" Carol asked.

Another sickly smile.

"Just where the hell am I?" Carol demanded.

"A resident home," the nurse answered.

"I was sure this wasn't the Plaza," Carol retorted.

"And your father's been downstairs since this morning . . . early this morning."

Carol rubbed her wrists and nodded. "Super. Now, if you'll gimme my clothes I'll see ya around."

The nurse moved between Carol and the door.

"Mr. Evans would like to see you."

"I would like to get the hell out of here," Carol mimicked. "And I'll 'visit' with dear old dad later."

"We wouldn't want another scene, would we?" the nurse insisted.

"Listen, honey," Carol said wearily. "Let's not go ten rounds. I want out. I like you, but I hate places like this. I'm not crazy, nor have I ever been crazy."

Carol stepped toward the door and the nurse leaned against it. "No one thinks you're insane, Miss Elliott."

"Oh brother!" Carol moaned. "Then what am I doing here . . . why was I strapped to the sack?"

"You weren't acting yourself," she explained.

Carol walked toward her bed and sat on the edge. "That's beautiful! I've heard bullshit, but that is the best! What do you people call insanity? Exhaustion?"

"It *is* a form of exhaustion."

Carol smiled broadly. "I love it!"

"Why don't you have some lunch with your father in the guest dining room?" the nurse suggested.

"Like this?" Carol replied. "It ain't m'size and the back's a little drafty."

"I'll get you a robe. Pink, or aqua?"

"Your choice, Florence," Carol replied.

Instead of shrieking at Thornton for locking her up in a booby hatch, Carol was furious about the expense, and lit into him right after their food was served.

"How can you be so dumb?" she asked. "We . . . I can't afford this place! I don't even have insurance! This is really one of your stupidest ideas!"

Thornton took the abuse quietly, and kept eating his chicken salad.

"Are you listening to me?" Carol growled.

"Not at all," he replied.

"I'm checking myself out of this hotel."

"And I'll put you right back in here," he answered without missing a bite.

"Damnit, Thornton," Carol hissed. "You have no right."

"Smile," he said casually, "or the two beefy waiters will escort you back to your quarters."

Carol churned inwardly and plastered her best phony smile across her face. "Thornton, you can't keep me here," she said lightly.

"But I can," he replied.

"I'm over twenty-one," she sang, and nodded politely at the attendants cum waiters.

"How well I know, my angel, but you're not in control of your 'faculties.' Therefore, I've taken it upon myself to 'temporarily' admit you to this 'residence.' " Thornton smiled at her. "Marvelous salad, isn't it?"

"I hope you choke on it," Carol sneered.

It was enough to pierce his bravery and Thornton began to cry. Not an attention-getting sob, but a slow, constant flow of tears that he daubed with his napkin. To the uncaring attendant/waiters it was merely an old man wiping his lips. Thornton was good at hiding things: coins in a palm, a pea in a shell, a series of hate letters, and most of all his own anxieties.

"Oh, Thornton, don't," Carol begged.

"I'm sorry," he whispered. "I thought . . . I wanted to do the right thing, but I guess. . . .well, I'm not one for making a situation better."

Carol put her hand on his arm.

"I didn't know what else to do," he continued.

Carol, you're a bitch, she thought.

"I was scared," he told her.

Thornton, Thornton, Thornton. I'm sorry. Tell him, she ordered herself. Tell him, you love him. Carol leaned her head on his shoulder.

"What do you want me to do?" Carol said hoarsely.

"Be safe," he answered. "Just be safe."

Monday night's explosion at the Q Club dissolved into Tuesday's tears, which faded into Wednesday's group session with several of the other "residents." It wasn't a bad "group," Carol thought. An ex-Major League shortstop, who was chronically depressed; an alcoholic wife of a bank president; a socialite, who thought stealing from department stores was "acceptable"; and a heavy-set woman in her early twenties, who wanted to be loved. Well, don't we all, honey, shouted the socialite.

Yes, it was a star-studded cast. However, first names only please. Of course, he or she never, and I repeat "never" was here. You bet, babe, and neither was I. Smile, smile. When's the reunion of those who were "never" here? Carol, she admonished herself, don't be so smart. You ain't in this here building for laughs.

Tap, tap, tap. Class come to order.

Oh Thornton, I'm only doing this for you.

"We have a new member," Dr. Pat Welch advised the group. "Everybody . . . this is Carol."

Smile, babe, you're on. Oh, my God, my hands are frozen. Keep smiling. Try to act normal. That's a laugh.

"Didn't I meet you . . .?" asked the socialite.

"I . . . I don't think so," Carol replied nervously.

"She thinks she's met everybody," groused the heavy-set girl. "She's like that, y'know."

Right, babe. Watch the fat one; she looks dangerous. Oh, Thornton, I'm suffering here 'cause I love you.

"However, Carol won't participate today," Dr. Welch advised the others.

Thank God for small favors, Carol prayed.

"Why not?" demanded the banker's wife.

"Oh, shut up, Hilly!" the ballplayer grumbled.

Yes, Hilly, shut up, and be a nice lush.

Tap, tap. Now, class let's not have any of this . . . we have work to do.

"Why don't you tell us about your feelings, Hilly?" Dr. Welch asked. "Let go of your hostility . . . rage, Hilly, rage."

Oh brother, what bullshit, Carol thought.

Thornton darling, get me out of here.

Welch turned to Carol and winked. "Group dynamics," he told her. "I'll explain it to you later."

Yeah, that would be super. Take a number. Be a patient.

Thornton, I'm trying. I'm really trying.

The group session was almost two hours of anger, friction, painful memories, and uneasy silences. Carol masked her nervousness with a sympathetic look. I'm not like these people, she repeated again and again. I'm sick, and I don't want to be sick. Keep smiling, babe, it's gotta end soon.

Angeline, the fat girl, brought it to a screeching halt with a verbal attack on her mother.

Gotta blame someone, Carol reasoned.

"Good, Angeline, Good," Welch affirmed. "Get it out." She did. They listened. Welch checked his watch. Sorry, sickos, time's up. Gotta run. Same time tomorrow, gang.

Pat Welch took Carol by the arm and bustled down the hall to his office.

Chatter, chatter. Come this way.

"How did you like the session? Nice people, aren't they? A lot of progress being made, yes indeed, a lot of good vibes there. Intimate groups are so positive, don't you think? What did you think? Difficult at first. It's tough to open up, isn't it?"

Carol held his tape recorder and notebook while he unlocked the door to his office.

"Well," he sighed, "now we have a chance to be alone." Carol hesitated. "Come in, come in . . . let's kick back and close the rest of the world out."

As Carol sat in the leather chair in front of his desk Welch locked the door behind her. He tossed the keys to Carol.

"Just unlock it any time you want to split."

Get me out of here. She put the keys on the edge of his desk. Smile, relax, and try not to be a wise-ass.

Welch placed his tape recorder on the bookshelf behind his chair, and depressed the "record" button without Carol knowing it. "I feel great today," he told her. "How about you?" he asked. Carol nodded stiffly. "Want some coffee?" he said brightly.

"No thanks," Carol replied softly.

"I thought show-biz people lived on the stuff!"

Carol smiled. "Always an exception to the rule."

"Have you always been an exception?" Welch shot back seriously.

The intensity of his tone caught Carol off-guard. "Meaning what?" she asked. "In the business? As a person?"

"You tell me," he said.

Watch him, babe, he's a sly fox. Think before you put both of 'em in your mouth.

"I would guess female comedians are 'exceptions.' "

Welch nodded. "How about Carol Elliott as a human, as a person?" Well, of course you're different, right Carol? That was really an obvious answer." Watch him. He's going for the jugular vein. "How do you see yourself?" he asked. "What does the inner Carol say about the public Carol?"

"Not too much."

Welch shrugged. "Meaning—?"

"It's an act. A put-on. The public image is an illusion. I'm no different than anybody else. A businessman is as much an actor as . . . an actor," Carol answered.

"Damn, that's incisive," Welch replied. "If you can see that . . . well, hell, we're all two or more people, aren't we?"

Score one for the not-so-dumb, ratty-looking blonde in the nuthouse. Carol smiled.

"If you had the chance to be someone else, who would you be?" he asked.

"Alpha Betty," Carol said immediately. Welch cocked his head. "She was a puppet I made . . . in another life."

"Why did you pick her?"

"She worked clean," Carol replied. "And everybody liked her."

"That's important to you, isn't it?" Carol looked puzzled. "Being liked . . . having approval." Welch smiled. "We call it 'validation,' " he said casually.

"Something like getting your emotions stamped?"

Welch nodded approval. "That's good. I'll use it at the staff meeting." He wrote the quip in his notebook. "What about Plato, don't you like him?" he asked without looking up.

"Plato's part of the act," Carol replied.

"You didn't answer my question!" Welch snapped.

"Of course I like Plato," Carol answered sharply.

"It doesn't sound like it."

"Do you want it in writing?"

"Plato and Alpha Betty are caught in a fire. Only one can be saved! Whom would you rescue?" he asked.

"That's stupid!" Carol shot back.

"Which puppet?" Welch insisted.

"I couldn't make the choice."

"Then you'd let both of them be destroyed?"

Carol shook her head. "No . . . Plato."

"Saved?" he asked.

Carol hesitated. "Burned," she whispered.

"You hate him that much?" Welch replied.

"I don't hate anybody!" Carol shot back. "Besides, it's only a game!"

"Was it a game when you tried to smother him?"

Carol glared at him. "Who told you that?"

"Does it matter?"

"I asked you a question, Doctor," Carol snapped.

"Were you this angry when you tried to kill your puppet?"

"I was overreacting," Carol insisted. "I was tired . . . a lot of garbage was layed on me. I had nobody else to talk to . . . everybody was dumping on me!"

"Including Plato?" Welch asked.

"Yes! Especially Plato!" Carol seethed. "Does that make you happy? I wanted to kill him, okay? Satisfied?"

"Are you?" Welch asked softly.

"Why are you screwing me up?" Carol screamed. "I don't need this shit! I don't like it! I want to get finished with everybody! Murray! Some frigging Diana! Plato, if it makes you happy . . . I hate it! I hate my life. I didn't ask for *any of this!"* Carol clenched the arms of her chair and rocked back and forth mechanically.

Asshole, schmuck, Carol thought. Easy, babe, easy. The hell with 'em. Idiot shrink. Count to ten, and then again. Treats me like a mental patient. Let's see how he'd handle this crap. Slowdown, kick back, cool it. Fat-faced freak sitting there like a frigging idiot. That's his thing. Whadda ya want? I want him to take a hike. Tuck-in, babe, play it safe. Schmuck! Ease back. Take a deep breath. Give 'em what he wants and get the hell out of there. Got it? Yeah, got it. Hit your mark. Ready? Chins up, honey. Thanks, babe. Lights. Camera, and . . . action!

"I'm sorry," Carol whispered. "I tried to handle it, but . . . I guess I can't."

Welch nodded. "I'm glad you trusted me."

"How?"

"By showing me the real Carol Elliott."

Oh brother, get me out of here. No, no! Smile and . . . action. "I've been very confused lately."

"I can imagine," Welch replied. "The accident didn't help matters either."

"No," Carol replied tearfully. What a ham! "I . . . I was terrified. The sound of the crash, the smell of burning rubber—"

"Oh, turn it off!" Welch bellowed. "You must

think I'm a fool. Stop the theater, your acting is pitiful."

Carol clenched her jaw.

"Carol, don't try to con me. Don't blow smoke," he told her ". . . burning rubber," he mimicked.

"Shut up!" Carol said quickly.

"That's better," Welch answered. "Get it out. Get finished with it. Tell me how you hate Carol Elliott. Tell me how much you detest Plato. C'mon. *C'mon!*"

"Okay! I hate him. He's a coarse foul-mouth—"

"You hate him enough to kill him?" Welch asked.

"Him? I hate me, Doctor. I hate being a smutty, disgusting woman. You know what my act's like?" Welch shook his head. "I tell filthy, disgusting jokes I say "fuck." I shock the audience. And sometimes I stand out there watching myself telling these horrible stories, and trading smut with the smutty audience . . . and I want to kill me!"

"And Plato?" Welch asked.

"Yeah! *And Plato!* I felt great when that little shit was strewn over the floor. I was glad I smashed him."

"But he came back," Welch replied.

"He had to . . . he's the meal ticket. The whole act . . . I'm just scenery. Y'know it didn't surprise me when he started to talk." Welch leaned forward. "I'm sure Thornton told you the whole story." Welch nodded. "You give something life, and it has 'life.' "

"Are you saying Plato is alive?"

"No," Carol answered sharply. "But after the accident . . . he was different . . . I could control him, and I couldn't."

"Almost like a dual personality?" Welch asked.

"Something like that."

"And it frightened you?"

Carol nodded. "Plato said it wasn't an accident." Welch studied her intently. "Then he kept repeating 'man, woman, man, woman' . . . words to that effect. At first I thought it was me . . . talking to myself, but it honestly was Plato."

"And his eyes moved?"

Carol nodded. "They did."

"Would you kill him now?" he asked.

"No," she murmured. "I want to kill me."

"Wouldn't that destroy Plato too?"

"No. He'd survive. I'd give him to the sisters."

Welch frowned. "Nuns?"

"No," Carol replied softly. "The doll ladies."

Welch eased himself back in his chair. "Doll ladies? Would you like to tell me about them?"

"Nothing to tell. I meet them once, and they asked us to tea. They wanted me to bring Plato." Don't tell him, Carol warned herself. Describe l'il Aggie and back to the shackles you go, babe. What about Papa purple-peepers? That would really blow his mind. Tuck in. Oh yes, dear God, I want to tuck in, and rest. Get me back to my room, and I'll be your dummy's dummy forever.

"Are you acting now?" Welch asked.

Carol looked at him intently, then smiled. "Doll ladies? Another Carol Elliott joke. Sorry, Doc."

"I almost believed you," he replied. "One last question." Yippee, thank you, Lord. "About Diana?" Carol froze. "Dear slut/bitch . . ." The smell of the burning rubber. "Man, woman, man, woman . . ."

"Yes?" Carol said nervously.

"What does she look like?"

She's out there. Hey, where ya going, lady? Follow her, babe, that's Diana. *Let go of me!* "Dear Slut." That's her, Thornton! Rush into the lobby. *Gone.* Run into the street. *Gone.* It's her!

Chick-a-boom.

Oh God, it was her!

Come on, Carol. Come inside.
Keep your rotten paws off me, Anz.
Let's not have a scene.
Chick-a-boom.

"What does she look like?" Welch repeated.

Carol stared him blankly. "Oh . . . she's blonde. A bleached blonde," she said mechanically.

"Your hair color?"

Carol nodded. "Yeah. Same color. Y'know, she's hard-looking . . . brassy. Yeah, brassy. Not a helluva lady. A little stocky too." Carol looked away. "She was at the club . . . at the bar . . . just eyeballing me the whole time."

"Did your father see her?"

Carol shook her head. "No. She took off as soon as I stopped the act. I would have caught her, but that damn detective. Aw, what the hell."

"Did Anz see her?"

"No," Carol said quickly. "Only me."

Welch thought for a moment. "Why do you think this woman's after you?"

"She's crazy, what else?" Carol replied.

Welch nodded. "Agreed, she's disturbed, but why has she singled *you* out?"

Carol shrugged. What the hell is he getting to? she thought. She's a nut. A kook. Oh shit, the tea party.

"What day is this?" she asked nervously.

"Wednesday," Welch answered.

Carol was relieved. "Could I go home tomorrow? Just to get some clothes, and my cosmetics?"

"We can get them for you," he replied.

Trouble, babe, they've thrown away the key. Be smart, be good. Play this dude for the open door.

"Right," Carol answered sincerely. "I can give someone a list . . . it'll be much easier that way." She smiled, and shifted gears. "What was the question? Oh yes, why am I target for tonight?" Welch nodded. "She has a deep-seated hatred for me, or women like me. Would that be fair assessment?"

"Indeed," Welch replied. "What do you think the threat about cutting off your breasts means?"

Metallic taste. Nausea, fear. She means it, babe. Who writes a dozen-plus letters for laughs? She's out there. Carol watched the heavy-set blonde move away from the bar, and into the lobby. Anz was holding her back.

"I don't know," Carol said nervously.

"Symbolism, Carol. It's very obvious that this woman wants to destroy you . . . you, Carol, as a female. What could be clearer?"

Sure! Right, Dr. Freud. My tits in her pocket are symbols. Oh, Thornton, get me outta here.

"Do you honestly believe Diana wants to cut off your breasts?" Welch asked.

Carol shrugged. "Of course."

"I don't agree. I think her threat is symbolic. She, that is, Diana . . . wants to destroy the feminine Carol Elliott. Additionally, she vows . . ." Welch opened a file marked ELLIOTT, CAROL and looked at a copy of a letter.

"Ah, yes . . . 'I will slit your breasts from your filth-laden body and stuff them in your vile mouth.' The same statement is repeated in all of the correspondence."

Nice reading, Doc. Glad you reminded me of the whole affair. Carol gripped the arms of her chair. Hold on, babe, this was supposed to be the last question.

"It seems Diana is telling us two things . . . first, she detests Carol Elliott as a woman and—"

"First!" Carol yelled, "she's going to kill me . . . and after that I don't care."

"Who said she wants to kill you?" Welch asked.

"Are you kidding?" Carol snapped.

Welch shook his head. "Diana never threatened to kill you."

"Oh? Those are love letters?" Carol replied.

"Let's analyze the intentions of the threat versus the breast-and-mouth metaphor."

"Don't talk in frigging riddles!" Carol said with annoyance. "A psycho broad wants to kill me and you're searching for deep meaning! For allegory!"

Welch pushed a copy of the letter toward her.

"This isn't a death threat," he said.

"Jesus! She sends me 'love letters' . . . a bra without cups, leaves a message with my service . . . and tried to kill me with her car! What the hell do you call that? Fantasy?"

"Interesting word," Welch said quietly.

"Oh please, this discussion is getting us nowhere. What do I have to do? Bring her here myself?"

Welch sat back, and thought.

"Leaving the symbolism aside for a moment," he reflected, "who consistently wants Carol Elliott dead?"

Thornton, why did stick me here? Carol asked herself. Be smart, be cool, and get out of there.

"I don't know," Carol answered.

Welch smiled. "Isn't it true you've constantly wanted to kill yourself?"

Carol looked away in disgust.

"This is really getting too heavy," she muttered.

"Isn't it a fact you tried to 'murder' Plato?" he asked.

"C'mon! He's a dummy. I told you . . . a lot of shit was coming down . . . and I took it out on Plato," Carol replied.

"And symbolically isn't he your alter ego?"

"Oh brother, this is too frigging much," she answered.

"But didn't you just tell me, er . . . I want to kill me'?" Welch asked.

"That's talk . . . everybody says that . . . or something like it. Yeah, yeah . . . 'I could kill myself,' but you don't. It's talk . . . meaningless dribble."

"Unless you really hate yourself. Wouldn't you like to destroy the foul-mouthed Carol? The brassy, smutty woman who tells dirty stories?" Welch asked.

"It's not me *up there,*" Carol snarled. "The real Carol isn't on stage."

"And you hate the stage Carol, right? You detest the vulgarity, don't you?" Carol nodded. "You'd like to be like Alpha Betty. She was nice . . . she worked 'clean.' She was respected."

"Get to the punch line, Dr. Welch."

"Who's Diana the Chaste?" he asked.

"I don't know," Carol replied.

"All right, let me ask you this. Why didn't Anz see her at the Q Club? Or in the street?"

Carol shrugged. "She ran away."

"Only you saw her, correct?"

"The bartender saw her," Carol replied.

"Possibly."

"What do mean 'possibly'? I know him. I'll ask him. Better yet, I'll have him give Anz a statement."

Welch shuffled more papers in Carol's file, and finally picked one up. "It seems Detective Anz has already. . . . Your bartender friend doesn't remember anyone blonde and heavy-set that night."

Carol shook her head in disbelief.

"Do you honestly believe she *was* Diana?"

"Yes," Carol muttered.

"And the same person who caused your accident?"

Carol nodded. "That's right."

"Why hasn't she killed you?" he asked.

"I don't know," Carol murmured. "She wants to punish me . . . make me suffer."

"Why?" Welch demanded.

"How should I know!" Carol snapped. "She's crazy . . . a sicko, yeah, she's sick and crazy."

"Don't they mean the same thing?" Welch questioned.

"Turn it off!" Carol yelled. "She was there!"

"But no one saw her."

"Do you believe I'm making this up?" Carol replied. "That I'm imagining everything?"

"Are you?" Welch answered.

Chapter Eleven

"*Are you serious?*" Carol shouted. "Do you honestly think . . . I've imagined this freaky broad?"

Welch shrugged. "Maybe," he replied.

"That's wild!" Carol answered. "Why? Why would I want to send threats to myself?"

"You've admitted you don't like yourself. The 'public' image . . . wasn't that the term."

"Y'know, you've been in this business too long, Doc. I think it's getting to you," Carol shot back. "Why would I send myself a cutout bra? Or leave a message with the service?"

"Dual personality," Welch suggested.

"Oh jeez!" Carol exclaimed. "I may talk to Plato, and myself, but that's as far as goes. I don't have three faces, or five alter egos."

"Are you sure?" Welch asked.

"Damn straight," Carol answered, "because I'd revert to someone else instead of this current, and all-too-painful, persona."

"Alpha Betty?" Welch remarked.

"No, babe, not her. Alpha Betty's mommy. The pure and unadulterated Carol Elliott—pre-Murray, pre-Plato."

"Maybe we'll see her yet," Welch replied.

Carol snorted disgustedly. "C'mon, Doc, I'm not

a chameleon. What you see, on the surface at least, is all there is, and there ain't no more."

"Maybe," he said quietly.

"You're big on 'maybe,' huh? I bet you'd love it if I had a split personality. I could stay in this bug house forever, huh? Free room and board, right?"

"You're wrong," Welch answered.

"Then why don't you accept Diana as reality?" Carol answered. "As a full-fledged kook who's on my case."

"I never discounted her," he said.

"Jesus!" Carol growled. "You talk in riddles. If she's real . . . meaning not me, why did we go through this little exercise?"

"I didn't say she was 'real' in that sense . . ."

"Terrific!" Carol replied. "It's all semantics, isn't it? All interpretation, huh?" Carol shook her head. "Is this session finished?"

"If you think it is," Welch answered.

"I can walk out of that door anytime?" Welch nodded. "How about this four-star asylum?"

"Not quite," Welch answered.

"Then I'm an inmate?"

"No . . . a guest."

"Super," Carol quipped. "How about my bill, and I'll see ya around?"

"You're a restricted guest," Welch countered.

"It figures. How do I reach the unrestricted list?" Carol asked.

"By cooperating with the staff, and progressing through certain phases of low-level therapy."

"Un-huh!" Carol replied. "To get along, little doggy, you gotta sit up and do talk, right?"

"This isn't a game, Carol," Welch replied seriously. "You need support. You need a structured environment. . . ."

And I *need* to get out of here, Carol thought.

Welch's reasoning spun away and Plato's voice echoed through her consciousness.

Play it slow. Make him a believer.

Right.

Give 'em a command performance, and split.

Right.

Let the tears and sob stories flow.

Right.

Make it high drama, and so long suckers.

Right.

Hit your mark. Look into the lens, and *action.*

"Carol . . . Carol," Welch asked cautiously, "who were you talking to . . .?" She looked away. "Was it Plato?" She shook her head. "Were you talking with someone else?"

"No," Carol groaned. "It *was* Plato, does that satisfy you?"

"Would you like to share the conversation?"

Carol agonized momentarily. Lovely, babe, Plato whispered. Pure theater. Hepburn couldn't have done it better.

"I was thinking . . . no, Plato suggested that I should stay here . . . for a while."

"Which Plato told you that?" Carol looked at Welch with surprise. "The Plato that's your alter ego, or the independent Plato?"

"Meaning . . . ?" Carol replied.

"You tell me," Welch answered.

"There's only one," Carol said nervously.

"Not according to . . ." he thumbed through a file for a moment ". . . a Dr. Evan Stampler. He said you told him—"

"I know what I told him!" Carol snapped. "I was out of control."

"Does that included trying to 'kill' Plato?" Welch asked.

"Oh come on!" Carol whined. "Everybody's blowing this out of proportion. So I beat on the dummy

. . . for God's sake, there was no one else. I went a little haywire, but that's over . . . *finished* . . . *gone!*"

"And what about your conversation with Thornton? Didn't you tell him Plato rolled his eyes, and said, 'It wasn't an accident' and something like 'man, woman.' "

"It was in my head, got it? The damn puppet can't talk, got it? I thought it spoke to me. I was wrong. I thought it moved its eyes. It didn't. I was screwed-up from the car wreck. Can you believe that, Doc?"

"For now," Welch replied.

"That's damn nice of you," Carol sniped. "I've always talked with Plato . . . better him than all those creeps in the club, or the losers in Vegas."

"Oh? Has this been constant, or a recent development?" Welch asked.

"Recent," she said softly.

"Weeks? Months?" Welch probed.

"Do we have to get into this?"

"Why do you want to avoid it?"

Carol laughed softly. "There's no winning with you, is there? A question countered by a question. Oh well," she sighed, "it was before my divorce."

"Murray Korn?" Welch remarked.

"You do your homework, Doctor. Yes, the infamous louse, and manager . . . Murray Korn," Carol said.

"Did Plato . . . the controlled Plato, ever talk to him?"

"Only when I couldn't face him," Carol replied. "It was an off-and-on situation."

"Meaning it got worse as your relationship deteriorated." Carol nodded. "Was there any point when you shut Murray out completely?"

Carol shrugged. "Probably after I found . . . well, my ex-husband liked to share his body . . .

with anything that was under twenty-five and breathing."

"That must have been difficult to cope with."

"Not for Murray," Carol replied. "It was a nice game . . . he booked me on the road, collected the performance fees, and spent my money on the lay-of-the-week. Y'know, I'd like to kill that bastard!" Hey, cool it, babe, you don't have to feed him all that. I gotta tell the truth. What's the big deal? We've talked about knocking off Murray before!

"An understandable emotion under the circumstances," Welch replied. "Does Plato want to kill him too?"

"It's not Plato's decision," Carol answered. "Besides . . . no matter how much I hate my ex . . . I could never murder him . . . or any of his Miss Quick-ones." Whadda ya mean *'not my decision'?* Jeez, babe, we've planned knocking off old Murray dozens of times. I can't tell the shrink that one! Well, tell him something else and let's blow this joint.

"You were talking with him, again, weren't you?" Welch asked. Carol nodded. "And this is very common, isn't it?" Carol nodded once more. "Would you say it was a constant habit?"

"Yes," Carol murmured. *Why did you say that?* Isn't it? *Yeah, But—!* 'But' nothing. Whatta ya screaming about? *Oh, the hell with it! Get finished.*

"Carol?" Welch questioned. "Are you talking to Plato again?"

"Yes," she answered dryly. "We're arguing. He's angry that I told you about . . . well, that we're always talking to each other." *Bitch! You shouldn't have done that.*

"Can I talk to him?"

"No. Only when I have him . . . hold him. That's the only time he responds to other people," Carol replied.

"I understand," Welch remarked. "Would you like us to bring him here?"

"If you want," Carol muttered. "I don't care." *Are you kidding?* Of course I am, dummy. This whole scene is a gag. *Holy jeez, and I fell for it. Con brio,* babe. It's not what ya say . . . it's the way ya sez it . . . with feeling. *Out of sight!* Stick around, we're going for the big jail break. *All right-t-t!* Remember m'boy, we have a date with two ladies. Yes sir, sister Jo is just your height.

"Are you still arguing?" Welch prodded.

"No," Carol replied. "I was thinking . . . that I'm really a case. Jesus, I didn't want it this way. I didn't want the damn act, or Murray, or even this frigging Diana character. It's the worst."

"Undoubtedly," Welch mumbled.

"I don't understand where I'm going," Carol replied. "I don't know what anything means . . . today, even yesterday. I'm falling down a tube and I can't stop."

Welh folded his hands and sat back. "We're going to help you 'stop,' " he replied.

Carol looked away, and shook her head.

"I hope so," she answered, "because I'm so damn tired of all of them . . . Plato, Murray, the lawyers. I'd like to sleep them away . . . wake up and start all over. Clean slate . . ." her voice trailed off. "Start all over again with Alpha Betty . . ." *Oh man, you are too much.* Be quiet! I don't want you to open that trap again. *And the winner in Hollywood is . . . !* Shut up! We're getting out of here.

Pat Welch moved from behind his desk, and stood in front of Carol.

"I think we've done enough for the day," he told her. "As a matter of fact . . . well, I'd prefer we met in private for the next few weeks . . ."

Weeks! Carol shrieked to herself. I can't afford

this joint. Oh, Thornton, your ideas are good . . . good and expensive. Careful. Don't slip out of character. What character, babe, you ain't got none. Smart, real smart mouth.

". . . I don't feel it's necessary for you to participate in the group meetings," Welch added.

"Whatever you think best," Carol replied.

Welch escorted her into the hallway, and to the elevator. "Why don't we continue this afternoon?" he remarked. "What about four . . .?"

"I'll be here," Carol said brightly.

The elevator door opened, and Carol stepped into the cab. Almost there, babe, almost free.

"Thank you, Dr. Welch."

The door started to slide shut, and Welch hit the rubber bumper. "Would you mind if I asked your father to bring Plato here?"

Thud. Thud. Thud. The door closing repeatedly on Welch's hand melded with the warning buzzer.

"Yes, that would be fine," Carol replied nervously. We're not gonna to do it. He's coming with me. Never gonna split. Oh jeez, would you let go of that frigging door.

Buzz. Thud. Buzz. Thud.

Don't panic. *I'm trying.* Be cool. *Shut up!*

"Fine," Welch said sincerely. "I'll call him later." He smiled, and let the door entomb Carol in the elevator. Oh jeez, I'm wringing wet. *Suck it in.* Yeah, yeah, I'm all right. *Punch 1.*

Carol pressed the "Main Floor" button, and the elevator descended slowly.

Be straight, babe, don't look right or left. Smile, say hello to the guards, and walk with assurance.

The door slid open, and Carol stepped into the hospital's lobby. One foot, two foot, smile, and split. She forced herself into a relaxed gait, dawddled for a moment at the staff bulletin board.

"How ya doing, Miss Newmark? How's things in the lab?"

Carol wheeled quickly. "What?"

"Sorry . . . I didn't mean to startle you," the attendant said.

She was face-to-face with a young man dressed in hospital whites. Carol tried to remain calm, though every muscle in her body strained, and perspiration seeped through her clothes. *Cool it. He thinks you're a staffer.*

"That's all right. Guess I was absorbed in my own thoughts," she answered.

The orderly laughed. "And this is the place for some real unusual thoughts, right?"

Play it to the hilt. Carol looked at him sternly. *That's it . . . The million-dollar icy stare.*

"I think that remark was out of line," she said.

"Sorry, I didn't mean to imply . . ."

The telephone started to ring at the reception desk. They know you're loose, babe. Don't panic. Carol shot a glance at the front door. *Ten feet, and that's it.* The telephone kept ringing.

"Why don't get your phone?" Carol suggested.

"Yeah, sure," the orderly said with embarrassment.

Carol pushed open the front door, and stepped into the street, as the orderly reached for the telephone. *Run,* Plato screamed to her, and Carol dashed across Park Avenue. *Don't look back,* he shrieked. She leaned against a building trying to catch her breath. *Move, girl, move.* She stumbled—ran up the side street and onto Madison Avenue. The galleries and boutiques were a blur.

Chick-a-boom. Rim shot. Hey, hey, let's get Carol. *Chick-a-boom.* Rim shot. Get the net.

Get Plato. Get Plato, kept pounding in her mind. *Go home* mixed subliminally with *Go to the club.*

Tea party . . . tea party . . . tea party swung in and out of her thoughts.

Never gonna make it. Never gonna make it.

The traffic, the noise swirled around her. Pat Welch lurked behind every corner. Carol hurried down Madison panicked by imaginary orderlies rushing at her from every store. *Run, run.* They're right behind you. *Run, run.* Here's nursie with the net. She lunged across Sixty-seventh street and was almost hit by a cab.

"You crazy broad! You ought be locked up!" the cabbie yelled.

Run, run. You'll be late for the tea party . . . the tea party . . .

Carol's lungs were exploding.

Welch looking at her understandingly mixed with Murray laughing. Murray, bastard Murray, sitting at the back of the room laughing at . . . always laughing at her.

Carol lurched forward.

I'll get you. I'll get you, she screamed to herself as she reached the side entrance of the Q Club.

She turned the door handle frantically, but it was locked. Damn, damn . . . *damn.* Suppose, just suppose they're waiting for you. No way. First, it's call Thornton, then check the apartment. Carol closed her eyes, and pressed the night button. No way. This wouldn't be the first place. Nothing, no answer. She jabbed at the button continuously.

"Hold your water," a voice groused from inside as the locks were clicked. Finally, Harold Farrar, the club's day porter, open the door.

"How ya doin', Miss Carol?" he asked. "Right early today, huh? Some rehearsin'?"

Carol stepped quickly into the murkiness of the backstage area. "That's right," she replied.

"Well, good for you," he answered and locked the door behind her.

"Thornton here?" Carol asked.

"No, ma'am. Not since yesterday. Just one of them dancers . . . y'know, boy dancers working out." Harold rolled his eyes, and smiled broadly. "Some sort of dancin', huh?"

"Right," Carol replied. "Listen . . . I'll only be here for a moment, but . . . don't tell anyone I came in."

"Gotcha," Harold replied knowingly.

"And Harold . . . if anybody calls, even Thornton . . ."

"You ain't here, right?"

Carol smiled weakly and watched the old man trudge into the darkened club.

She felt exhausted. The cramp in her side made her wince. I'd like to replay this one, she thought. Right from the top . . . and a five, six, seven, eight. Hit the mark, get born all over, and start fresh.

Maybe the Markhams would lock me in. Oh yeah, I'd like that, babe. Lock me in, and lock all the bad guys out. No more lawyers, or Murrays, or crazies. I'd take it in a minute, Carol thought as she walked through the wings toward her dressing room. Just l'il Aggie, sister Jo, Papa purple-eyes, me, and the dolls.

Suddenly, she stopped.

The door to her room was slightly ajar, and a narrow triangle of light split the wooden floor.

The bogeymen returned.

Carol's fears welled in her mouth and pressed against her stomach.

Thornton? No. Harold would have told me.

Welch and company. Doubt it.

She wedged herself between two flats straining for a sound. Diana? Oh jeez, don't!

A high-pitched giggle curled into the darkness and faded into the spotlights.

Carol inched from behind the scenery into the hallway and peered carefully at her dressing room.

Another falsetto laugh.

". . . And who's little boy are you?" filtered through the shadows.

Carol pushed her door open. Latino was holding Plato on his lap, while he stroked his face.

"What the hell are you doing?" she asked.

"Look who's back," he replied.

Carol took Plato from him instantly. "I asked you something, buster?"

"And I heard you, busty!" Latino quipped. "We were having a chit-chat. Don't get bent out of shape, honey."

"Get lost, fruit," Carol replied. "Don't ever let me catch you in this room again . . . or touching him!"

He clucked his tongue, and smirked. "But you can come in my room anytime, hon. My makeup would do wonders for those bags, and sags, dearie."

"Thanks. When I run out of eye shadow, you'll be the first."

"Oh?" Latino replied, "don't they let you have those goodies at the sanitarium?"

"Get out, creep!" Carol ordered.

Latino lounged against the door. "Sorry, hon, I was going to send you a cake with a hacksaw."

"Shut up! Keep your filthy remarks to yourself!" Carol told him.

Latino laughed at her. "Filthy remarks?" he mimicked. "You're one to talk. Jesus, the queen of smut turns lily-white! My goodness, aren't we getting dainty."

"Get out of my dressing room," Carol snapped.

"Don't get high and mighty with me, bitch! You and that sicko puppet should have your mouths washed out. No! Better yet . . . have your tongues cut off!"

Carol recoiled in fright.

Diana! The bra, the letters . . . 'cut off your breasts and stuff them . . .' Everything rushed back, and she was terrified. He glared at her.

Latino kept up his invective. "I never heard such filth come from any woman's mouth . . . *woman?* That's a joke. No woman talks like a goodamn sailor. Aren't you ashamed of yourself?" He glared at Carol. *"Aren't you?"*

"Yes, yes," she replied quickly.

"Bullshit."

"No, I'm ashamed. I really am," Carol said nervously. "I never intended to be like this. I was different."

"Sure, sure," Latino replied sarcastically. "I'm so pure," he mocked. "I'm so nice." He pushed over her chair. Carol groped for something to defend herself with from the dressing table. Rattail comb, brush, hand mirror, anything. Latino looked at her with disgust, and shook his head.

"You're a pitiful excuse for a female," he snarled. "You disgust me . . . and the other dancers. You make us feel dirty, and I hate you for it." He stepped toward Carol, and she moved behind a chair.

"Don't—" she begged.

"Don't what?"

"Keep away from me."

"I wouldn't dirty my hands on you, bitch. You're scum . . . plain old gutter scum. Touch you?" he laughed. "I wouldn't give you the thrill."

Latino stared at her, then walked out of the dressing room. Carol closed her eyes, and sunk into a chair. She heard her heart pounding, and felt the blood racing through her veins. A bead of perspiration inched down her cheek. What was that faggot doing here? That flaming queer was up to something. Bastard! Carol growled. Only when the pressure against her chest made her gasp for breath did she realize that was clutching Plato. She laid the dummy on her dressing table, then rested her head in her arms. Gotta get out of here. Move, Carol, split the scene before he comes back. The low pulsating of disco music wafted into her room. *Chick-a-boom. Wah, wah, wah!*

Carol struggled to collect herself. She glanced at her traveling clock: 12:37. Never make it to the apartment. *You have to!* an inner voice screamed back.

Chick-a-boom. Latino's tape recorder blared as he ground the routine to phantom groupies. *Wah, wah, wah.* He threw a pelvis to the unheard screams.

Carol pressed herself against a backdrop as she edged toward the stage door.

Slowly, slowly, she begged herself. Another few feet, another few feet.

Chick-a-boom. Latino gyrated into his final macho pose and spread his arms to the adoring ladies.

Wah, wah, wah resonated through the club as Carol slid past the manager's desk, One foot, two foot, and you're free.

Suddenly Latino wheeled. "Sneaking out, huh?" he laughed. "Bye, bye, Mr. Plato. Take care of the bitch."

Carol froze, then rushed toward the stage door, wrenched it open, and ran.

Chapter Twelve

The Markham sisters were exceedingly agitated by Carol's disheveled appearance.

"She weep all the way," Papa Noir explained. "Can make no sense. She hide around corner of the building. I almost not see her, then she slapdash into *mon* taxi. She weep, and weep. It is *mal, sœur* Josephine. Not good at all."

"Pity, pity. Poor child," Jo answered. She took Carol by the arm and led her into the doll shop.

"I'm all right, really I am," Carol replied hoarsely, then convulsed into tears.

Sister Aggie shook her head.

"Some *mals* been chasing her, I think," Papa told her. "She flibberty-gibbet about a doctor, and dancing. It make no sense. The *histoire* isn't straight."

"Oh my," Aggie answered as Jo eased Carol into a Victorian settee. "I knew it wouldn't last. Oh my, too soon, dear Papa, too brutal."

"Indeed so, ma'am. She cry about this Diana. Hard tears about that *mal* lady. It a heavy time for missy."

"Yes, yes," Jo replied as she held Carol's hands.

Carol lowered her head, and wept softly.

"Now it's all over," Aggie advised her. "Isn't

that right, Jo? Poor Carol. My dear, did you imagine for one moment we would abandon you?"

Carol shook her head. "Guess not," she whispered. "It seemed I would never get here."

"That's ancient history," Aggie assured her. "You're safe and sound with us . . . and of course, Papa." Aggie patted Carol's hand, and smiled warmly. "Sister Jo and I will take care of you from now on, isn't that right, Jo?"

"Absolutely, dearest Carol," Jo added, "you won't have to bother with all those nasty people."

Carol returned the sisters' smiles. "I wish it were true," she said.

"But it is!" Aggie replied emphatically. "Unless you don't want to accept our custody."

Carol squeezed Aggie's miniature hand lightly. "Thank you, but I couldn't impose on you . . . I couldn't stay here."

"Oh, we didn't imply that, my dear," Jo replied. "You'll have to maintain yourself a bit longer . . . what Aggie mean was . . . well, we'd like to offer you a temporary shelter . . . for the next few hours . . . until you regain your equilibrium . . . isn't that correct, Agnes?"

"Chatter, chatter, chatter, Jo Markham. Don't you see she's all a-bother, and needs to renew her energies."

"Of course I did," Jo answered indignantly.

"The poor child's near exhaustion, aren't you?"

Carol smiled weakly.

"We'll show you to your room," Jo told her.

"It's quite lovely," Aggie remarked. "A perfect setting . . . when the time is proper."

The Markhams stood in front of Carol beaming with delight. "And when you're ready we'll have a nice, long chat about the predicaments," Josephine added.

"Maybe she'd like to freshen up, Jo?"

"Of course, of course! Would you like to take a tub . . . a nice, long soak?"

Carol shrugged. She felt grimy and the idea of a hot bath appealed to her. "If it's not any trouble!"

"Trouble?" shrieked Aggie. "It would be our pleasure. A superior bath . . . and you'll have some fresh clothes.

". . . and Aggie can do your tresses," Jo added.

"It would be so much fun . . . and you'll wear the ball gown," Aggie insisted.

"A ball gown for high tea? Are you serious?"

Aggie gave a pixieish smile. "It is a party, isn't it? And Carol would look so beautiful. The gown's wine-colored velvet trimmed in Alençon lace with teeny seed pearls and—"

Jo cut her off sternly. "You do prattle on, Miss Aggie. Let Carol select her own frock."

"I was merely making a suggestion," Aggie insisted. "Carol can wear whatever she wants . . . the closets are brimming with clothes."

Papa Noir coughed discreetly to halt the sisters' bickering. "Miss Carol tired," he reflected. "Think it best she *parle avec tout le monde* later."

"Indeed so," Aggie pouted. "Come this way, my dear, I'll show you your room and bath."

Carol smile wearily, and followed Aggie to the staircase. "Yes, I would like to relax for a moment," she said.

"And so you shall," Aggie comforted.

"However . . ." Josephine suggested, aren't we forgetting, or missing . . . someone?" Aggie looked puzzled. "I mean . . . Carol dear . . . did you . . . bring your little man with you?"

For a second Carol was confused, then recovered. "Oh yes! I think . . . wasn't he in the taxi?"

"C'est vrai," Papa replied. "Put him in the front with me. Remember, missy? You lie down on seat and I take him!"

"Of course," Carol answered.

"I get him, *mes sœurs,*" Papa added, and left the shop.

Carol leaned against the bannister to steady herself. Hold on, babe, she begged.

"That's a lovely picture," Carol remarked pointing to a turn-of-the-century photograph in a silver frame.

"It's Josephine. She was twenty," Aggie replied. "Such beautiful auburn hair. She was the rage. All the galants clustered about her. There was always a stir when she entered the cotillions."

"Yes, she's beautiful," Carol remarked. "Her eyes are so lustrous."

"Aren't they?" Jo remarked.

"And who's this?" Carol asked, pointing to photograph of a young woman dressed in a cycling costume.

"That's Carlotta," Jo replied. "She's Aggie's friend. Dear, dear girl. So gifted."

Papa Noir stood at the foot of the stairs holding Plato. *"Ici, le petit homme,"* He held Plato toward Carol. "You want to take him upstairs, missy?"

The sisters surrounded Papa Noir before Carol had a chance to answer. They fussed and clucked over Plato, touching his face, examining his clothes, and smoothing his wig.

"Did you make his outfit, dear?"

"Where did you get the hair for his wig?"

"Is it real hair?"

"Do you have other little men?"

"I told you he was a sweetheart, Aggie!"

"Now don't get carried away, Jo."

". . . but his clothes. Oh dear, we must attend to his garb. Could we create a new wardrobe for him Carol?"

"Certainly . . . of course," she replied.

"I have the perfect item, Aggie. Remember the

smoking jacket we made for . . ." Buzz, buzz. Whisper, whisper. Carol smiled at Papa Noir pretending not to intrude on the sisters' trading secrets.

"Missy Carol uncomfortable, *petites soeurs,*" Papa reminded them. The sisters were shamefaced, and apologized. Papa nodded approvingly. "Sometimes the ladies get very, very taken," he remarked to Carol. "Right so, Miss Aggie?"

"Indeed, indeed," she answered. "But it's not every day we have someone . . . this special."

"*Two persons* who are special," Jo added.

"Didn't mean to exclude our dearest Carol," Aggie bickered. "I wasn't ignoring her."

"But you did," Jo said coolly. "You're all ga-ga with her little man, and it wasn't polite . . . and you started the whispering."

"Did not!" Aggie pouted.

" 'Tis so. Admit it!" Josephine countered.

Papa Noir coughed again, and the sisters stopped. "Suppose I put Monsieur Plato in the music room, while Missy Carol in her *chambre?*"

"Quite so," Aggie said imperiously. She handed Plato to Papa, who winked and nodded at Carol.

"Let me show you the way," Josephine replied. "At least I know how to be a gracious hostess."

Aggie, exasperated by the reproach, turned on her heel and disappeared into the drawing room.

"Don't mind us," Josephine remarked as they climbed the stairs to the second floor. "Sometimes we argue like fishwives."

"Yes," Carol replied forcing another tired smile.

"Be there soon," Josephine promised.

Carol followed her down a narrow hallway. Rows of pictures lined the fabric-covered walls. Women in long skirts and wide-brimmed hats. Gentlemen in bowlers. More pictures of Carlotta. Groups of men and women casually sitting around picnic baskets. Memories of a more civilized era, and people long since buried.

Aggie opened the door to Carol's room.

"Here we are," she said delightedly. "Do you like it? There's another room if you'd prefer."

Carol was stunned by the elegance of the room. A canopied four-poster stood against the wall. Lace curtains framed the window. A wicker rocker was flanked by Victorian planters. Streams of pink, and yellow, and white meshed together in the highboy, the dresser, the delicated vanity table. Carol walked about the room gingerly touching the myriad of appointments that filled the shelves, the burea top, and the wicker desk. A polished sea-lemon-yellow parasol leaning against the chaise.

And dolls were everywhere. The room was filled with valuable bisque- and wax-headed dolls. Jumeaus. Brus. Kestners. A Carrier-Belleau was seated in her own high chair. Carol couldn't believe the quality and the quantity of matchless little women staring at her from every corner.

"The private room is here," Jo said casually.

"Thank you," Carol mumbled.

"You'll find the bath sachets in the medicine cabinet, and the soaps in the crystal vases. I think . . . well, I know there's magnolia, and lily-of-the-valley . . . no matter, chose wh which ever one you wish."

"I will," Carol replied softly. The bathroom was another time warp. Claw-legged tub, brass faucets on the china sink, wicker hamper.

"And in the closets," Jo giggled, "select any dress you desire." She lingered at the bedroom door for a moment. "Take your time," she said, "we'll be in the drawing room."

"Yes," Carol replied slowly. The room, the dolls and the ambience of the surroundings had numbed her. "I'll be right there."

Josephine nodded, and left the room.

Carol sat on the edge of the bed, and leaned her head against a post. Exhaustion seeped through her body. Her arms ached; her legs felt leaden. She sprawled backward and stared at the white-lace canopy. Plato, Thornton, Welch, and all the horrors of the street tumbled away as Carol spiralled into a fathomless sleep.

Sister Jo poured a cup of dark mocha java from a Meissen coffeepot and handed it to Papa Noir. She waited expectantly as he sipped the ebony-colored brew.

"Ah-h-h, *sen-sationnel!*" he exclaimed. "Truly, sister Josephine, you have a gift for concotion. Yes, ma'am, it is the finest."

Josephine was quite pleased, and sat back contentedly. "Thank you, Papa. I put a touch of French roast in, and it seems to bring out—"

"Hush!" Aggie interrupted. She strained to hear beyond the drawing room.

"Is it Carol?" Jo whispered.

Aggie held up a hand to silence her. Papa listenly intently as did Josephine, however, whatever noise filtered from the second floor was beyond their hearing. Aggie closed her eyes and concentrated.

"Poor child, she's asleep."

"Hasn't been easy for her, has it?"

Aggie shook her head. "Not at all."

"And her little man hasn't made it easier, has he, Papa?"

Papa Noir nodded. "*Le petit* is more than one person, I tell you that indeed. Them eyes . . . many, many secrets layered within them eyes."

"What else, Papa?" Josephine asked.

He laughed softly. "No, no, ma'am, you know that ain't me specialty. I cannot read like *soeur* Agnes."

"Do you think he's lived before, Aggie?"

She nodded. "Get him, Jo."

Josephine moved the tea cart aside and walked into the living room. Plato, inert, almost broken, slouched against the arm of a chair.

Josephine picked him up carefully, straightened his collar, and brought him into the drawing room.

"Make him comfortable," Aggie suggested. Josephine placed Plato upright in the middle of the sofa, folded his arms across his waist. He slipped to one side and she righted him. "What a pretty boy," Aggie cackled.

"Maybe, and maybe *au contraire,*" Papa remarked.

"Go ahead, Aggie," Jo urged.

Papa Noir and Josephine nodded, and took seats on either side of Plato.

Sister Agnes stood in front of the dummy. She closed her eyes and lowered her head. Agnes's breathing became deep and rasping as she drew herself into an alpha-trance. She swayed slightly, then caught her balance as she moved further into a twilight consciousness. Papa Noir placed an undersized caneback chair behind Aggie, and gently seated her. She sat rigid for a moment, her breathing became rhythmic, then with a jolt she sat upright and her eyelids opened. Aggie stared directly into Plato's eyes.

"This is not your first incarnation, is it?"

Plato didn't move.

"Oh, I know you can hear me," Aggie said. "He's a clever one," she told Papa Noir and Josephine. "A sly fox . . . and very naughty boy."

"Who was he, Aggie?" Jo asked.

She closed her eyes and concentrated. "Bobby," she said mechanically. "Yes, Bob Backsomething . . . not very clear. Definitely not a nice individual . . . always carping about other people . . . teachers, or officials. It's slipping away . . ." Aggie's voice faded into an inaudible whisper, and she sat silent again.

"Goodness gracious, Papa Noir, that wasn't very spicy. Thought Aggie would at least regress him to a murderer . . . or a pirate."

Papa smiled broadly, and put a forefinger to his lips.

"Well, it *wasn't* exciting!" Josephine said quietly. Papa wagged his finger at her, and she turned away indignantly.

"Can't go further than the Bobby persona," Aggie told them. "No ancestors . . . no tracings . . . Bobby to the present little man . . ." she said in a singsong voice. "Just Plato . . . and Plato . . . and Plato and—"

"And Plato!" Plato bellowed.

Both sisters and Papa Noir were startled by the dummy's outburst.

"It was Bobby Backbite, little lady," Plato announced. "And that's as far as the tree grows."

"Oh, Aggie, you're wonderful. How did you do it? We've never had any of the marionettes communicate with us."

"I'm *not* a puppet, lady!" Plato sniped.

"Then what are you, ma-an?" Papa Noir asked.

"I don't talk to niggers!" Plato spat out.

In contrast to Josephine's horror, both Agnes and Papa Noir were calm, almost expecting Plato's slur.

"Horrid person!" Jo exclaimed.

"You ain't so hot yourself, turkey neck," Plato jested. "Don't be so shocked, toots, it's the truth ain't it?" Jo pretended not to hear the comment. "Well, this is really dull . . . you wanted to talk to me . . . it's your nickel, troops."

"Is Plato your real name?" Aggie questioned.

"Good as any! It don't make no difference, honey;

besides, what yer named ain't got nothing to do with your powers . . . or abilities, right? Plato, Bobby B . . .? All the same. Even the one you missed, sis . . ."

"Oh?" Aggie replied. "I didn't imagine you had a life beyond Bobby . . . Bobby who?"

Plato cackled insultingly. "Bobby Backbite! Yeah man, he was m'granddaddy, m'sponsor all rolled into one mean-ass character. He was all I needed to get through. Y'know, reentry isn't all that hard. It's easy . . . ya see, to get into the present ya gotta have a wedge . . . something like a door opening . . . and old Bobby was m'man. Yes, ma'am, as soon as Carol threw him a personality . . ."

"Obviously, a unlikable one," Joe added.

"So all right, he wasn't Mr. Charm, but that's all I needed. It was only a matter of time before I emerged."

"Pity!" Jo said imperiously.

"Josephine . . ." That wasn't worthy of you," Aggie replied. "We hardly know Mr. Plato, and you've made a judgment. It wasn't very ladylike."

Josephine pursed her lips and looked away in disapproval.

"Go on, Mr. Plato," Aggie added.

"Sure thing, honey. After Carol bombed with Alpha Betty . . . some cockeyed hand puppet that was going nowhere, I put a little zip into her life . . . Bobby B, that is, who made gags about other people. He was a ballbreaker. Not a good word for anybody and could cut you down before ya had a chance to run for cover. Tough monkey, old Bob."

"Monkey is *right!*" Josephine quipped. "Poor Carol! How she could have ever let you loose!"

"Don't think she was aware," Papa Noir added. "Seems Mr. Plato would have arrived no matter, eh?"

"Right on, big daddy slick!" Plato replied. "Y'know despite yer flesh tones you got some brains."

Papa Noir laughed. "At least I got skin instead of pine and glue."

"A temporary inconvenience, Rastus," Plato shot back. "Pretty soon . . . like the others, I'm gonna be mingling with the crowd. All pink, and inhumane like the rest of 'em. So don't boogie outta line 'cause a new day's creeping over them hills and the time's growing short, boy."

"We see. We see," Papa Noir answered.

"This is getting much too personal," Aggie interjected. "Remember, Mr. Plato is our guest," she said politely, "and we must accord him some respect."

"I wish you hadn't regressed this . . . this creature," Jo retorted. "Why don't you force him back, Aggie?"

"Now that's close to impossible, ain't it, Miss Shorty?" Plato quipped.

"Indeed," Aggie replied.

"Like Daddy Darky says . . . I woulda made my debut no matter," Plato explained. "Carol was only the carrier. In fact, the perfect vehicle . . . SST, rocket to the moon, Seven Forty-seven . . . to slip me back into circulation."

"And how was that?" Aggie asked softly. "I never could fathom the transfer process."

"As old Bobby? Or me? Whatcha talking about, honey?" Plato asked.

Aggie thought for a moment. "Your emergence as an independent personality. I'm assuming you've had a confrontation with Carol?"

"It scared the shit outta her," Plato laughed.

"Vulgarian!" Josephine whispered.

"It was right after the wreck. Y'know she was in

a total. Bad accident to you, toots. The car was blasted. Oh yeah, *whammo!* I went spinning, and landed flat on my ass. It was lights out, sister!"

Josephine looked at Papa Noir and shook her head.

"Was the accident planned?" Aggie asked.

"Probably, but I really dunno," Plato replied. "The usual schtick is some kind of trauma. A rape. A shooting. Yeah, yeah, the wreck was 'planned,' " he reflected. "And it was beautiful! *Kapow!* Poor Carol thought she was dead."

"And how soon afterward did you emerge?"

"In the hospital. M'peepers shifted. Like this." Plato moved his eyes left. "And then like this." He moved them to the right, and locked them in the center.

"Can you see?" Josephine questioned.

"Not yet. That's in the future," he replied. "But I can hear pretty damn well. Man, can I hear."

"Are you always brought through by violence?" Aggie wanted to know.

"It's the only way to go, honey. A death experience is the best . . . or an assault. Jeez, that is wild."

"Not for the victim!" Josephine replied.

"Hey, who cares? It's all over for that personality. *Finito! Kaput!* If they didn't want to be taken over they wouldn't have put themselves in jeopardy, right?"

"Like Carol?" Aggie asked.

"Straight-A, toots," Plato snapped. "She hated herself, and couldn't kick it, so why hang around? Listen, Carol was prime for me! She wanted to kill herself . . . and I'm glad to help."

"Too bad she couldn't reciprocate!" Jo replied.

"She nearly did, honey! And I'll pay her back for that one," Plato snarled. "Put a pillow over me head! Scraped her frigging nails down my face! She'll pay. Oh yeah, honey, that's something I won't ever forget. She'll pay!"

"You're an ugly little demon," Aggie retorted.

"Well, that's show biz," Plato mocked.

"You still haven't expanded on the transfer . . . I mean 'reentry' factors. Is it a continuous process?" Aggie asked. "Have you had other lives?"

"Yes and no," Plato thought. "You can have the same character repeated century after century.

"One lifetime certainly would be enough, if not too much," Josephine said haughtily.

"It's simple," Plato bragged. "Carol, for example, was the ideal set-up. As soon as them badass thoughts popped outta Bobby B's mouth I knew it was a matter of time. Why, hell's bells, Miss Shorty, old Bob was a laugh riot . . . just like me, so we pumped him up with some lines, and the audience went wild. It was a damn sight more profitable than boring Alpha Betty."

"We?" Aggie inquired. "There are more personalities attached to Carol?"

"Naw, naw. The 'we' is the other guys hanging out there waiting to reenter. We help each other out . . . on occasion. So-and-so comes back, in a minor way, and helps shape the landing pad. Old Bob lingered in Carol's head for a long time. He was everything she wanted to say . . . y'know, all the remarks ya never have the guts to make. Anyhow, he started growing . . . and pretty soon instead of a brain trip . . . there he was . . . a hand puppet telling the other teachers about Mrs. Fatface . . . and making them laugh. He had great material, which we supplied."

"I can't believe our Carol would stoop to such cheap theatrics!" Josephine blurted out.

"Sorry to disappoint ya, honey! When in doubt

and unhappy . . . and up-a-wall, ya gotta blow some steam. Carol's no different, 'cause all them goody-goody phonies were getting on her case."

"We're all entitled to mistakes, however, your emergence certainly was a monumental calamity!" Jo replied.

"Yeah?" Plato shot back. "You ain't seen nothing yet!"

"Please! Let's conduct ourselves in a civilized manner," Aggie suggested.

"Quite *le vrai,*" Papa Noir said calmly. "Monsieur Plato," Papa asked, "I don't *comprends* your term 'carrier'?"

"That's simple even for a darkie," Plato snapped. "Carol spawned the minor-league bad thought in Bob Backbite. Gave it shape, and form, right? That's all we needed to spring me into the unreal world. I took over from old Bob . . . I kept Carol on a roll with more material, more gags, more bits of schtick. She started getting laughs with a word here or there . . ."

"You mean a *foul* word!" Jo corrected.

"Right, sweetie. I gave her the blue act, the hot one-liners, the whole bit. Let's face it, troops, I made Carol Elliott into a star," Plato announced pompously. "And when I'm finished with her . . . well, that's another matter," Plato cackled. "Just hang around 'cause you ain't seen nothing yet."

"You plan to dominate her completely?" Aggie questioned.

"Ha! I have, honey!" Plato said sarcastically. "I've worked on her for years. I've written the dialogue. Oh, she still thinks I'm an inert schmuck, but that's the way we want it for the moment. I'll play the game, but I'm dealing. I got her so ga-ga she thinks she's talking to herself."

"And that's what you want, isn't it?" Aggie asked. "You want to drive her insane."

"Natch, babe. That's how we make the next transfer. Didn't you realize that all the nuts, the wackos, the schizoids . . . all the loonies are carriers? *Yeah man!* The crazies are the transfers.

They think they're hearing voices! *Bullshit!* They *do* hear us . . . we've taken them over . . . we've used them. *The frigging voices are real!*"

Papa Noir and the Markham sisters looked at each other worriedly.

"This has to cease," Aggie said softly.

"No way!" Plato told her. "You can't stop us . . . I mean, who's gonna believe you, huh? Three weirdos talking to a dummy? Ya gotta be kidding. Gentlemen, get out your nets."

"Then we'll advise Carol," Jo remarked.

"And tell her *what?* You've been talking to me? She'll think you're creepier than you are, sis! Besides I'll tuck in . . . I won't talk . . . I'll be a good boy and not bug her. Listen, honey, she still thinks she controls me, and we know that's a gas. A real gas!"

"You *mal, un vrai mal,*" Papa replied.

"No kidding," Plato sneered.

"We'll see what Carol has to say about this," Josephine suggested.

"Agreed," Aggie concurred.

"Indeed so, *petites soeurs,*" Papa Noir remarked. "I think ma'am Carol has enough energy to force a change . . . and make this *mal* return."

"Yer blowing smoke, folks," Plato interrupted. "I got her by the brain . . . I'm deep in her head, and there's no letting go. Beside if you make one rotten suggestion . . . I'm placing her right in front of the firing squad, and yer sweetie gets a pair of mams chopped off."

"Which means?" Aggie replied.

"Man, woman, man, woman . . . the big D is

gonna get her," Plato mocked. "And I mean get her sooner than I planned." He cackled maliciously.

"You're more despicable than I realized," Aggie replied.

"Can it, honey!" Plato growled. "I'm warning ya . . . not a peep about our delightful conversation. I didn't talk, and you didn't listen. This never happened. I'm just dummy Plato . . . and we let Carol think she's still in control. Got it, babe?"

Chapter Thirteen

Popcorn. Cotton candy. The Ferris wheel kaleidoscoped into Thornton's face. "Let's go on the whip, Daddy" echoed through the tunnel and reemerged "Here's Carol Lane, and *Mr. Plato.*" Traffic lights blurring into neon. Someone's behind us. Step on it! She's coming closer. The sweaty faces screaming for Latino's thighs. "You've got a foul mouth, lady!" *Ice storm.* Burning Rubber. *Explosion.* Ragdoll time. "Is she dead, Harry?" Swim, swim. Lights, and twirl. *Chick-a-boom.* Down the tube. Falling deeper into the blackness.

Carol convulsed into a fetal position.

"Thornton!" she screamed, and woke herself into reality. The down pillows, the four-poster, the smell of rose sachets edged into focus. Stuffed pillows, and lace. An ivory comb-and-brush set and a beveled-edge mirror. The grinding crash and the whipping police lights faded into perfumed safety. It was her room and she was safe. Carol dragged herself to a sitting position trying to shake the smell of rubber, and fright. She stumbled into the bathroom. The bloated eyelids reflecting from the mirror weren't appreciated.

"Carol, you've outdone yourself," she muttered and splashed water into her face. No amount of water's going help, she told herself. Babe, you're a wreck. Bags, sags, and crags, Carol worried as she dried her face. Well, that's the breaks. Carol leaned against the sink and stared at herself in the mirror. Bummer, washed-up tramp. What are you doing in the garden? Don't know, gazed back. You look like hell, kid. Bleached hair and frown lines reflected at her. Carol turned away from the mirror, and walked into the bedroom.

Everything you wanted . . . want . . . will want is here. She touched the ribbons streaming down the canopy.

In the next life, Carol reasoned. Sure, next time you'll come back as doll. As a Jumeau with pouty lips, and pudgy cheeks. And all the little old ladies would make clothes for you. And all the little girls would rock you to sleep.

Sure thing, babe. It'll never happen 'cause knowing your luck some cat would spray you.

Yeah, that's the story of my life, sister Aggie. Just when you reach for it—Aw, what the hell, Carol thought. She stared at herself in the vanity mirror, ran the comb through her hair a few times. God, you're haggard.

It's the best I can do.

That's pitiful, an inner voice called out.

Sorry, fella, I wish it was different.

Yeah, me too, the voice replied.

You'll have to live with it, Carol shouted back, because *I* have to live with it.

Carol hesitated before leaving the room. Chicken? an inner noice asked. You better believe it, shot back. However, she turned the knob, pushed open the door, and walked into the hallway.

"Did you have a nice nap?" Aggie called from the foot of the stairs.

No hiding sleep-puffed eyes. "Yes, I did," Carol replied.

"That's good," Josephine added. "Come, come, there's still time for some tea . . . and I'll put a flame under the scones." She scurried into the kitchen immediately.

Plato was sitting where Carol had left him, and the chairs were returned to their former spaces. It appeared the session with Plato had never taken place. Carol walked into the living room and casually sat in an oversized wing chair.

"I'm sorry. I just couldn't keep my eyes open. It was very rude of me," Carol apologized.

"Under the circumstances I could imagine you would sleep for a month. All that horrid business crisscrossing your path. I don't see how you've born up this far."

"Because she's strong," Jo suggested as she entered the room carrying a silver tray laden with pastries and the "tea" that was coffee. "And here's a bit of sustenance to aid in the battle." She set the tray in front of Carol. "Rasberry tarts, blueberry muffins, or apple torte? Have one, have all!" She poured Carol a cup of coffee, stirred in some cream, and handed it to her.

"I love tea parties," Josephine squealed.

"So do I," Aggie added.

The Markhams launched into banal chatter to mask their inner feelings, and carefully skirted any mention of Plato, or Diana, and the anxieties that lurked beyond the doll shop. It was a perfect tea party filled with talk of bisque-headed dolls; of "How did you make that?"; of comparisons of silks to the "horrid, absolutely horrid" twentieth-century fabrics; of three ladies laughing; of two spinsters delighted; of one scarred performer shedding her armor in the sweetness of an era.

And then the gaiety exploded into reality.

"He's worried about you," Aggie commented.

Carol was stunned. The remarked pierced the illusion and all the fears returned.

"I think he's been in touch with the police."

Carol's hands became icy.

"Sorry, my dear, I think it's time for you to go back."

"I don't want to . . ." Carol stammered.

"It wouldn't be proper," Aggie replied.

"Not at this time, dear," Jo added.

"You see, Carol, we can't assist you right at the moment," Aggie concluded.

Carol was stunned. The knot in her stomach forced up another metallic taste.

"I thought . . . well, I imagined I was going to stay with you." The sisters shook their heads. "And what about Plato? Didn't you want to talk to him? You asked me to bring him!" Carol felt herself pleading.

Aggie clucked her tongue. "I think it was an error, isn't that right, Jo?"

"How true. We felt . . . that is, Aggie sensed a presence, but it wasn't your little man. I'm sorry, dear."

"Sometimes I tune into many spirits," Aggie added. "Oh, it's so difficult to cull one's way through the other side."

"You're hiding something," Carol insisted.

The sisters looked at each other, and shrugged.

"Did I say anything to offend you?" Carol asked nervously. "I know I have a bad mouth . . . I mean, I say things that I don't mean . . . it's a bad habit. If I did I apologize."

"No, you didn't offend us," Jo answered.

"Then why are you putting me out?"

"There's hardly anything to be afraid of," Aggie replied. "I wouldn't be troubled. Oh no, not at all."

Carol felt herself being hustled toward the front door. "I can't go!" she insisted. "What about the kook . . . yeah, the crazy out there, who wants to kill me?"

Josephine placed Plato carefully in Carol's arm. "You won't have any problems if you're careful."

"How can you say that?" Carol whined. "She's a wacko . . . I don't know when she'll go for me . . . the club, the street . . . I want to stay here. At least I'm safe with you."

"The older man with the *T* in his name will secure your safety," Aggie informed her. "He's very upset. Oh pity, pity, I can sense his quandary. Poor thing, he's so worried about you."

"I don't want to be with Thornton," Carol snapped.

The sisters looked at each other again.

"Well," reflected Aggie," if he gives his permission we'll consider the matter. It's not a promise, only a point of deliberation."

Carol felt relieved. "I'll discuss it with him."

"You do that, dear," Jo replied. "Now Papa will return you to the apartment house."

Aggie opened the door, walked Carol to Papa Noir's taxi. "Miss Carol would like to return home," she told him.

"*Absolutement,* ma'am. I transport her *vite,*" he answered and helped Carol into the backseat. "No worry now, missy, Papa take you straight away."

Sister Jo slammed the door, and nodded to Papa Noir. He wheeled the taxi quickly down the street, and sped up Columbus Avenue. The anxieties swelled, and crested over Carol immediately. Hide the truth or tell Thornton about the sisters? Right? Wrong? How would she face Thornton? I can't go back to that nuthouse. Papa Noir drove faster. Please slow down. I don't want to go to the apartment just yet. Pat Welch's face. It isn't in my head. Pat Welch smiling, and agreeing. Don't humor me, you bastard. A subliminal picture of the bra. Anz holding it and shaking his head. The accident. The paramedic shaking his head. Carol leaned against the armrest. Why is everybody shaking their heads?

"You say somethin', Missy Carol?" Papa asked.

"Nothing important," she mumbled.

He stared at her through the rearview mirror.

"Don't fret," he replied. "*Toutes les choses* work out for the best."

Carol smiled weakly.

"You being tested."

"That's for sure," she answered.

"*Les petites soeurs* understand many, many things. They watch over you as does Papa." His facc broke into a wide smile, and his violet eyes radiated. "Trust all," he said confidently. "And never trouble 'cause Papa *est ici.*"

"Thank you," Carol answered dryly.

He pulled the taxi in front of Carol's building.

"Home sweet home."

"I'm not too sure of that," Carol replied.

Papa Noir wagged a forefinger at her. "What you think is not," he said cryptically. "And take care of your little man. He's very important, you know."

Carol glanced at Plato, then Papa Noir. "Yes, he is." She wanted to stay in the taxi. "Did anything happen . . . I mean, did Miss Agnes read him . . . while I was asleep?" Carol stammered.

"Not at all. *Soeur* Agnes did in no manner 'read' Mr. Plato as you say. On that I am sure. Maybe in the future, but that is to be, *n'est-pas?*"

Carol smiled weakly. Stall, she begged herself. Ask another question. Take a ride in the park. Stall. Don't go in. Don't get out of the cab.

"I know you don't want to depart," Papa Noir said thoughtfully, "but . . . got to be."

Carol caught a glimpse of the doorman rushing toward the cab. "Drive away! Take me back to the doll shop," Carol demanded. Papa shook his head. *"Please!"* she whined as the door of the taxi was wrenched open.

"Hey, where ya been, Miss Elliott?" John asked. "Yer fadder's been goin' bonkers lookin' for ya!"

Carol looked pleadingly at Papa Noir, but he shook his head.

"Come on! He's upstairs."

Carol slowly stepped out of the taxi.

"Come on, Miss Elliott," John repeated. He slammed the cab door, rushed her through the lobby, and made certain she was sealed in the elevator.

She had never seen Thornton look so haggard.

"Where the hell have you been?" he blurted out. "I've turned this goddamn city upside down! *Where the hell were you?"* he screamed.

"Please, Thornton, don't!" Carol begged.

"Don't? You must be joking! Anz has men searching for you! Dr. Welch is frantic. And I'm a wreck, so don't tell me 'don't'!"

Carol put Plato on the couch, then stared out the window. "I'm sorry. I couldn't stay there another minute."

Thornton checked his rage. "Was it that terrible?" Carol nodded. "Why didn't you call me?"

"I was only gone a few hours," she replied.

Thornton crossed his arms, and held them, trying to stop himself from shaking. "I don't want you ever to do that again," he said deliberately.

"Oh *please!"* Carol shot back. "I'm not five."

"I imagined you . . . you had committed suicide." Carol looked away with annoyance. "Don't give me that look. In your condition it was . . . well, Welch felt the chances were—"

"Welch?" Carol interrupted. "I spent less than an hour with that creep, and he's filling your head with idiocy! Do you honestly think I would kill myself?"

"I don't know," Thornton whispered.

"Thanks for the vote of confidence."

"Under the recent circumstance it wasn't an outlandish assumption," Thornton retorted. "Considering the accident, the Plato episode, and the incident at the club, you couldn't be classified as 'stable.' "

"You forgot to mention my delusions about the wonderful and charming Diana," Carol replied.

"And that too."

"Did Welch suggest . . . that she's a figment of my imagination?"

Thornton wanted to avoid the subject. "We chatted about it," he replied. "Briefly, yes briefly. It wasn't paramount."

"I had to get out . . . to get as far away from that loony bin as possible . . . and I'll tell you another story," Carol said firmly. "I'm not going back . . . *ever!*"

"All right! All right!" Thornton backed down. "We'll make other arrangements.

"No!" Carol snapped. "Listen," she said calmly, "I have friends that are willing to help me." Thornton looked puzzled.

"What friends? Do I know them?" Thornton asked. Carol shook her head. "Another psychiatrist, or a therapy group?"

"Not at all," Carol replied. "It's difficult to explain."

"I have the time."

Carol agonized. How could she explain little

Aggie, no less sister Josephine? Or Papa Noir? Thornton would throw the net himself.

"Yes," he asked questioningly. "I'm waiting."

"Remember when we had the argument?"

"There have been several these past days."

"The one after we left Robb James's office . . ."

Thornton shrugged. "I don't, but anyway . . ."

"After I left you . . . I thought I was being followed." Thornton held himself rigidly. "It sounds crazy, but I was . . . anyhow, I had another argument . . . with a cabbie, and I ran out of his taxi . . . and it was raining." Thornton forced himself to smile, and nod. "It was a downpour, and I ran under an awning . . . in front of a doll shop. Well, the owners asked me to come in, and I did."

"Quite nice of them," Thornton suggested. His patience was strained. "Go on . . ."

"It's owned by the Markham sisters . . . Agnes and Josephine," Carol explained. "They dress . . . in Victorian clothes . . . long gowns, broaches, lace handkerchiefs . . . and they're very nice. Agnes . . . well, she's a midget and—"

Thornton burst out laughing. "This is incredible," he roared. "In the middle of all this you're starting with jokes."

"I'm not!"

Thornton's amusement shifted quickly into anger. "Don't you know I was goddamn worried! Half of New York is hunting for *you! And you* have the gall to start telling me stories!"

"Would you listen?" Carol seethed.

"To the truth!" Thornton replied.

"These sisters were very kind to me. They're special, very special. And I ran to them . . . God knows they're the only ones I could turn to at this time. I was away from you! From Welch! From everybody! And, Daddy dear, it felt grand . . . for the first time in years I didn't have to be foul-mouthed Carol Elliott . . . and he," Carol said pointing to Plato, "didn't utter a single four-letter job. I'd go back there in a minute if they'ed let me."

"Those are your friends?"

"Yes," Carol replied softly.

"And you've known them a few hours?"

"If you want to put it that way," she answered.

"How else can I put it?"

"There's a special quality about them. It's as if I belonged with them . . . or I've met them before. Can't you accept that?" Carol begged.

Thornton mustered all the control he had left. He pleaded with himself to be calm, to rationalize the incident, to let her "get it out" as Welch suggested. Whatever it took to defuse her emotional state he was to do, and if it meant agree, then he would agree. Now he was faced with the situation and he was straining to cope.

"I guess I'll have to accept it," he replied.

"Don't humor me!"

"I'm not," Thornton answered. "This . . . this hasn't been one of my better days. The past few hours certainly haven't been fun."

"I didn't mean to worry you. I wanted to call, but they don't have a telephone."

"Where . . . where is this doll shop?"

Carol laughed softly. "I really don't know. In the Seventies off Columbus, or the low Eighties. Yes, it's Eighty-third . . . no, maybe Eighty . . .? "Isn't that dumb! I honestly don't know where they are."

Thornton showed more restraint. Where was she? he thought. Certainly not at a doll shop. What was Carol hiding? Drugs? Not likely, but it couldn't be ruled out. Impossible, he corrected himself, but he looked into her eyes trying to detect glassiness.

"Why are you looking at me like that?" Carol demanded. "Don't you believe me?"

"Of course," Thornton recovered. "I was only thinking . . . well, I should call Welch—"

"Why?" Carol interrupted.

"To tell him you're safe. Isn't that reasonable?"

Carol nodded. "Sorry, I thought you might . . ."

"Not at all," Thornton answered. "If you don't want to stay . . . well, the hospital was only a temporary measure."

Carol smiled at him warmly. "Suppose I call Dr. Welch, and explain what happened?"

"That would be—"

The telephone rang and cut Thornton's suggestion in midsentence. Carol picked up the receiver immediately.

"Hello."

"Well, where the hell you been, lady?" Nick Anz bellowed. "We nearly had people dredge the river for you!"

"I was with some friends," Carol replied.

"Jesus . . . next time tell someone, huh?"

"I'll try," she answered. Carol covered the mouthpiece and informed Thornton it was Anz.

"That would be nice," Anz shot back. "Listen . . . you ever met a guy by the name of . . . Arnold Cohen?"

"I don't think so," Carol replied. "But that doesn't mean much, I'm rotten with names. He could have been associated with Murray or someone I met in Vegas. What does he look like?"

"He's about five ten, swarthy, dark curly hair. About twenty-five . . . and built like one of them musclemen," Anz described.

"If he's unmarried, I'll be right down," Carol quipped.

"If his name's . . . stage name's Latino, does that make a difference?" Anz countered.

Carol gripped the telephone tightly.

The confrontation in her dressing flooded back. Latino playing with Plato. Latino strutting in front of her. Latino telling her what he thought, how he despised her. Diana, Latino, Diana, Latino. "He's one of the go-go dancers at the Q Club."

"Was," Anz replied dryly. "It seems someone's opened his stomach with a knife. Why don'tcha come back to the Q Club, huh? I got a couple of things I want to ask you."

Chapter Fourteen

In contrast to the upbeat, hold-back-the-reporters Hollywood scenario, the murder scene at the Q Club was muted, almost detached. Detectives stood in small groups comparing facts, and noting them on pads. Monotone voices seeped into the backstage as the coroner's men probed Latino's body. Camera shutters whirred and snapped, recording another angle of the body. Anz and his men huddled like track officials at the finish line comparing stopwatches.

There was nothing to get excited about, just another routine New York murder. Arnold Roger Cohen, professionally known as Latino, occupation: dancer, lay sprawled across centerstage. The death technicians hovered around him instead of screaming admirers. More pictures. Another angle. Another flash. The adoring crowd had given way to clinicians probing the gaping wound in his midsection, picking fibers off his tights with tweezers, carefully dusting the doorjambs for fingerprints. It was an exercise in precision. Nothing would be left to chance. The coroner's men examined Latino's nails, hoping to find bits of skin, or threads, but came up empty. Nevertheless his hands were "bagged." More notes, more paperwork. It was routine. The death spot was chalked, the body crammed into an official green bag and removed. No one wept, or gagged, or flinched. The pros had seen worse.

Nick Anz carefully paced splotches of Latino's blood from middle of Carol's dressing room to the larger pool at centerstage.

"I don't see how he got this far, Harry!"

"Pulled himself across the stage," the younger detective replied. "The coroner's people found slivers of wood in his knees."

"Bled like a sonofabitch, didn't he?"

"Yeah, Nick. The doc says he was just about dry."

"Shitty way to go." He studied the distance again. "Where's the janitor?"

"Down front," the detective replied.

"Right," Anz said.

Anz retraced Latino's final entry into Carol's room. C'mon, c'mon, he muttered to himself. Where are ya? He poked through Carol's cosmetic table. Where's the mistake? C'mon, where the mistake? The whatever? Don't hide from old Nicky. Anz got on his hands and knees and lightly fingered aside the nap on the carpeting. He edged around a moist patch of blood searching for a hint, an aberration, anything that would link the dead man with his killer. Anz stood up and clutched his back. "It's in here somewhere," he told the detective. "Go through the room again, Harry. And this time pull up the carpeting, right?"

"The boys been through her room twice."

"Good," Anz replied, "you make it a lucky three and find what those clowns missed."

"Aw, Nick!"

"Do it!" Anz commanded. "The mistake's right in front of us. I'll be with . . . whatizface?"

"Farrar. Harold Farrar."

Anz retraced Latino's path again, then walked down a side ramp leading into the main room. Harold Farrar, the club's handyman-porter, sat nervously at a table.

"Rotten business, huh?" Anz asked.

"We never, *never* had anything like this since I been here. We had fights," he intoned, "we had ladies clawing at each other, but nothing, *nothing* this bad. And I had to find him . . . it was my day off, and I had to come in . . . just to check, just to make sure this place . . . well, it was bound to happen, but why did I have to be here?"

"Whatta ya mean 'it was bound to happen'?"

"Pshaw! All that nudity . . . women stuffing money in that boy's underwear. This place used to be respectable. None of the carrying's on . . . men running around naked! *Pshaw!*"

"Yeah," Anz agreed, "it's tough to handle."

"We never had one speck of trouble until . . . well, the new owners . . ." he said confidentially, "made it this way, but don't say I told you. Turned everything upside down . . . no more jazz, no more improv groups . . . only Miss Elliott and that dummy stayed . . . and you know what kind of mouth God gave her. Pshaw! It was bound to happen . . ."

"Yeah, it's a pity," Anz agreed.

"I remember when this was called the Zebra Room. It had class . . . people dressed to the nines. Remember?"

"Vaguely," Anaz replied "Now, what time did you let Mr. Cohen, er, Latino, in."

"About eleven, maybe a little after," Farrar answered. "He always came here Thursdays . . . to practice that kind of dancing. Put on the music and started moving around . . . it was something else. But I told the officers all of this," he protested.

"And what time did Miss Elliott arrive?" Anz questioned.

"Here we go again!" Farrar muttered. "I guess it was about noon. It's just as I said . . . she was alone, I went about my business, and I didn't hear her leave."

"And there was no one else? Not even the manager? Or any of Latino's friends?"

"No sir!" Farrar replied.

"Didn't you hear anything? Telephone call? Men talking? Did Miss Elliott see Latino?"

"Of course she did! I told your people I heard them arguing! Or talking loud! How many times do I have to repeat myself?"

"What were they arguing about?"

Farrar shook his head. "It was too far to hear. I was behind the bar and they were in the back . . . I didn't hear anything 'cept some hard talk."

"And Latino was shouting at her?"

"They both were at each other!" Farrar corrected. "Then he turned on some of that music, and that's all I know."

"And no one else was in the club?" Anz asked.

"I told them policemen that!" Farrar erupted.

"Was the stage door locked?"

"Yes sir," Farrar snapped.

"You're positive?" Anz shot back.

"Absolutely," he replied. "I've been locking this place for fifteen years. It was locked."

"But Mr. Cohen could have let someone in, right?"

"Yeah, yeah," Farrar answered.

"Or Miss Elliott."

"I don't know if they did, or didn't. Besides someone could have been in the club all night . . . just waiting for that boy. Tain't that so?"

Nick Anz chuckled. "It's a possibility."

"Anyhow, the only thing I know for damn sure is

. . . I didn't let nobody in here 'cept Miss Carol and that . . . that dancer."

Anz saw Carol and Thornton enter the main room. "Thanks, Mr. Farrar, we'll get back to you."

"Sure. Y'know the pity of it is we'll probably be open tonight. Damn shame. Them owners never want to miss a beat," he groused and walked slowly toward the bar. "How ya doing, Miss Elliott? Mr. Thornton?" Farrar muttered as he passed them.

"What happened, Harold?" Carol asked softly.

"Nasty business," he replied. "Bound to happen, bound to happen," he whispered and disappeared into the gloominess of the club.

Thornton and Carol exchanged anxious glances as they followed one of the detectives toward Anz.

Carol glanced furtively at the chalked blood stains, and the outline of Latino's body. "Unbelievable," she whispered. "I saw him . . . I don't know . . . about noon, one o'clock. Horrible."

"Yeah," Anz replied. "Someone did quite a number on him. The poor bastard bled to death."

Carol stared blankly at the maroon patches on the stage.

"He was attacked in your dressing room, Miss Elliott, then stumbled out here . . . and that's it!"

Carol stiffened. "I didn't kill him," she replied.

"I wasn't suggesting it," he answered.

Carol nodded, and looked away.

"However, you two argued, didn't you?" She nodded again. "What was that about?"

"Plato," Carol answered. "He was holding Plato when I walked into my room."

"Oh? That provoked you?"

"I don't like people touching him," Carol answered.

"That's not unreasonable," Anz replied.

"He was sitting in my room . . . holding him . . . pretending to talk with him," Carol said with annoyance. "I told him to get out, but he wouldn't. We had words . . . no, no, it was a shouting match."

"About Plato?"

"That and other things," Carol replied.

"Such as . . .?"

"He . . . he made some remarks about my act."

Anz nodded. "Uncomplimentary remarks."

"Yes . . . I can't remember. It was a flurry, and I grabbed Plato from him."

Un-huh, Anz thought. "Was there anyone else here . . . besides the janitor?" Carol shook her head. "You're sure of that?"

"No," she answered. "I don't know."

"About the incident with Mr. Cohen. His remarks made you angry, right?" Carol nodded. "More specifically, what did he say?"

"Different things," Carol replied nervously.

"Like what?" Anz insisted.

"About my condition . . . being in the hospital."

"Anything else?"

"Of course, but I can't remember them . . . it was a scene. I yelled something at him, then he started on me . . . about my act."

"For example!" Anz asked.

"I can't remember . . ."

"Try!" Anz insisted.

"That it was blue . . . that I was, yeah . . . 'queen of smut' . . . I should have my mouth washed out . . . and maybe have our tongues cut off . . . it was creepy. I mean, he started to sound like . . . Diana, the letter writer . . . at one point I was scared."

"Scared enough to protect yourself?"

"I didn't kill him!" Carol replied forcefully.

"Did he threaten you?"

"In a way," Carol answered.

"So he did touch you."

"He *never* touched me, but I had the feeling . . . well, it's what he said, his tone. I was damn glad to get out of there . . . damn glad."

"You ever have any trouble with him before?" Carol shook her head. "But you knew him before?"

"He was here when I left for the Coast."

"Didja ever date? Go out afterwards?"

Carol laughed. "No way! Not him! Latino? He looked macho, but he was all fairy underneath that facade."

"You're positive?" Anz replied.

"C'mon on!" Carol quipped. "Everybody knew it!"

"So how didja get out of the club?"

"Latino went on stage. I heard his music. I picked up Plato and ran. That's the last time I saw him."

"Did you see Harold before you left?"

Carol thought for a moment. "No," she replied.

"About what time were you here?"

"Between twelve and one. No! I was looking for a cab about twenty of one. I was running down the street and I glanced at the clock on the Chase Bank."

"Where were you going?" Anz asked.

Carol hesitated. The Markhams? Papa Noir? It would be another absurd story. No address. No phone. Tell him, she begged herself. A darker voice screamed no.

"Miss Elliott, where were you heading?" Anz pressed. Carol stared at him blankly. "*Where,* Miss Elliott?"

"I had a luncheon appointment," Carol stammered. "With two friends . . . two sisters . . . on the West Side."

"And you took a cab from here?"

"No," Carol answered, "I went home first."

"Why, because you wanted to avoid your father, or the doctors?"

"They were going to pick me up at the building," Carol explained. "It's complicated . . . I was late . . . you wouldn't understand . . . it's all complicated."

"Try me!" Anz replied. "I'll listen."

Carol looked down and shook her head.

"Miss Elliott," Anz replied quickly, "this isn't a game. We've got a dead man, no witnesses, and two immediate suspects. I want you to talk to me, huh?"

"You think I killed . . . are you saying—?"

"I'm saying nothing. However, Mr. Cohen was stabbed once . . . a nice clean shot that ripped his stomach open, which means that either he knew the killer, or wasn't afraid of the person. One stoke in the stomach. No sign of a struggle. No evidence of a fight."

"I *didn't kill him!*" Carol said forcefully.

"Is there anything you haven't told me?"

"No!" she answered.

"Is there something you may have forgotten?"

"Of course . . . I don't recall the exact conversation . . . or the time! He was here . . . in my dressing room and we had words . . . I was scared, and I ran."

"Did he lunge at you?" Anz asked.

"No!" Carol replied. "I said . . . it looked like he would, but *he didn't!*"

"Did he ever come into your dressing room before you went to the Coast?" Anz asked.

"No! Why would he?"

"Just a thought . . . maybe you and he were friends. Something like that," Anz suggested.

"I already told you. He was a fag. A prancing queen!" Carol replied. "I didn't like him."

"Did you ever have another confrontation with Mr. Cohen? Other arguments? Did he threaten you before?"

"Dammit!" Carol yelled. "I never associated with him! He didn't threaten me!"

"Aren't you contradicting yourself?" Anz asked.

"Will you climb off?" Carol shouted. "I didn't kill him!"

"You always anger this quickly?"

"No! You're making accusations," Carol said quickly. "Everything's coming down on me, and I can't handle it. This is getting heavy . . . too frigging heavy. Yeah, I get angry . . . especially when someone's trying to railroad me."

"She doesn't have to answer any of your questions," Thornton interjected. "Carol's entitled to—"

"Oh shut up, Thornton," Carol growled. "I've had enough with the damn lawyers.

"Just trying to help," he replied.

"Good. You can help by saying nothing." Carol looked at Anz suspiciously. "Am I a suspect?"

"Yeah," Anz replied. "You and Mr. Farrar are both suspects."

"Outrageous!" Thornton shouted.

"Hey, Nick, we got something!" a heavy-set detective yelled as he walked quickly across the stage. "Ya gotta take a look at these!"

"Whadda ya got, Howie?"

The detective slapped a stack of typed pages into Anz's hands. "Letters, a whole stack of letters to the dancer. Look, look at that! Hot stuff, huh?"

Anz skimmed through the correspondence.

"Outta sight, no? Is that coincidence, or is it, huh? We fell into this, Nicky."

"Lemme read, all right?" Anz grunted a few times as he went through the letters quickly.

"Pretty creepy, huh Nick?"

"Yeah, Howie," he said slowly. "Pretty creepy."

Anz looked at Carol as he slid the letters in a

evidence bag. "You might be interested in those letters."

"I doubt it," Carol replied.

"On the contrary, Miss Elliott, you and Mr. Cohen got a mutual pen pal . . . Diana the Chaste."

Chapter Fifteen

Latino darling,
I love you with all the passion of
of the universe.
Diana the Chaste

Latino darling,
I hunger for you.
Diana the Chaste

Latino darling,
I watch you every night, and know
you're mine alone.
Diana the Chaste

Latino darling,
I want you throbbing within me.
I love you.
Diana the Chaste

Latino darling,
Thank you for everything, my celestial.
Your beauty will linger in my soul.
Even the slut/bitch cannot befoul
our wonderful air.
Diana the Chaste

Nick Anz closed the file on his desk and slumped in his chair. "So tell me, Howie," he said to the detective seated across from him. "What did the geniuses come up with?"

"We got approximately two hundred latent fingerprints. It took Brownstone and Baer nearly three days to lift any clean ones. It came up zero, Nick, they matched all the people at the club . . . dancers, Farrar, Elliott. It's a dead end. Not even a smudge that could be used as evidence."

"Terrific!" Nick Anz groaned.

"Next time pick a more intimate spot for a murder . . . like the men's room at the stadium. Y'know how many prints were in that joint, huh?" Lederer asked.

"Terrific!" Anz repeated. "Next item."

"The wound pattern is similar to those inflicted by a bayonet . . ."

"A bayonet?" Anz shot back.

"That's right, Nick. Penetration was in excess of five inches, the width approximately one to one and a half, and the thickness about a quarter of an inch. It wasn't your ordinary steak knife, or a Buck knife. One shot entering Cohen above the pubic bone and ending below the sternum. Just like a zipper, Nick!"

"Jeez!" Anz replied. "No defensive wounds?"

"Nothing."

"Gotta be, Howie."

"Wanna see the autopsy report? One shot. No wounds on either hand, or the forearms, or the back."

"Yer telling me Latino stood there and took one right up the gut . . . without moving?"

"The bastard never knew what hit him. Someone pulled out the bayonet and . . . *zip!*"

"Zip your ass! How does the murderer get *that* close, make a hit, no defensive wounds, no clues."

"Not our department," Lederer replied.

"Swell!" Nick snorted. "No prints! No sign of a struggle! No witnesses! All this topped off with a single wound. It stinks, Howie, it reeks."

"Ya got yerself a real strange lady out there, Nick."

"And that doesn't figure either. A bayonet isn't a female-type weapon. No way! Plus the wound! One penetration. It isn't a typical crime of passion. If she was so incensed she would have covered Latino's body with wounds! It stinks! It doesn't add up."

"Yer dealing with a creep! An out-of-control creep. It's only theory that she used a bayonet—"

"All right! Give me the rest of the report. What about the letters, or weren't they typed?"

"Clever, Nick, very clever."

"C'mon, Howie, tell me what else the crime lab and the staff psychiatrist found."

"A pretty solid profile," he replied. "Same typewriter, same paper. She's right-handed. The *l's* and *o's* are heavier than other letters. Good speller, no typos. All the letters were written at the exact moment . . . same rate of speed."

"I'm so glad she's a good speller," Anz quipped. Lederer smiled and continued. "The Elliott letters conform with the Cohen letters. Your Diana sat down and reeled them off. However, the 'slut/bitch' in the Cohen letter is etched deeper into the paper. Miss Diana was really upset when she typed that one."

Anz compared Carol's last letter with the one Lederer mentioned. "Heavy pressure on the Elliott letter too." he remarked.

"All of them have heavy pressure. The writer is pounding on the keys . . . typing rapidly. Check the smears on the right edges of each letter. The venom's flowing, Nick. You got a weird one out there."

"Thanks, Holmes," Anz shot back. "Fingerprints? Watermarks? Special paper? Anything?"

"Sorry, Nick," Lederer replied. "Only Cohen's

and Elliott's prints. Five-and-dime paper. You got all of it."

Anz glanced at the stack of letters. "Square one. Starting point. Nothing. Zero. A big fat zero, Howie."

"I haven't finished," Lederer replied. The staff psychiatrist has analyzed the typing patterns—"

"Ah, bullshit!" Anz groaned.

"—*and* came up with some variations."

Anz shook his head.

"Our Diana is one screwed-up chick."

"That's beautiful!" Anz exploded. "Jeez, they really know how to make conclusions downstairs. Of course, she's crazy! You gotta be nuts to shove a knife in someone."

"Lemme finish, huh? Their report suggests Diana has a dual personality . . ."

"Like a ventriloquist?" Anz replied quickly.

"They don't think it's the Elliott woman."

"Why not?" Anz asked.

"At first . . . it was under consideration. However Diana shows a lot more masochistic tendencies *and* is working out a sexual-psychological problem."

"She's a schizoid, huh?" Anz asked.

"That's what they think," Lederer replied.

"Think! But don't know, huh?"

Lederer shrugged.

"So how 'bout this, my friend? Carol Elliott, a confused woman to be sure, could fit into the profile. Ventriloquist . . . under emotional pressure . . . under psychiatric care. She's not too stable, my friend. And there are a bunch of holes in her story. Think of it . . . she escapes from a nuthouse, runs to the Q Club for the dummy, has a face-to-face blow-out with the deceased, and runs away again! Where? She's purposely vague on that. Why?

Another blank. Schizoid? Her own shrink nods on that one."

"She doesn't fit the profile," Lederer insisted. "The letters dump that idea."

"In one personality, okay. But the other . . .?"

"No way, Nick. Diana isn't Carol Elliott. Too many personality deviations. The letters show her under tremendous strain. She's ready to break loose because she's frustrated . . . filled with hate. The Elliott woman may 'hate' herself, but would never project it into a murder."

"Nice theory. Tight! Convincing, but I don't buy it, Howie!"

"Up to you, boss, but it ain't Carol Elliott. The shrinks know she wants to 'kill'—'kill' in the abstract sense—herself, but not in the physical sense. Listen, Nick, she'll do another number on the dummy . . . masculine image, huh? A little antipathy to men, huh? No, she's got other problems, but murder isn't one of them."

"So what motivates . . . Diana, huh?"

"Rejection!"

Anz frowned.

"Yeah, Nick, men don't like her. She's not attractive. She's a go-go groupie! The Q Club. The other places. We think she's been to all of 'em. She gets her rocks off fantasizing. And that's the extent. Latino was idolized. Maybe other dancers in other clubs have been approached?"

"Could be," Anz reflected. "But—"

"She's not getting any wham-bam, Nicky! This broad's a toad. She can't get herself laid, or she's too hung up to try it! She's living in a dream. Cohen was everything she wanted."

"He was a fruit!" Nick replied.

"How did she know. He looked sexy, masculine. She sends him letters, but he doesn't respond. We know he's a beefcake, not Diana! Not her! She's saving herself for him! Diana the Chaste, huh? Finally, she meets him, he teases her, puts her on, but that's it, and the infatuation grows out of proportion. She sees him after the show, still zip! She's a dog, he's a fruit, so you see, it's nothing but frustration. In the end he rejects her, maybe belittles her. She goes to the club, and cuts him up."

"And Carol Elliott, what's her part? Why is she dragged into this?"

"Diana sees her as competition," Lederer answered.

"It doesn't feel right," Anz replied. "Too many ifs and maybes."

"Suit yourself," Lederer replied.

"Suppose it's a fruit? Take your entire idea and replace Diana with a homosexual, huh? A thwarted love affair. Gays in conflict. A falling out. It could explain how the killer got into the club. Cohen had an appointment, opened the door, got stabbed."

"Don't think so, Nick. The psychiatrist says—"

Anz cut him off.

"I'm still going to check the other dancers, Mr. Cohen's buddies, and the rest of the people. I'm not ready to accept your Diana bit."

"Why don't you test it out, Nick? They think Diana hasn't finished. Remember she's still after Carol Elliott. Take the wraps off . . . let her go back to work . . . make it appear she's an easy target."

"You gotta be kidding! I'm not gonna set her up!" Anz replied.

"Nick, the lovely Diana is coming back. Let's get her under controlled conditions.

Let's finish the case. Let her think she's got a clean shot at the Elliott broad, and we'll nail her."

"No way! Too risky!"

"Nicky, we're dealing with a psychopath who

won't be satisfied until she's completed another pattern of abnormal behavior."

" *'She?'* You're always refering to this crazy as a woman. I don't buy it! How do you *know* it's not a fruit?"

"We didn't find a trace of ejaculate," Lederer countered. "Nothing . . . not a shot."

"Okay, I gotcha," Anz replied understandingly.

"It was the first thing we looked for. Believe me, Nick, I thought it was another guy for sure, but the pattern didn't fit. Naw, it's a screwed-up broad, and we gotta shut her down before Carol Elliott is next."

"Yeah," Anz said thoughtfully.

"I'm sorry, Nick, I wish it was different."

"It's all right, Howie, I know we can't protect Carol Elliott forever . . . better we force the issue." Anz leaned back in his chair. "Y'know she'll never go for it. . . ."

"The shrinks disagree, Nick."

Anz shook his head. "No, I mean Carol. I doubt she'll ever go back to that club. And her father will certainly veto the idea."

Lederer stood up, and stretched. "Use your innate charm, and personality."

"Thanks," Anz snorted.

"Nicky," Lederer warned, "tell her the truth . . . either way she's on a downer 'cause Diana won't forgive or forget. It's the pits no matter how you slice it."

Chapter Sixteen

"Out of the question!" Thornton bellowed. "I won't let you step on that stage." Carol ignored him and kept staring out her window. "Did you hear me?" She nodded. "The idea is absurd! Absolutely preposterous! I've called Anz's superiors. I want another detective to handle this matter. . . ."

Carol watched the tankers glide slowly up the Hudson River. Her own thoughts intercepted and blocked out Thornton's outrage. I wonder how long they're at sea? she thought. Six months? Possibly. That's a long time. Probably more like a year. She watched the tanker disappear, then fixed her gaze on its wake.

"Carol," Thornton insisted, "I want you to call Jack Lanzetta."

"Yeah," she muttered softly.

Thornton was surprised. "You'll go to Vegas?"

"Maybe."

"Now you're making more sense."

"I want to talk with Anz first," she replied.

"Why?" he snapped.

"Because I want to!"

"I've asked him to be removed from the case."

"Nice," Carol replied as she walked into her bedroom, and shut the door in his face. She curled into a fetal position in the middle of her bed. The half-lit room cast angular shadows, and the wind sweeping across the Hudson rattled the windows. Carol pulled the down comforter over her and burrowed into the safety of her cocoon.

A week without a letter from the Markhams. Why? And why had they rushed her out of the shop? Disfavor? Maybe they had sent a letter and Thornton had— Paranoid, babe, she told herself. The "why" lingered and flowed into the fear that Diana might be behind her.

A week with fitful sleep. Nightmares of Latino, the bra, and the blood-splattered stage. You used to have Murray as the center attraction, she thought. Murray! I'd settle for that aggravation now, Carol laughed. Bastard Murray, you only wanted my money.

A week of "protective custody." What the hell is that, Anz? You'll have protection, echoed back. For the rest of my life? Not exactly.

I'm a goddamn prisoner, Carol thought.

This isn't anyway to live, she told Anz.

Sorry, echoed back.

Ya know, he told her, there might be another approach.

Oh? You want me to have plastic surgery. Good idea, Anz, I'll pick a face. How about Raquel? Or Bo? I'll be old Raquel, or old Bo. Not funny, huh?

The wind shook the windowpanes again and Carol wound herself tighter into the warmth.

"You mean you'll never catch . . . this freak," reverberated through her mind.

"It's a strong possibility," Anz echoed.

"You've got to . . . got to!" Carol had pleaded.

"Well . . . there is an option. . . ."

Helluva option, Carol thought.

"I'll think about it," she had told him.

Carol tried to squeeze Anz out of her mind. Sleep, she begged herself. Escape, and sleep, but her wish wasn't possible as old apprehensions fueled new fears. Finally, she tossed aside the comforter, reached for the telephone and dialed Anz's number.

"Nick Anz," he boomed.

"It's Carol Elliott," she replied. "I've been thinking about our . . . discussion."

"Oh? So what's the story?"

"Suppose I was to get out of New York for a couple of months. Go to Vegas. They'll let me hit the lounge circuit for two, maybe three months."

"Still no good," Anz told her.

"Can't the locals protect me?"

"The police or the privates?"

"Both," Carol suggested. "Or I can hire a bodyguard. At least I'll be away from the Q Club. . . ."

"What's to stop Diana from following you? Miss Elliott, the police psychiatric report is pretty . . . here, lemme read it to you: 'The party known as Diana is obsessed with the thoughts of cleansing, i.e., premediated homicide, the negative object, i.e., Carol Elliott. This is indicated by the paragraph underlined in Police Exhibits 54-3AB, and the Cohen letter marked Police Exhibit Z43-72PG."

"The letters?" Carol questioned.

"Right," Anz answered, "and to further drive home their point lemme read you . . . 'I believe Diana is continuing to work out a homicidal obsession, and will not stop until she has taken a definitive action.' Signed, *L. Stuart Christopher, M.D., N.Y. Police Department, Department of Psychiatry.*"

"Pretty grim, huh?"

"Pretty grim," Anz replied.

"She'll come after me here, or Vegas."

"That's right, Miss Elliott."

"I guess I haven't a choice."

"Slim to none," Anz quipped. "And I can't protect you forever," he added.

"Un-huh," Carol replied. "I figured as much. It's a helluva risk. Suppose you screw up?"

"I don't intend to," Anz replied.

"And suppose she doesn't take the bait?"

"We think she will."

"They've been wrong before," Carol said.

"It's still your decision. You can run, and she'll be behind you, or you can play it out hoping to nail her," Anz replied. "It's a downer either way."

"What the hell did I do to deserve this?"

"You offended her," Anz answered. "The staff psychiatrist believes your act brought out some latent hosility."

Carol chuckled. "And I thought it was for laughs."

"Well . . . it's a pretty tough routine," Anz told her. "Some people might take exception to your sense of humor."

"Meaning my language?" Anz didn't reply. "I understand," Carol replied. "Sometimes it upsets me too."

"Whatever you said triggered the outburst . . . of letters, and the bra."

"And Latino? How did a poor fag get it, or are we into the age of surrogate murder?" Carol asked.

"He probably rebuffed her, and the rest you know," Anz replied. "You see, we think she fantasized a 'pure' relationship with him, and when that exploded . . . so did she. She's a weirdo, Miss Elliott, and you're a player in her sick game."

Carol regripped the telephone. "When do you want me to perform?" she asked.

"This weekend. Give the club time to promote your return. Ads, and junk like that. Let's advertise."

"Right . . . 'come and get me,' huh?"

"It's the only way," Anz replied.

Harold Farrar had been right. It was as if nothing had happened. No bloodstains. The bar wasn't draped in black bunting, neither did the waitresses sport armbands. A muscular youth, costumed in flesh-colored tights, and billed as Mr. Sleek, had taken Latino's spot. The beat went on, and the not-so-lovely ladies never missed a pelvis-grinding performance. It was a rim shot and *chick-a-boom.* Hang in there troops, 'cause tonight marks the return . . . the very special return of The First Lady of Blue. Yes, I'm talking about Carol Lane and little Mr. Hard One himself . . . the one, the only . . . *Plato.* Oh shit, Helen, I thought they got rid of her. *Naw.* Wasn't that last comic super? *Yeah.* So cute! I woulda liked to see him in tights. *Maybe.* What's the matter with you? *I dunno.* Sometimes, Helen, yer such a pill.

At first Thornton refused to appear at the Q Club or take part "in this travesty," but he relented, met Carol at the stage door, rushed her into the dressing room, and sat anxiously beside her as she applied mascara.

"Thornton, would you stop looking like death warmed over?" Carol requested. He forced a smile. "I can't function when you're staring at me!" she told him. He pretended to read *Variety.* "Would you give me some space?"

"All right. I'll wait outside."

"No!" Carol barked. "Sit in the audience. Take a walk. Stop hovering. I can't stand it anymore."

He looked at her disdainfully, and left the room. Carol tossed her lipstick at the mirror.

"Damn you, Thornton!"

"Tsk! Tsk!" Plato replied. "It ain't his fault, you know."

Carol glared at Plato's reflection in her mirror. "You're not hooking me, babe. I know I'm talking to myself. She combed her hair, and sprayed it. "No way, José. Not now . . . I got enough trouble."

"Ya really think it's all in yer head?" Plato asked.

Carol wiped a smudge of rouge off her cheek. "Ya gonna ignore me, huh?" She readjusted the neckline of her dress. "Fine with me, babe. If that's the way ya want it . . . well, you're on yer own."

Carol carefully reworked the mascara brush against her lashes, staring directly into the mirror.

Chick-a-boom seeped through the club followed by adoring screams. Latino flashed subliminally through Carol's consciousness.

"More, *more, more,*" pulsated into her dressing room. *Chick-a-boom* and rim shot.

Carol glanced at Plato. The little bastard *didn't* talk. Welch's smiling face appeared and vanished.

Chick-a-boom. Bump-and-grind music laced with panting screams.

Suppose she's here? And she gets by Anz's men? The thought was chilling. A tinge of fear crept from Carol's shoulders up her neck.

Chick-a-boom and rim shot. "And let's hear it for our newest addition . . . c'mon, let's give it to *Mr. Sleek!*"

Nick Anz rapped on the door, and opened it.

"All set?" he asked.

Carol glanced at him in the mirror. "I guess so," she replied.

"The dancers are almost finished. Why don'tcha wait with us in the wings?"

Carol sat Plato on her arm, tugged his collar, and followed Anz to the offstage area. *Chick-a-boom.* It was final pose time, which was punctuated with screams, and cheers. Not a trace of Latino's blood as Mr. Sleek pranced at centerstage. Farrar was right, the club owners never missed a beat.

"You okay?" Anz asked.

"I have to be," Carol replied.

"We've got men spotted around the room, so don't worry," he told her.

"Sure," Carol snorted. "And what about after the

show? What happens if it doesn't work?" The vision of Diana charging at her with a knife welled up and disappeared. "I don't give a shit about this place! It's afterwards. You got that covered, chief?"

"And now-w-w-w-w," the new emcee blared as the dancers muscled offstage, "back with us once mor-r-r-re . . . that fabulous lady of filth . . ."

Carol cringed.

". . . that doll of the double entendre with her prurient partner of pine . . ."

Anz shook his head.

"Nice, isn't it?" Carol remarked.

"I wish there was another way," Anz replied.

"I was talking about my intro. It gives the emcee a chance to use his mind," she laughed. "In Vegas I'm called . . . lemme see, Carnal Carol, or worse. Real class, huh?" Carol shook her head. "Yep, it's a sophisticated act. No wonder I've gone so far," she said sarcastically.

"Ever thought of quitting?" Anz replied.

"How often do you breathe?"

Anz shrugged. "So . . . why not pack it in?"

"Money. It's only a means to an end," she snorted. "Every paycheck get me closer to the top of the hole. . . .Another five grand and the lawyers are out, another seven clears up debts . . . oh shit, it's endless."

Rim shot and cheers filtered from the stage.

"Y'know those bitches don't even remember Latino," Carol growled. She stared at Plato. "Well . . . I've got my own problems, huh? Especially with this little guy. I thought he was talking to me before you came in . . . it's just nerves, right, Detective?"

"Probably," he replied.

"I know he didn't talk . . . now or after the accident. It's all in my head . . . split personality, the bane of ventriloquists. I'm really screwed-up

. . . maybe I'll get lucky and our friend will finish it for me. That's the only way I'm gonna break free."

"Listen, Carol," Anz said pointedly, "one bad vibe, one inkling that our friend is out there, and I want you to get offstage. Don't pull any stunts! Don't have the dummy talk to her, right? Just pull the whole frigging act, and get off! *Capishe?*"

"Yeah. Guess so," Carol muttered.

". . . let's put our palms together, and give a big welcome home to the one *and only* . . . *Carol Lane* and-d-d *Plato!*" Carol froze as the emcee beckoned to her.

"You okay?" Anz questioned.

"You kidding?" she replied. "I'm scared shitless."

Not losing a beat the emcee firmly led Carol on stage. "It's all your-r-r-rs, Carol-l-l-l-l Lane," he crooned, then dashed into the wings.

Rim shot.

Carol froze for an instant.

Another *rim shot* shocked her into place. The vintage gags, dirty jokes, and innuendos, spewed forth.

"Hey, didja hear the one about the two faggots and the parrot?" Plato asked. A three-sixty, and eye roll.

"I don't want to!" Carol shot back.

"Super! Just 'cause ya asked . . . this raggedy-assed parrot. . . ."

Anz flinched at the crude punch line.

Carol followed it with gags 734 through 761. It was the standard Q-Club routine. Set-up, punch line, and laugh. Observation, suggestion, punch line, and laugh. Nothing had changed. The day porter was a prophet. Carol and Plato moved uncaringly through the scrubbed-out bloodstains. Anz watched her as she delivered another raunchy gag without missing a beat, or flinching, or shaking, or thinking that Diana the sick was alive.

Anz recoiled at her language.

"She's outdone herself tonight," Thornton whispered as he stood behind Anz.

Rim shot. Smut line. Grab 'em by their dirty minds and make 'em laugh.

"Yeah," he answered dryly. "She's got some act. Some *rotten* act." He shook his head and moved away from Thornton.

Rim shot. She was laying 'em out in lavender. Anz's men lounged casually against the bar, half listening to the smutty patter, half watching the maze of women clustered about minuscule cocktail tables. Blonds? Several. One of them Diana the crazy? Doubtful. Hey, Frank, check the babe over there. Whadda ya think? No way, Harry.

Jeez, Harry, check the tits on that one. Holy shit, my old lady would kill me if she knew where I was. Maybe your old lady's here, Frankie?

"Let's play a game," Plato announced.

"Which one? Doctor?" Carol replied.

She manipulated his head side-to-side. "Naw! Let's play . . . pick on a plump one . . .!"

The audience cheered wildly.

Carol rotated his head slowly, looking for a target. "No, she's too thin," Plato commented. Finally, Carol spotted a heavy-set woman and Plato stared directly at her. "*Aha!*" he screamed in glee.

Victim time. "Hello, fatty!"

Insult time. "How ya doing? The chairs okay?"

Rim shot, and roars.

"Now, folks!" Plato insisted. "Don't be cruel 'cause this lady is a celebrity. That's right, she's Bo Derek's sister . . . I wantcha to meet 'Dough' Derek!"

Rim shot and laughter.

The woman withstood the attack as Plato heaped insult after abuse on her.

"C'mon, folks," Carol suggested, "let's give her a big . . . and she likes it big . . . round of applause for this gal."

Drum roll and mocking laughter.

"Bad taste," Anz growled at Thornton. "Sometimes your daughter goes too far, y'know?"

Thornton nodded and looked away.

Carol was about to move into the audience for the last part of her act, but a sudden rush of fear welled up and she stepped back. Millisecond flashes of Latino, the accident, shattered glass, and the hospital churned and exploded.

"And now the moment you've waiting for," Carol announced. "For my final number . . ."

Rim shot and jeers.

"Get off, bitch!" a young man shouted. "We want the mudwrestlers."

More jeers, and the chant went up as expected.

"Mud, mud, mud!"

"Take a hike, foul-mouth," was shrieked across the main room. "*Mud,* not the dud," joined the rhythmic clapping. "*Mud, mud, mud . . .*"

"Get off!" screamed a dumpy blonde. "*Get out!*" The fury in her voice shocked the audience into an uneasy silence. "Get out!" And take that disgusting dummy with you!"

Anz's men lurched out of their amused complacency, moved toward the stage.

". . . As I said before I was rudely interrupted," Carol replied.

"Someone oughta sew your filthy mouth shut," the woman snarled. "You make me ashamed . . . you tramp!"

Carol tried to hold her composure. "Moving right along, folks . . ." she countered.

"Why don't you?" the woman yelled.

Anz's men hustled thorugh the maze of cocktail tables as the woman pushed her way toward Carol.

"She's coming for ya!" Plato whispered.

Carol stared at him blankly.

"That's right, babe, I'm talking to you."

Carol froze. An icy, metallic taste welled in her mouth. Her skin was bathed in perspiration.

The woman grabbed a beer bottle from one of the tables and threw it at Carol. "*Get off!*" she screamed. The bottle slammed into Carol's neck, and she sagged to her knees. Plato was suspended for an instant, then bounced across the stage. Anz rushed between Carol and the woman as she charged across the stage.

"I'm gonna kill that bitch!" the woman yelled. She lunged at Carol, but Anz grabbed her arm and twisted it behind her back.

"I'm gonna cut her tongue out!"

Anz's men jumped on the stage, and helped him push her into the wings, while Thornton helped Carol stumble/walk off stage.

Drum roll, and *rim shot.*

The emcee hurried into the spotlight with an upbeat staccato of patter. "Some excitement, troops . . ." He picked Plato off the floor, looked at him, then tossed the dummy to a stagehand. "Hey, that's really a finish right? *But now* . . . it's time . . . *showtime* for our lovely ladies of ooze. . . ." *Rim shot* and cheers. "Yes, it's time for the mud."

"Not the dud!" was called out. The audience laughed nervously.

"Absolutely," the emcee replied. "And now let's meet our gorgeous gals of grime . . . if you please . . . come out and give us a look. . . ."

The incident, and the violence of the moment, was shovelled into memory as four bikini-clad women saunter on stage.

Drum roll and *rim shot* blend into the mud wrestlers theme.

"Here's the lovely . . . Candy. . . ."

"Jeez, Helen, that was wild."

"It's only an act, Joyce, the whole thing was a fake. A set-up!"

"Ya think so, Helen?"

"Y'know, Joyce, you're so gullible it's pathetic."

Chapter Seventeen

"Once more, Jo," Aggie begged. "Try the the cards again."

"It's absurd. I won't play another hand," she replied. "I'm exhausted . . . besides, there's nothing clear. Higgledee, piggledee, all the time. I shan't lay out another hand, Aggie!"

Agnes frowned, then smiled coyly at Papa Noir.

"Oh no, Miss Aggie, if'n *sœur* Josephine feel she all scattered, and the cards make no sense, I not going to advise otherwise."

"Well, I didn't ask you, Papa," Aggie pouted. "I merely smiled."

Papa Noir grinned widely. "I know that face, ma'am, and too many times that charm allied me to you. No, no . . . if the cards are tiring Missy Jo, then it tain't me place to intervene."

"Fiddlesticks, you always take her side," Aggie replied.

"Bicker, bicker, bicker!" Jo interjected. "I can't stand your persistance, my dear." Jo shook her head slowly. "All right . . . one more hand, but that's it!"

Aggie clapped her hands. "Goody. This time I'll be quiet."

"And don't touch the cards!"

"Not a one," Aggie replied.

"And no singing!"

"No singing, Jo. I promise."

Josephine eyed her carefully. "Doubt that," she snorted. "You always sing when I'm moving the wrong card . . . or what you believe is the wrong card."

"I won't even hum," Aggie promised.

"Bicker, bicker, bicker!" groaned Papa Noir.

"How true, Papa," Jo remarked as she shuffled the deck of playing cards.

"I think there's an ace on the bottom," Aggie said.

"Do you mind, *sister?*" Jo replied.

"Sorry," Aggie squealed, and smiled at Papa.

Josephine shuffled, and cut the cards several times, then placed the deck in front of her. She stared at the cards, then said, "Ten, six, and a queen."

"The queen again," Aggie whispered to Papa.

"This is 'solitaire,' dearest," Josephine snapped. "Meaning . . . singleness, *and* quiet!"

Aggie gave a pixieish shrug, and put a forefinger against her lips.

Josephine picked up the deck, cut it again, then dealt the cards onto the table in front of her:

Nine of clubs, flip, flip, flip, flip, flip, flip.
Ten of hearts, flip, flip, flip, flip, flip.
Queen of clubs, flip, flip, flip, flip.
Six of spades, flip, flip, flip.
Ace of diamonds, flip, flip.
Jack of diamonds, flip.
Jack of clubs.

"They're all there!" Aggie exclaimed. "Just like you predicted. Queen of clubs, again."

"Please, my dear!" Josephine asked.

"Merely assisting," Aggie quipped.

"Always assisting!" Jo remarked as she swiftly

played the jack of diamonds on top of the queen, then the ten onto the jack of clubs, which was covered by the nine. Lastly, Josephine placed the ace of diamonds to side. "Double jacks," she whispered. "This is the fifth time Carlotta's received double jacks."

"You mean Carol!" Aggie replied.

"That's what I said, dear!"

"No, you said 'Carolotta', Jo."

"Did not!" Josephine looked at Papa Noir for confirmation, but he nodded. "Well . . . it was a slip. I'm playing for Carol, and I made a mistake."

"Of course you did," Aggie replied sympathetically, "Now turn the cards . . . let's see what's hidden from us."

Josephine sighed. "This spread is for Carol, *not*. . . . Carlotta."

"I understand," Aggie answered. "Turn the cards, dear."

Josephine thought for a moment, then turned over a queen of hearts, a jack of spades, and a jack of hearts. She moved the jack onto the queen uncovering the the queen of spades. She shook her head, then placed the jack of hearts on the queen. The queen of diamonds appeared, and the jack of clubs was moved on top of it. Finally, Josephine turned the last two cards to reveal the six of hearts and the six of clubs.

"Blocked, again," she muttered.

"All those queens, and jacks," Aggie remarked. "You're already turning jacks onto the queens."

"Could be knaves," Papa added.

"You think so?" Josephine asked.

"Many, many knaves been appearing. Too many little men scampering through the games. You ain't turned a king since the first try. Strange . . . missing the kings all this time. Tain't a good sign, *mes sœurs*."

"I know," Josephine replied. "Poor Carol's plagued with . . . jacks, or knaves."

"Working with all those sleazy creatures it's no wonder she's surrounded by petty half-men," Aggie retorted. "It's not a place for a lady."

"Half-men?" Papa asked.

"Of course," Aggie answered. "Not grown-up enough to be *real* men. Anybody in that milieu certainly isn't fully developed."

Josephine stared at the cards. A predominance of queens and jacks had appeared in the games.

Always the jacks on top of the queens. However, the queens seemed never to be placed on the kings. At first the pattern was annoying, but as Josephine played game after game the absence of kings became irritating. Queens without kings. Jacks after queens. It was apparently a force rather than circumstance that was dictating the course of the session.

Josephine stared at the four queens holding the four jacks. Papa had been right. The queens were blocked at every turn. It was a bad sign.

"He won't let go," Josephine whispered. "Her little man never leaves her."

"Maybe the jack is a knave, and not her dummy?" Agnes suggested.

"Could be," Papa Noir said. "Too many knaves . . . I think it's the *mal* that's pursuing missy. The card is ever after her, not blocking her. No, no . . . *je pense* the missing kings are her puppet. He's a sly one . . . always hiding always appearing when it's too late."

Josephine studied the spread in front of her.

"Carol's blocked, and hunted. There seems little chance for her to elude . . . her detractors. I agree, Papa, Mr. Plato is the king, and that wretched Diana is the jack."

"Maybe! Maybe not!" Aggie remarked. "It doesn't feel right. I've never sensed Diana as a knave."

Josephine swept the playing cards together, shuffled them several times, then placed the deck in the center of the table.

"It's the best I can do," she replied, "if you want more information you'll have to illuminate the cards."

"Oh, dear Jo," Aggie pleaded, "I wasn't casting any doubts on your interpretations."

"You were!" Jo pouted.

"My dear, I merely suggested that the knave didn't impress me as a woman."

"It's definitely not Carol's ex-husband!" Josephine retorted.

Papa Noir rubbed his face, and sighed. "Bicker, bicker," he moaned softly. It wasn't the first time the sisters had been at odds with each other over cards. "*Incroyable,*" he ingested. He shook his head, and coughed politely. "Pardon, *mes sœurs, peut-être* Ma'am Agnes should 'read' the deck?"

"Yes!" insisted Josephine. "Let's see how much further *you* can see," she sniped.

"Oh, Miss Jo," Papa crooned. "No one does better with the cards than yourself. I only suggest a different approach to clear missy's path. It's reasonable, no?"

Josephine relented, handed the deck to Agnes, who cut the cards twice, than gave them to Papa Noir. He held held the cards for an instant, then placed them at the center of the table.

"I shall turn, *mes soeurs,*" he said softly.

The first card was the queen of hearts, and the second was the jack of spades.

Josephine placed them in front of Agnes.

The tiny woman placed a palm on each card, closed her eyes, and drew herself into a beta-trance.

Her breathing became deep and labored as she

forced her consciousness into another realm. Her head twitched several times, then hung limply over her chest. Finally, the breathing became rhythmic, and she settled into a relaxed state. Her hands slipped away from the cards, and dangled by her sides.

"Man, woman, man, woman," she muttered.

Papa Noir's violet eyes peered at her intently.

"There are two," Aggie whispered, "man, woman, man, woman. There are two," she repeated.

"Who are they, Aggie?" Jo asked.

Agnes shifted the cards twice. "Two acting as one," she said mechanically. "The man is the woman, and the woman is the man."

Papa Noir looked at Josephine and shook his head. "And Missy Carol? Is she this pair?"

Agnes drew several deep breaths.

She let her fingers run lightly over the queen of hearts. "Carol . . . Carol . . . the pair isn't in Carol. The man hates the woman, and the woman hates the man," she whispered.

"Do you see the woman?" Josephine asked.

Agnes placed both hands on top of the queen.

"Yes, I see her," she replied.

"Is it Diana?" Papa questioned.

"Part is Diana," Aggie whispered.

Josephine shrugged. "This isn't a proper reading," she told Papa Noir. "It's too obscure. I really believe Aggie isn't concentrating."

Papa disagreed. "Her sight never vary, ma'am. Me thinks this *histoire* follow the cards exactly. Too many knaves on queens all night. The pattern is constant," he suggested. "I ask about the *mal*. Who is queen, ma'am?"

"Diana," Aggie replied.

"And who is knave?"

"Diana," Aggie answered.

"Indeed so, Miss Jo, it confirms all. The knave

mixed into the queen makes two into one. Oh yes'm, Miss Agnes see Diana in truth."

"And Mr. Plato?" Josephine asked. "Is he the hidden king?"

"No," Aggie replied. "Her little man is not the king, or even a jack. Mr. Plato . . . is not within the pack."

Aggie pressed her fingertips against her eyes. "I see her," she muttered. "Indeed, I see the queen-knave. She's blonde . . . yes, blonde and rounded. It's Diana, I know it. Man, and woman. All in two, yet both in one."

"What else?" Jo urged.

"I see a room . . . her room. Oh, it's beautiful, and very neat. Very tidy."

"Where is it, ma'am?" Papa asked.

"Don't know," Aggie said mechanically. "In the city . . . high up, she lives high up. Very tidy, yes, an extremely well-ordered room. Almost too orderly for a woman."

"What's she doing, Aggie?" Jo whispered.

"Being beautiful," she answered. "Diana's sitting in front of a mirror . . . a very large mirror . . . many cosmetics . . . many wigs . . . perfumes abound. She likes a special fragrance. She's painting her face. I see her face . . . I see her . . . I see her. . . ."

Aggie lowered her hands onto the cards, and stared at them blankly.

"Many cylinders of lip paint," she said slowly, "and rouges . . . and powders . . . very meticulous . . . she's wiping her fingers . . . tubes of nail paint, all neatly aligned.

Aggie shifted the jack on top of the queen.

"Her face and her body seem . . . seem unmatched. She's rounded . . . very rounded, but the face is narrow . . . she's older than she appears

. . . yes, much older. The body betrays the face . . . soon the lines will show . . ."

"What else, ma'am?" Papa asked.

Aggie leaned against the table, her hands pressing on the playing cards to steady herself.

"I think sister's returning," Jo whispered to Papa Noir.

"Now she's walking down a hall . . . filled with pictures . . . pictures of young men. Many, many handsome young men," Aggie said hoarsely. "Some are nearly undressed . . . some in bathing costumes . . ."

"Confusing *très extraordinaire,"* he told Josephine. "Soeœur Agnes maybe getting two messages?"

Aggie lifted her her hand from the queen of hearts. "Walking to the bathroom . . . she's putting surgeon's gloves on her hands . . . thin rubber gloves . . ."

Papa Noir and Josephine exchanged worried glances.

"Diana has Carol's picture . . . she's cutting it up with a pair of scissors. . . .Yes, cutting it into small pieces . . . cutting! Cutting! She's cutting Carol's face!"

Suddenly, Aggie swayed, and collapsed.

Chapter Eighteen

"Would you mind taking your feet off my coffee table!" Carol demanded.

The heavy-set detective grinned sheepishly. "Sorry about that, Miss Elliott."

"Right!" Carol shot back. "And try not to make another mess in the kitchen, huh?"

"Sure thing, Miss Elliott."

"Miss Elliott! Miss Ellot!" Carol screeched. "Can't any of you call me Carol? I do have a first name. I've been caged in this frigging apartment with you and the other clowns long enough . . . so call me anything, but not goddamn 'Miss Elliott,' okay? Simple? *Capishe?"*

"Sure thing . . . Carol."

"Was that so difficult?"

"Anz doesn't like—"

"The hell with Anz!" she snapped. "He doesn't show up anymore. He doesn't give a shit, does he?"

"Aw c'mon, Miss—, er, Carol . . . the boss wants to get this outta the way . . . as much as you."

"Then why hasn't find Miss Creepy?"

"He's working on it."

"Right!" Carol answered. "He's downtown busting his ass, huh? No way, fella . . . I'm just out-of-the-way . . . 'under protective custody'!"

"If he could nail your lady he would," the detective replied. "Listen, it's no great shakes sitting in this apartment either."

Carol smirked. "That's for sure," she countered.

"Look, we're working on this . . . so the gal at the club was just a drunk. Anz made a judgment call, and it didn't pan out."

"At my expense," Carol reminded him. "And so we sit here . . . day after rotten day. For what? What's Brilliant Plan Number Two?"

"I don't know."

"Neither does your boss, fella."

The detective bit his lip, and nodded. Bitch, he thought, I don't like this detail any better than you. And that goes for my relief, and his relief, and everyone. You're a pain in the ass, *Miss Elliott!*

"Hey, listen, wanna play some pinochle?"

Carol shook her head.

"Just a thought."

She stared at him disgustedly, then walked into her bedroom and slammed the door.

"Up yours, fruitcake!" he muttered, and picked up the deck of cards. He shuffled several times, then dealt out a hand of solitaire. The face cards were all queens and jacks. He grumbled to himself as he flipped through the deck. Not a move. Not a match. Shit, he said to himself and swept all the cards together. The hell with you, he groused at the door, then put his feet back on the coffee table and began to read the newspaper.

Carol lit a cigarette, then crushed it out. I can't stand it! she thought. I can't take another week of this. Prison, babe, it's prison.

She looked at Plato, who was sitting in the corner of a small sofa.

"And I can't take another word from you," she snapped. "I don't want to hear 'babe' or 'toots' or anything."

She stared out of her window. Tramp steamers and tugs. The Hudson was calm. That's what it's about, she thought. Getting on a boat, and getting the hell out of here. Some chance, no chance. It's a never-to-be. Everything nice, everything she wanted: never-to-be. "What happened?" Carol moaned. "How did it get this way? What the hell did I do to deserve . . . Murray, oh, bastard Murray . . . or Mr. Foul-mouth . . . and now this bitch. This crazy bitch! Who needs this aggravation, babe!" Carol shook her head. No use, she thought. My luck, I'll never get clean. Clean, babe? Turn back the clock? Be a pissy-mousey grade-school teacher married to a schmuck? Carol set her jaw. The thought was appalling. Any thought of what might have been, or what was now, was appalling.

She walked over to Plato, righted him, and tugged his collar. "Y'know, fella, the only place I honestly want to be is—"

She placed the dummy on her lap, put her hand through the back of his jacket, set her fingers on the eye and mouth rings, and turned his head. "Where's that?" Plato asked. Carol watched her performance in the mirror above her dresser.

"Oh no!" she muttered. "My mouth moved. You could see everything. I can't even do this!"

She stared at herself. "Where's that?" she repeated. Her lower lip tightened as she said "that."

"Where's that?" she tried again.

"It no good. I opened my mouth."

She laid Plato on the dresser and practiced "Where's that" over and over. Your mouth's still open; your jaw moved; you're pursing your lips.

"I gotta get out of here," Carol thought.

The detective quickly pulled his feet off the coffee table as Carol burst through the bedroom door.

"Whazzamatta?" he demanded.

"I'm getting out of here, fella," Carol replied as she pulled a coat out of the hall closet.

"Wait a minute! Just old on!"

"No way," she answered. "This place is closing in. I'm going for a walk. A hike. A drive. A plane trip."

The detective blocked the front door.

"Move it, buster!"

"Let's be reasonable, Miss Elliott."

"Why?"

"I can't let you leave."

"Why?"

"Anz's orders."

"Screw Anz."

"Don't be a hardhead, Miss Elliott. I've got authority to handcuff you."

"Go to hell!" Carol shrieked.

"Sit down, Miss Elliott."

"I want to talk to Anz."

"Okay," he replied, "but please sit over there, and I'll make the call."

"You know how to dial?"

"Just be a nice girl, and put your ass on the sofa, and we'll get this straightened out."

"Right!"

The detective made certain he was between Carol and the front door as he dialed Anz's number, and waited. "Yeah, Nick. It's Carl. We gotta small problem. Miss Elliott wants to take a hike."

"Put her on," Anz replied, and he did.

"I'm getting out of here," she told him.

"Can't do it."

"That's what you say."

"Listen, Carol, another couple of days."

"*No*!" she bellowed. "Not another minute."

"You wanna die?"

"Why didn't he catch my buddy?" Carol asked sarcastically.

"*You wanna get killed?*" Anz yelled. "You wanna have this creep slit you up the gut? Or cut off—"

"*No!*" Carol replied.

"Then sit still . . . just a bit more."

"Can't," Carol moaned. "This place is closing in . . . just let me take a walk with one of your gorillas. *Please!*"

"What do you need? We'll get it for you."

"I've got to get out. Just let me go to Saks, or Bloomingsdale's. An hour."

"Too risky.

"The Metropolitan," she suggested.

"No, no. You'll give us the shake."

"I won't. I promise!"

Anz thought for a moment. "No, no way!"

"The market," Carol begged. "Can you trust me in the Grand Union, or Gristede's?"

He paused. "Yeah, that's okay. Put Carl on."

"Here, gorilla, it's for you—"

"I'm sorry," Carol said softly.

"It's okay. I been called worse," the detective replied. "Don't sweat it."

"I'll let you push the cart," she quipped.

"No thanks."

Carol shrugged, yanked a grocery cart from nest of chrome-and-plastic, then marched toward the meat section of the Broadway Gristede's. "What if somebody sees us together?" she joked.

"Let's just get this over with," he replied. "If your buddy Diana is here I can handle it."

Carol smiled. "Not her! Me! Suppose your wife sees you with a bleached blonde?"

"She knows about you. I ain't worried."

"So much for my sex appeal," Carol sniped. "Jeez, the price of meat. Oh well, there's nothing I can do about it!" She jabbed at a roast beef, frowned, picked it up, then put it back. "Too much. Let's see the special." They walked along the meat aisle, but either the quality was poor or the prices exorbitant. "Well, this year I'm going vegetarian," Carol remarked.

"That's nice," he replied flatly.

"You've really got a lot of charm. I bet all the girls tell you that?"

"I don't play around."

"Right!" Carol agreed. "Suppose your mother-in-law spotted us?"

"They live in Queens. What would she be doing on the West Side, huh?"

"Following you," Carol joked. "Waiting for you to step out with a chickie, and blow the whistle."

He shook his head. "Listen, I wuz on the special guard detail for the Playboy Bunny Convention two years back, and my wife never batted an eyelash. Y'know why . . . cause . . ."

Because you're a schlubb, fella, and your wife knows it, Carol thought. She smelled, nodded, picked up a can of pitted olives, was annoyed by the price, and put them back. Push, push. Too expensive, too expensive. The detective rambled on. ". . . and three years ago. Remember when they had all them Hollywood starlets here?" Yeah, yeah, you walked away a virgin. How great, fella, Your wife can trust you anywhere. Another aisle, the wheel on the cart scrapes, and wobbles. Whaddja expect, babe? Not much, she thought. Upward and onward, gal. Stick to the shopping. How about some cottage cheese? Skimmed milk? Or yogurt? The pits. How about sausage, and green noodles?

"Oh yeah, Miss Elliott, I love green noodles," The detective remarked. Carol was startled. "Especially with lots of Parmesan cheese."

"Why did you say that?"

" 'Cause you were talking about Italian food."

"I was?"

"Sure."

"I thought I was talking to myself."

"Maybe you were, but it was kinda loud," he replied. "Maybe you were mumbling."

Carol forced a smile. Did my mouth move?" she quipped. "Or did the carton of milk talk?"

"That's a good one," he laughed. "Hey, why don'tcha try to freak out an old lady? You stand to the side, and throw your voice. Make like a talking cereal box."

"Right!" Carol said wryly. "Then I'd really be put away. Stick to crime, fella, it's a growing business."

"C'mon! Just for laughs," he suggested. "We'll go up to the detergents, and you throw your voice."

"I won't," Carol replied, halfheartedly. "One of those women might have a heart attack."

"Let's see . . . try it out."

"Forget it!"

"Have some fun, Miss Elliott. I tell ya what . . . I'll go up to the bin with the soaps, okay? I'll pick one up . . . smell it . . . and you talk!" Carol smiled, and shook her head. "You say . . . er, 'I'm half soap, half cleansing soap, and I smell . . . smell like jasmine."

Carol stared at him blankly. "It wasn't jasmine," she replied in a monotone.

"Okay, so it's something else. . . ." his words tumbled into a fade, and echoed into nothingness.

It wasn't jasmine, Carol thought. It was stronger. The visuals and the scent swelled and crested, then exploded in her memory. The club. *Chick-a-boom.* The stench of the sweating dancers. *Ice storm.* A tinge of the sent clung—the odor of burning rubber. *Chick-a-boom.* The club again. Carol fought off the detective's mindless spiel. The scent. What was it? Where was it? *Wah-wah-wah.* Latino grinding out his routine to an empty club. Again, it clung to the stage. The club. *Flash.* The car. *Flash.* Where else? Carol stared at the shelves blankly. Strong perfume. Unmistakable. Expensive. Heavy. An evening scent. Her mind churned. *The ice storm.* It *was* there. Couldn't be, shouted back, *The club.* Impossible, but the idea was fixed. Yeah, babe, it *was* at the club. *Chick-a-boom.* Carol relived the not-so-lovely ladies. Who? The faces swam, and melded. *Remember! Remember!* Who! Where! Carol felt her hands tighten against the cart. Oh jeez, *the letters.* "Slut/bitch." the scent clung to the vemon. . . . "Your putrid ashes." The perfume was pressed into the words. . . . "Slit your breasts." Same as the club. Same as the car. Same as the day Latino was—

"Did you check the letters for perfume?" Carol asked wildly. "Did Anz check them for perfume?"

The detective was startled. *"What?"*

"The same perfume . . . Diana uses a *special* perfume."

"I don't understand!"

"*Perfume,* you asshole!" Carol shrieked.

Now the old ladies were paying attention.

"Look, Miss Elliott, why don't we go back to the house, huh?"

"Don't humor me, you idiot!"

"Okay, okay, just cool it . . . lower your voice, and we'll talk, huh!"

"The same perfume," Carol growled, "it was at the club, it was on the letters . . . the letters she sent."

"Sure, it's possible," he remarked, and tried to guide Carol toward the checkout counter. "I'll call Anz when we get back. It's a good lead . . . solid lead. You say it was on the hate mail, huh? We'll check it out."

Carol shoved the cart against him. "Bastard! You think I'm crazy?" she shouted.

Carol's voice carried beyond the aisle just enough to attract a pimply boxboy, and assorted grocery-groupies.

"I didn't say that," the detective replied. "Let's take it slow, huh. We'll call downtown when we get—"

"Did they run a chemical test on the bra?"

He took Carol's arm, but she yanked free. "Let's not have a scene, Miss Elliott."

"Did your geniuses test the letters?"

"I dunno," he replied. "How about discussing this outside?"

Carol glared at him. She clenched and unclenched her fists. She wasn't imagining the connection. The blonde running out of the club. Same scent. The bra, and the box, and letters, and envelopes. *Same scent.* Latino's blood staining the stage. Same scent. Anz will listen.

"Say what, Miss Elliott?"

She stared at the "gorilla" blankly.

"Let's go home, huh?"

"Anz has *got to listen!* Carol thought. Get to Anz. Carol tried to settle herself. Okay, babe, count to ten, and then again.

"Just leave the cart right here, Miss Elliott."

"Don't patronize me," she shot back.

"Didn't mean anything," he replied.

Carol nodded. She swept past two women pretending to shop while eavesdropping. "Hope you enjoyed the performance, girls."

Carol's pace quickened. She push her way through a crowded aisle. Nosy bitches! The faces were a blur. *Chick-a-boom.* Diana was there. *Wah- wah-wah.* Latino's mocking laugh as she ran from the club. Papa Noir's eyes, and the Markham sisters kaleidoescoped into Plato's face. Plato being surly. Plato threatening. *He didn't talk.*

"What's that, Miss Elliott?"

Carol nearly broke into a run.

"Hey, wait up!"

The clue was there all the time.

It's her fragrance, babe. Tell Anz.

Carol felt a welling sense of nausea. You're smelling everything, babe. Diesel fuel. Miss Complimentary Drink. The apartment. Vomit still hung to the carpeting. It's all in your head, babe. There ain't no scent. The club. God, those women smell. The dancers dripping with sweat. You reek, Mr. Sleek. *Chick-a-boom.* The letters. Oh yeah! The bra. *Rim shot* and *drum roll.* Here's nursie with the net. The hospital smells staggered Carol, and she leaned against a shelf.

The detective put his arm around her. "It's okay. I'm going to take you home," he said gently.

The scent jolted Carol. "Smell that," she demanded. He shrugged. "Just . . . just concentrate. It's the same perfume. It's hers . . . hers," Carol whispered. The detective looked at Carol intently, trying to figure out his next move. Handcuffs? She's flipped out. Reason with her? No, it wouldn't work. Twist her arm behind her back, and out we go. Too much action; she'll start screaming. "She's here," Carol whispered. "I know she's followed us."

"Who, Miss Elliott?"

"Diana," she replied. "Let's be smart about this . . . we'll act like we don't know." Carol's eyes danced wildly. "Let's pretend we're shopping. No, I forgot something . . . it'll give us an excuse to go through the store."

"Yeah," he agreed. "We'll do it nice and easy." Jeez, she's a real fruitcake, he thought, but I'll work it out. Got to get her into the nuthouse. Jeez, she's a case. Cool it, he told himself, or she'll start throwing things. "Tell ya what . . . I'll get another cart."

"*No!*" Carol replied sharply. She inhaled repeatedly, trying to detect another wisp that conjured Diana's presence. "We'll go down this aisle, then around the store."

He nodded, forcing himself to smile, to relax, to play the game, and all the while thinking how disturbed she was. They casually walked passed the cereal section. Nothing. Carol's nostrils dilated, relaxed, dilated. Nothing.

"Whadda ya think?" he asked. She shook her head. Jeez, her eyes were nutty. Look at 'em dart. Ya think something's coming at her from the frozen foods. Jeez, she's a psycho. Gotta get her outta this joint.

"See anybody?" he asked.

Suddenly Carol stopped. She grabbed him by the sleeve. "The scent's stronger. She's up the next aisle."

"Yeah," he replied softly.

Carol hesitated. *Chick-a-boom.* The blonde ran out of the Q Club. *Wah-wah-wah.* Latino grinds another one and laughs. *Ice storm* and *explosion.* Why didn't we die? "Slut." It's lavender. "Bitch." *No,* it's jasmine. "Slit your tits." The waft of perfume curled around the aisle. Carol froze.

"She's in front of us," she whispered.

Jeez, Miss Elliott, you're a nut.

"Let me walk up a bit. Where's your gun?"

Oh man, you're crazy. He patted his jacket.

"Okay . . . but don't let her get too close," Carol told him. The detective nodded, and was directly behind her as she paused, then walked up the aisle.

Nothing. No Diana. No women. At the end of the detergent section a short, plump man in his early fifties was reading a label on a box of soap.

"It's her!" Carol whispered. "Smell her perfume."

The detective was stunned. "Can't be . . . that's

a guy. C'mon, Miss Elliott, maybe it's the next section."

Carol shook her head vehemently. "She's in disguise. *It's her!*"

"Please, Miss Elliott!"

"Hello, Diana," Carol called out.

The man looked up.

"I know it's you!"

"C'mon, Miss Elliott," the detective pleaded.

"Your perfume gave you away," Carol continued, "you shouldn't have made that mistake. It's on the letters . . . it's on the bra. . . . I'm going to have Anz trace everything."

"What are you talking about, miss?" the man replied. He backed away as Carol moved forward. "Who are you?"

"You know damn well," Carol replied.

You cra-zy?" he replied. His voice had an effeminate, singsong quality. "I don't know you-u-u. Listen, honey, I don't want to know you-u-u."

"Liar!" Carol shouted. "You're Diana."

"Jeez, Louise," he answered. "They let any-body on the street today-y-y!"

The detective stepped between Carol and her prey. "Listen, this has gone too far," he told her. "That guy's an old fairy . . . he's a queen, Miss Elliott. Let's cool it!"

"It's her!" Carol insisted. She tried to push the detective out of her way and lunge at the man.

"It isn't!" he replied. "He's a fruit!"

"He's Diana!" Carol screamed. "She's the killer! She's the one that's trying to kill me!"

The man shoved his shopping cart at Carol and ran. Carol pushed the detective against the displays and charged after him. "*Diana! Diana!*" she shrieked. The man fled, his shoulder brushed against a pyramid of canned corn and sent it crashing into the aisle.

"*Manager!* Help! There's a looney here!" he clamored. "*Manager!*"

"*Stop her! Stop her!*" Carol shrieked, but the shoppers, and clerks were frozen by the madness of the instant. No one reached for the man as he elbowed his way through a checkout line. No one spoke as Carol screamed curses at him. The thrashing insanity of the incident shocked the store into silence.

Only Carol's convulsed sobbing echoed through the aisles. She braced herself against a rack of shopping carts.

"It *was* Diana!" she pleaded. "Her perfume," she wept, "is on the letters" Somebody stop her! Please!"

No one spoke, no one moved as the man dashed into the street and disappeared.

Chapter Nineteen

"You stupid sonofabitch! How did let this happen?" Nick Anz roared.

"She just went bananas, Nick! One moment she's talking about perfume, and the next thing I know she's chasing an old fag through the supermarket," the detective explained. "She's a frigging nut, Nick! You oughta have her in a jacket!"

"Shut up, Carl!"

"Listen, I wuz lucky to get her out of that store. Y'know, she grabbed onto a shopping cart. I had to pry her hands off it, huh! She's holding on, and screaming, 'Diana! He's Diana!' Some scene, Nick!"

"All right, you couldn't help it," Anz replied wearily. "Shit! This has gone too far. Did you speak with her father?"

"Naw, but I left a message at the Q Club, and with his service."

Anz nodded. "We're gonna give him two choices: She goes into a private hospital again, or he moves in here. Either way it stinks!" Nick Anz shook his head. "What really made her freak out, Carl? C'mon, level with me."

"A bar of soap!" Carol said sharply as she walked into the living room.

"I didn't know you were up!" Anz replied.

"You calling the gorilla a 'sonofabitch' woke me

. . . no that's not true. I couldn't rest," she remarked calmly. "I was trying to pull myself together."

"You seem . . . better."

"You mean 'sane' or 'normal,' huh?"

Anz nodded. "Carl says you had a little problem at the market. Wanna talk about it?"

Carol sat on the couch. Cool, calm, collected, she told herself. Just suck it in, babe, and pitch the story line. No hysterics, no emotion. "I know you think I'm crazy," she started.

Anz exchanged worried glances with the detective.

"I wouldn't blame you," she continued. "It's not normal to get bent out of shape at the market even if the price of eggs has doubled," she quipped.

Anz forced a smile.

"Sorry," Carol said quietly, "not one of my better jokes. It's clean, anyway." Anz smiled, and shrugged. "The punch line is 'perfume,' " Carol explained. "I remembered the fragrance when your pal here suggested I throw my voice from a bar of soap."

"What the hell was that?" Anz snapped at the detective.

"It was a prank, Nick. I suggested . . . well, she talk to some old ladies . . . make like the soap was speaking to them. Like a commercial. It was a gag!"

"Some gag!" Anz replied.

"No, it was all right," Carol insisted, "because the soap . . . its scent . . . triggered a detail. A link," she said calmly, "between the accident, the letters, the bra . . . and the murder." Anz looked puzzled, but held his composure. "Diana . . . my buddy wears a certain perfume. It's heavy . . . something a woman would put on for a date, an evening out . . . it's a formal scent. Follow the pattern . . . it's not crazy, even though I went wild at the market . . . What's the difference if an odor triggers the fragment of an idea, or clue, out of my subconscious . . . we have something that isn't a dead end. Now does that make sense? Am I being logical?"

"You know the name of this perfume?" Anz asked.

"No," Carol replied, "but I've smelt it before . . . maybe Bergdorf, maybe Magnin's in Los Angeles. It's a particular manufacturer, and I know it's expensive . . . very expensive. A super-luxury item."

"We can track it down," Anz replied.

"And I'm sure it's on the letters, and the bra," Carol added.

"We'll see what the lab group uncovers," he said quietly. "I'll take care of that today." Anz hesitated; the episode at the market had to be discussed. "What about the guy in Gristede's? What happened? What was that all about, Miss Elliott?"

"I went haywire," she replied. "It was a combination of things . . . I can't explain it. I thought . . . I don't really know . . . at the time I felt he was watching me."

"He wasn't even near you."

"It was a sensation. A feeling," Carol tried to explain. "I knew he was there."

"And the 'he' in this little saga is 'Diana'?"

"Yes," Carol answered hoarsely.

"C'mon, it doesn't make sense," Anz snapped. "First, you can't see him; now it's a man."

"An old fruitcake," the detective added.

"Whatever!" Anz commented. "Why would he/she follow you to the supermarket?"

"Why would Diana come to the club?" Carol answered sharply. "With hundreds of people around her? Did you really expect her to run through the audience with a knife? Didn't you tell me if I had 'any inkling,' or 'one bad vibe,' I was to get off . . .

and obviously direct you to our gal?" Anz nodded. "Well, I got that 'bad vibe' in Gristede's."

"But you tuned into a man! A guy!"

"And experienced a scent . . . a possible clue."

"No way," Anz insisted, "Maybe you smelt cheese, or fruits, but not perfume."

"You don't believe me."

"No, I don't, but that's unimportant 'cause *you* believe it. *You* think he was Diana, and I'm not gonna touch that with a pole."

"What about the perfume?"

"It's a possibility," Anz admitted. "However . . . you mind if I take your perfumes, and cosmetics, to the lab also?"

"They're on my dresser," Carol replied sullenly. "Help yourself."

"Please, Miss Elliott, don't get bent out of shape. We want to resolve this business too. I'll accept the perfume angle, but not the man. It's too—"

"Irrational?" Carol interrupted.

"Illogical," he countered. "The pattern doesn't conform to her phychological profile."

"Meaning what?" Carol demanded. "She doesn't exist? This is a figment of my imagination? Putting it more concisely . . . Carol Elliott is plain, frigging crazy?"

"Did I say that?" Anz replied.

"You implied it!"

"Okay, up to now we've played the game, and you've been the star. The letters are a fact. Sender unseen. The bra is a fact. Sender unseen. The dancer's murder is a fact. The killer unseen, and unknown. Maybe Diana! Maybe not! There's a correlation between you, the dead man, and Diana, *but* the killer's M.O. doesn't match with your pen pal's. That's as straight as we have it. There's more unknown than known. . . .

"If you want to help, talk to someone . . . your

father . . . a professional. Anybody! But try to get your head together instead of meddling in our business."

Anz's outburst created an uneasy silence. Carol stared out the window. The detective ran his fingers across the back of the sofa. Anz, emptied by his tirade, slumped in an easy chair.

"I didn't think I was meddling," Carol said softly. "I guess I stepped out of line."

"You've been under quite a strain," Anz replied. "Your accident, the threats, finally the murder. It's a heavy trip, and God knows what you haven't told us."

Carol smiled. Right on, Sherlock, 'cause you don't know the flip side. How about them Markham gals? One of them beauties is a midget. And don't forget Papa purple-peepers. That's the right, Watson, he's got a matching set of violet nonviolent eyes.

Hear that, Carl? She's a weirdo, Nick.

But that's nothing, fellas. I ain't spread the word about your friend and mine, old Mr. Plato. Didja hear the one about the talking dummy. Oh yeah, troops, he talks *without* my hand up his spine. He talks not walks, just like a real, live inhuman. And here's the punch line: He threatened me!

Didja catch that, Nick? Get the net, Carl.

"We want to help you," Anz continued. His tone soft and sympathetic. "We understand what you've had to deal with . . . all the anxieties, and fears."

Keep that ever-loving smile plastered across your face, Carol urged. Let him run the soft-soap line. He's not buying the perfume bit. Why should he? You've been acting plain old nuts. They want you away babe.

"Why don't you discuss this with your father?" Anz suggested.

Rim shot. Great idea. Key to door. Passport. Anything to get out of this place. "I'd like that," Carol replied. "The walls keep closing in . . ."

"Why don'tcha stay with him?" he added.

Drum roll. You bet, fella. I'm packing. "Do you think . . . well, would it be safe?" Oh, the sob in the voice! What a performance, babe.

"Yes," Anz replied. "A change of scene wouldn't hurt. We'll keep a surveillance team here as a dummy. The more Anz thought about his idea the better he liked it. "Yeah, moving would give us some time. Why don't we get you out of here today?"

Fanfare. Ten-four, good buddy. You take the perfume, and I'll pack m'duds. "All right," Carol agreed. The phrasing was beautiful. Such emotion, babe, such meaning. "Let me get a few suitcases from the trunk room."

"We'll take care of it," Anz replied.

"I'm not running away," Carol answered. "I'll pack, but you can carry the bags, and take them out later."

"Okay," Anz relented. "Carl'll go with you."

"Please, that's carrying it too far. I'm going downstairs, John, the doorman, will take me into the trunk room . . . because he's the only one with a set of keys and—"

"Go ahead," Anz said casually. ". . . but don't leave the building."

"Only with you," she answered, "Scout's honor. Cross m'heart." Carol crossed the living room, picked up the building telephone in her kitchen. "John? It's Carol Elliott. . . . No, I don't want a cab. Would you meet me in the trunk room? . . . Okay, a couple of minutes." Carol hung the receiver on the hook. "Satisfied, fellas?"

They weren't. Anz walked her to the elevator.

"Isn't this getting out of hand?" she asked. Anz shrugged, and relented, allowing the elevator door to close him out. Carol leaned against the back of the cab. Her first instinct was to run. First floor, and out. Where? Markhams? You don't even know their address. Maybe Papa Noir's waiting? Fat chance, babe.

Stick to the game plan. At least the gorilla won't be hovering or messing up your house. No, Thornton will take his place. Hover, hover. Want an apple? Some hot milk? Oh, Thornton, get off my case. Oh, Carol, he's just trying to help. Poor Thornton, he always gets the shaft, she reflected.

Carol tensed as the elevator stopped on four.

Subliminal visions of Latino's blood knotted her stomach as the door slowly opened. Surprise! An old woman with a shopping bag.

"Going to the first?" the woman asked.

"Basement," Carol answered.

"Musty down there." The woman jabbed "Lobby" twice, folded her arms, and stared straight ahead.

Four, three, two . . . lobby.

"Nice talking with you," the woman said and marched toward the front door.

The basement *was* musty. A dankness mixed with the odor of soot. Curls of dust trailed Carol's footsteps as she walked through the dimly lit corridor toward the large floor-to-ceiling wire bins. Five-A was neat; their cartons were clearly marked. CHRISTMAS ORNAMENTS were stacked upon MIKE'S BOOKS. Seven-C wasn't neat. A three-wheeler rusted beside lawn furniture. Messy people. Eleven-G was almost empty. An old steamer trunk plastered with labels. THE ILE DE FRANCE, THE CUNARD LINES. Travelers lived in Eleven-C. Step. *Click.* Step. *Click.* Carol's high heels echoed through the aisles. The smells blended with the hint of heating oil, and the roar of the building's furnace drowned her steps.

More history! Nine-B kept a wooden sled. Flexible Flyer, all wood, leaned against packages labeled SUMMER SLIPCOVERS—LIVING ROOM.

The whine of an elevator stopped, and a door opened. Carol hesitated. "Miss Elliott?" John called.

"Yeah, John!" Carol shouted back.

"Hold on. Gotta lock the car."

"I'm down here."

Carol heard him hook the sliding door, and pull the wire gate closed. "Okay, okay." Carol laughed. His keys jinkle-clinked with every step. "Damn cold down here," he muttered. Step, *click*, step, *click*. "Boy, this place gets dirtier every year. Got your key, Miss Elliott?"

She did and he took it.

"My bin's down here," Carol replied.

Their steps flattened the dust, and echoed off the walls. "This whole place should be cleaned out," he groused. "Half-empty, always dirty. Well, what the hell!"

They walked down another poorly lit aisle of wired bins. "Look at this," John groaned, "Junk! People got more stuff they don't need. Y'know, the Salvation Army should come in here . . . and shovel everything into their trucks. I've been after the super for years . . . but he don't give a damn. You down this way?"

"Yeah," Carol answered.

"Another light out," John remarked. "I mean, this place is just the worst! Even the exterminator says it's nothing but a breeding ground. Not that we have any rats in the building," he added quickly.

"No . . . of course not!" Carol chided.

"Aw, here we go. Jeez, you got pretty much stuff in here. Well, entertainers need lotsa of valises and junk, huh?"

"Right!" Carol joked.

"Gimme yer keys." Carol's lock snapped open, but the building's security lock was frozen. "Sonofabitch," John cursed. "This beauty's all jammed." He struggled with it, then Carol tried. "Damnit, and it's the right key."

The buzzer for the service elevator whined. "Typical, huh?" John shook his head. "*All right!* Hold your water," he shouted. "I remember when this building had a back elevator man too! Remember that, Miss E." The unseen hand kept a thumb on the buzzer. "Pain in the ass! *Shut up!*"

"Go ahead," Carol suggested.

"He can wait," John replied. "Probably another one of those jerks from Crown Plumbing. Those guys get under my skin." The buzzer stopped, then picked up with an annoying staccato. "*Aw shit!*" John yelled. "*Turn it off!*" He turned his key in the lock, but the tumblers wouldn't move.

"C'mon, we'll get some graphite, and I'll take care of that guy," John gripped. "Can you believe this?"

"Let me fool with the lock. Go ahead," Carol replied.

"I don't wanna leave you here alone," he replied.

"Oh please," Carol answered, "I'm not going to run out of the building."

"Just ride with me," he asked. "I'll get the stuff for the lock and let the plumber, or whoever that idiot is, *out!*"

"Would you mind?" Carol replied. "I'm not entirely helpless, and you'll be away . . . two minutes? Three?"

He relented and handed Carol the keys, yelled his way toward the service car, and crashed the gate closed. The whine of the elevator partially drowned out his stream of curses. "Go get 'em, John," Carol muttered as she struggled with the lock. She tried another key. No good. Another. Same result. Gotta have at least twenty on this ring, she thought. Well, there's only one way. The whine of an elevator stopped, and the cab door opening distracted her.

"How many keys do you have on this ring?" she called. The elevator slid closed. "John?"

There was no answer.

"John? Did you bring the graphite?"

The basement was still except for the constant roar from the boiler room.

Carol whistled. "Hey, John!" She shrugged, slid a new key into place, and with a half turn the lock snapped open. "It's open," she called. "You were using the wrong key."

A wisp of perfume wafted through the trunk room and curled on the wire cages. Carol froze. Her fingers clung to the diamond-shaped openings. The scent mixed with footsteps, which moved nearer, stopped, then edged closer. Carol felt a bead of sweat inch down her cheek. Don't move, she screamed inwardly, don't make a sound. The steps continued, then a slight grinding of dirt, and they moved away. Don't breathe, she begged herself, don't breathe . . . she's moving away. Diana's moving away! Carol pressed her face against the cage; her fingers clutched the wires. The steps had stopped. Nothing. The boiler cut off, and the trunk room was naked in the empty silence. Nothing.

Carol's fingers ached. She felt the thick strands of wire pressing diamond shapes into her skin.

Suddenly there was a cough. A bolt of fear arced through Carol's mind.

Movement again. The sliding crunch of a shoe stepping on paper resounded through the trunk room.

"Carol-l-l, I know you're here." The voice was high-pitched, almost a falsetto.

Run, babe, *run!* Carol tried to pry herself from the bin. *Get outta there.* Where? She pressed her lips together, attempting to stifle a scream. *Nau-*

sea. It's the *ice storm* again. The grinding, squealing, and the burnt rubber mixed with a strong scent of perfume.

Another shuffle. Another step forward.

Take off your high heels, babe. Too much noise. She doesn't know where you are. Carol dropped the rest of the keys as she tried to remove her left shoe.

"I heard you, slut-bitch."

Carol ran toward the end of the row, and stopped.

"I'm never going to let you out of here," the voice mocked. "I'm going to cut your breasts off, and you'll bleed to death. You won't be a woman anymore . . . you won't!"

"*What did I ever do to you?*" Carol screamed.

"Everything! Diana shouted.

Carol turned the corner toward the elevators and Diana lunged from a section of bins. Carol stumbled, caught herself, and ran down another aisle.

"You dirtied him," Diana shrieked. "You let him touch you . . . I know all about it."

Carol's heart pounded. The blood surged faster and faster through her body. She felt as if her hands were swollen, and her face on fire. Get me out of here . . . get me out of here . . . John, come back. Her lips were dry and her voice refused to become more than a rasping croak. "Anz," she begged. "She's here, Anz . . . somebody . . . somebody."

Diana appeared at the end of the aisle. A swinging light bulb above her cast frantic, choppy shadows across the floor.

"You stole him . . . like you stole the others," Diana hissed. "You put your sweaty hands on his thighs . . . you let your fingers caress his beautiful stomach."

"I never touched . . . I never came near Latino,"

Carol replied hoarsely. "You've got to believe me," she sobbed.

"*Liar!*" Diana screamed.

Carol edged away from her.

"You defiled our love."

"I didn't . . . I didn't!"

"I'm going to cut the woman out of you," Diana said menacingly. She reached under her skirt. The bayonet gleamed in the dim light. Diana held it in front of her, then made jabbing motions as she slowly moved toward Carol.

"Somebody . . . *Somebody!*" Carol screamed.

Diana slashed the air with the bayonet. "Run, Carol, run . . . it makes it more exciting. And I like things that are exciting, don't you?"

Carol edged away, then rushed around a corner.

"You'll never be free," Diana mocked. "You'll pay for your sin. You'll redeem my loss."

Carol leaned against the wall of bins trying to catch her breath. Can't go any further. It's all over. She's nailed me, Carol thought. Finished! Dead! She lunged across the aisle, and held onto the door of an open bin. Jeez, I'm back at square one. John's keys hung on her lock. *Keys.* Step. *Lock.* Step. *I'm dead.* Step. Suddenly an inner voice screamed at Carol . . . "Get inside, lock yourself in." She yanked the lock off the hinge, scurried into the storage space, and snapped the padlock shut. Diana lunged at her, but Carol threw herself against the back partition.

The bayonet flicked and jabbed wildly through the wire diamonds.

"You slut . . . you whore!" Diana shouted as she maniacally hacked at the lock.

Carol huddled in a fetal position as the bayonet chinked and slapped against the wire and the lock.

"I've waited too long," Diana seethed. "Every day I've watched this building . . . every day I've waited for you. At night I've walked outside your door . . . I've waited in the stairwell hoping to catch you alone." Diana seized the wire door and shook it violently. "*You dirtied my love! You'll pay!*" She slammed at the lock with the bayonet, then stopped. Carol covered her head with her arms. Don't let her do this, she begged over and over. Dear God, don't let me die, she pleaded. I'll do anything . . . *anything*. The stillness was underscored by Diana's breathing. Her outline was etched into the wall of wire. The scent of perfume mixed with perspiration. Carol dug her nails into the palms of her hands. Don't let me die, she begged.

Diana tapped the edge of the bayonet against the lock. Carol jammed herself in a corner of the bin.

Tap, tap, tap.

"Why aren't making some jokes, Carol?"

Tap, tap, tap.

"Talk, Carol! Say something funny!"

Tap, tap, tap.

The bulb suspended from the ceiling dimmmed as the boiler clicked on. The elevator whined, stopped, and a door slide open. Diana cocked her head. Footsteps.

"*Help!*" Carol screamed. "*John!*"

Diana pressed against the bins, then slashed at the bulb, but missed.

"Anz? She's here, Anz!"

As the footsteps drew closer, Diana moved toward the far end of the row. The bulb swung lazily above her, casting shadows through the aisle.

"*John? Anz?*" Carol sobbed.

It was neither. The muscular frame of Papa Noir emerged from the darkness.

"Get her! Ger her!" Carol begged.

He stared at Diana, but didn't move.

"It's Diana!" Carol moaned.

"I know," Papa answered softly.

"*Stop her!*"

Diana glared at him as she backed away. For an instant the bayonet glinted in the light, then it was lowered to her side. She stepped into the darkness and disappeared. A door near the elevators scraped open, then slammed shut. Diana had escaped.

"*Why didn't you stop her?*" Carol cried.

"Ain't the proper time, missy," Papa replied. "The sisters know when the hour is right. You near the end, missy," he suggested. "Soon the clock will be yours," he said gently, then vanished into the murkiness of the basement.

Chapter Twenty

"I wuz gone two minutes," John whined.

Anz grabbed the doorman by the collar and slammed him against the wall. "I oughta break your frigging neck, fella!" he snarled.

Blood streamed from John's nose. "I swear it, mister, I didn't do it!"

Anz volleyed a fist into John's stomach, and he crumpled on the floor. "Tell me you didn't lock her in that bin?" John shook his head. "You want to play practical jokes, huh? Okay, fella, I'm gonna show you a few myself." He grabbed John's hair and bounced his head off the basement wall. "Let's go over it again!"

"Didn't do it!" John replied. He wiped his face on his sleeve, leaving a blood smear. "I got a call . . . it wuz no one . . . I came back . . . and she wuz in the bin." Anz raised his fist, but held it back. "*I didn't do nothing!*" the doorman screamed.

"Ya left her alone, ya schmuck! That's what ya did," Anz fired back.

"I wuz gone two—"

"Yeah, yeah," Anz replied. "That was enough."

"I'm sorry," John cried.

"A lot of good that does . . . she's upstairs, hysterical. I can't get any sense from her and you're 'sorry.' "

John shied away as Anz made a motion to kick him, then pulled his leg back. It's not this bastard's fault, he thought, it's mine! Never should have left her alone. We should have gone with her. The "should"s and the "why didn't I"s knotted his stomach.

"Get up, asshole!" Anz shouted. John scrambled to his feet, and moved away. "What did you see? Think . . . think clearly. Who was here, besides Miss Elliott?"

"Nobody," John answered. Anz looked at him carefully. "Not a soul, I swear it!"

"Didja hear anything?"

John shook his head. "Only Miss E. She was sobbing . . . maybe she said, er, 'Papa something,' and the rest I didn't catch."

"Papa, huh? Terrific!" Anz groused. He eyed John again. "Get outta here . . . and John—You fell down, right? One wrong word to the wrong people and we really give you a trimming."

"Yes sir!"

"And John, if your pea-brain gets a flash, and you remember something . . . anything . . . call me at the Ninth Precinct."

"Yes sir!"

Anz rubbed his hands across his eyes as he waited for the elevator. The case was going sour. Carol Elliott was an emotional vegetable. The frigging pen pal was *still* at large. He leaned against the back of the car. Now he had to go upstairs and piece out Carol's incoherent story, and placate Thornton.

"It's my fault," he told Thornton.

"Goddamm right!" Thornton shot back. "How stupid. You jeopardize my daughter! You let some maniac get at her! I've had just about enough of your methods!"

Anz let him rage. You deserve this, he told himself. The old man's right: You've screwed-up. The ploy at the Q Club drew a blank. The protection broke down at the market.

"*All right, shut up!*" Anz exploded. "I've frogged up the case. You made your point!"

The outburst shocked both men into an exhausted silence. Thornton threw himself into a chair, and Anz looked out the window.

"What are we gong to do?" Thornton questioned softly.

"I dunno, Mr. Evans, I honestly dunno."

Thornton shook his head. "Sorry about the tantrum. You've tried your best," he said quietly.

"I've made a hash of this," Anz replied. "We should have let her go to Vegas . . . get out of New York. I dunno. Nothing makes sense."

"She told me it was an accident. She locked herself in the cage," Thornton remarked. "I don't believe her."

"Neither do I," Anz answered. "The hack marks on the lock blow holes in that story."

"Do you think it was Diana?"

"Who else?" Anz replied.

"Then why . . . why in God's name won't she tell us? She holds on to this bizarre story, when she knows damn well neither of us buy it."

"I dunno, Mr. Evans. Maybe the real story is more fantastic than that one?"

"Hardly," Thornton snapped.

"I don't know who we're dealing with anymore," Anz replied. "There's the stage Carol. The private Carol. Maybe there's a dozen more? What's real for one could be fantasy for the others. Mr. Evans, I don't want you to take this wrong, but—"

Thornton nodded quickly. "I know. It's been on my mind for weeks. I don't even know her myself.

She's different . . . secretive, almost withdrawing from reality. There's a vacantness in her eyes. She's there and she's drifting. Only that damn puppet comes alive . . . and the act. How I hate *that disgusting act!* I cringe every time she steps in front of an audience . . . but *she* blossoms, and the dummy radiates! It's as if they were melding . . . and had boundless energy." Thornton looked at Anz sadly. "I'm not making any sense. I'm rambling, and it's not helping her, is it?"

"Can either of us help her?" Anz asked.

"No," Thornton replied pensively," Carol needs *professional* help. She's beyond fatherly advice."

"But it didn't work out the first time."

Thornton nodded. "She's always been able to straighten herself out . . . even before this episode. Well, the problem was quite different."

"With her ex-husband?" Anz asked.

"Yes," Thornton answered. "It was a very bad time. Murry was a liar, a cheat, and a thief. He took her for everything. Yet Carol didn't bat an eye. The act went on, unfortunately. The act! Cruder! Tasteless! And that damn Plato was coarser!"

"Too bad," Anz replied, " 'cause she's a different person underneath the glitz and smart talk. There's probably a little girl screaming in pain."

Anz's insight caught Thornton by surprise. "Yes, the public Carol is quite dissimilar from the real person, but now I don't know who she is," Thornton replied sadly. "It's quite painful to watch my child grow insane."

The two men, absorbed in their thoughts, sat quietly. An occasional car horn, or gust of wind rattling the picture window, punctured the solitude.

"Thank you for listening," Thornton said. "Please excuse me, perhaps Carol would like something." Anz smiled and nodded as Thornton disappeared into the bedroom. He leaned his head back, and closed his eyes. A rotten case, he thought. Nothing made sense. "Watch your child grow insane" echoed in his mind. The whole scene stunk, and he had made it worse.

Carol was huddled in the middle of her bed. She heard the door open, and close, but didn't move as Thornton rearranged the comforter over her shoulders; then she sensed him standing above her, wanting to be helpful, yet almost helpless. Poor Thornton, Carol thought, always picking up the pieces, but never able to put them together.

"Anz still here?" Carol asked softly.

"Yes."

"He doesn't have to hang around."

"He wants to," Thornton replied.

"I can't answer any more questions."

"That's not why he's stayed."

Carol turned over, and faced him. "I'm not leaving the apartment again," she answered.

"He feels responsible," Thornton told her.

"That's ridiculous."

"Nevertheless it's true."

Carol sat up. "Could you open the blinds? I can't function in this gloom."

Thornton restrained himself from asking the numerous questions that pressed against his curiosity. Instead he directed himself to badger her with stupidity. Are you going to shower? Want some clean clothes? How about a cup of tea? Why not? Are you hungry? Banality subjugated concern. He hovered, and knew she hated it, but it displaced the dark questions that either Anz or his man had asked.

Thornton's cleverness, his contrived irritations, sufficed for the moment, but could not prevent the discussion.

"Do you want to talk?" Carol asked.

"About what?" Thornton replied.

"Oh, Thornton, you're such a rotten actor," Carol answered, "but you're a wonderful father."

"I'm *that* transparent?" Carol nodded. "So much for any thoughts on a second career."

"It wasn't Anz's fault—"

"You don't have to talk about it," Thornton suggested. "It's not necessary right now."

"It was my fault," Carol continued. "I could have taken my overnight bag. There's enough of them in the apartment, but I had it in my mind to get out of here . . . everything was closing in. Anz! That gorilla! The parade of detectives marching in and out. Can you understand that?"

"Yes, of course."

"He suggested we go to your place, or I suggested it. It doesn't make any difference. It was better than sitting in this trap day after day. I went to the basement with John, he tried to open my storage bin . . . well, he used the wrong key then got a call . . . and the next moment her perfume flowed through the basement."

"Diana?" Thornton asked tentatively.

Carol nodded. "I saw her."

"You're sure?" he asked.

"Of course!" Carol snapped. "Don't you believe me? Diana followed me into the basement . . . Diana's always following me . . . she'll never stop . . . don't you understand, she's always going to follow me."

"Yes, yes," Thornton replied nervously. "I know . . . and Anz understands."

"He doesn't!" she replied fiercely. "After the scene at the market he doesn't believe one word . . . and that's why I didn't tell them about the basement . . . about Diana." Carol beckoned Thornton to move closer. "Listen," she whispered, "I saw her. I know I saw her, Daddy."

Thornton nodded. "Yes," he replied calmly," I'm sure you did, and you have to tell Anz all about it, dear. You have to give him a description of Diana."

Carol shook her head violently.

She's insane, he thought, then bit his lip. I've got to get her back to the hospital. How? What do I have to do? Thornton concealed his anxieties, and fought to keep his own emotions under control.

"Carol, er . . . why don't you tell me . . . all about . . . well, what does she look like?" he stammered.

"It was too dark to see her features, but she's small, yes, small and dumpy. I covered my head when she lunged at me. She's blonde! Yes, blonde . . . a heavy-set blonde."

"That's good," Thornton replied, and immediately regretted the stupidity of his answer. "Yes, a blonde like the woman in the club."

Carol nodded and smiled.

"Anything else?" he asked.

"She kept screaming at me. She blamed me for Latino's death. She said "I dirtied him." I ran, and she kept chasing me through the aisles . . . screaming about Latino. Finally, I locked myself in the bin."

"Yes," that's right," Thornton agreed.

"And she had a knife . . . no, it was longer than a knife. And she kept chopping, and hacking, at the lock, and wires. It was a nightmare. A horrible nightmare."

"My God . . ." Thornton whispered.

"But then Papa Noir appeared, and she stopped."

"Who?"

"The sisters' protector. Papa Noir."

"I . . . I . . . I don't know who Papa Noir is," Thornton stuttered.

"I've never told anyone this," Carol replied. Thornton sat on the edge of her bed. "Remember the Markhams . . . the doll ladies?"

"Vaguely," Thornton answered.

"Papa Noir protects them," Carol replied.

"From who?" he asked.

"From anybody . . . from the world, and he saved me from Diana."

"But . . . but who is this man?"

"Papa is a West Indian. Haitian? One of the islands. He's a taxi driver . . ." Carol said hesitantly.

"And *he* was in the trunk room also?"

"When Diana was attempting to break the lock he appeared, which made her stop. He stood at the far end of the aisle, and she froze, then ran."

Thornton tried to disguise his fears. The story was beyond any bounds of sanity. Taxi driver? Papa Noir? Incredible, no, worse: deranged. Stampler. The Resident Home. Treatment. Where to turn? Who to call? Alarms and fears crowded into his consciousness, only to be masked with a sincere, and intent, expression.

"Did he . . . this Papa Noir try to stop her?"

"No," Carol replied. "I begged him to catch her, but he said it wasn't time. The sisters said it wasn't the right moment."

"The Markhams?"

Carol nodded. "Then John came back, and the rest you know."

"And *he* saw Papa Noir?"

"No. He was gone before John got over to the bin."

"I see," Thornton replied. "No wonder you didn't want to tell Anz. So much happened, and it was quite confusing."

"You don't believe me, do you?" she asked.

Thornton had prepared himself for her question.

"On the contrary," he lied. "Anz found evidence of four people. The dust on the cement floor . . . well, you can't hide anything from a good detective. That explains the other set of heel marks, doesn't it?"

Carol seemed pleased. She curled deeper into the blankets. "Is the offer still open for a cup of tea?"

"And toast?" Thornton replied. Thank God, she bought it, he told himself.

"With strawberry jam," Carol added.

Thornton tucked the comforter under the foot of her bed. "Be back in a moment. Don't go anywhere," he joked. His hands shook as they closed the door to her bedroom, then motioned to Anz to follow him into the kitchen.

"Jeez, you're ashen," Anz remarked. "You having palpitation? Chest pains?"

Thornton steadied himself against the stove. "What . . . what is the legal procedure to have an adult placed in an institution?" he asked.

Carol sat Plato on the pillow beside her.

"Well, sport, we're going to get some action," she turned his head to face her.

"They think yer nuts, babe," he shot back.

I'm not starting this again. I'm talking to myself; he didn't speak; his lips didn't move; I'm not going through this number another time.

"Suit yourself, babe," Plato whispered, "but I'm givin' you the square. Thornton's plotting how to stick you in the booby hatch. Nursie with the net, you bet!"

She smiled, and jabbed him on the nose.

"I'm you. You're me. I talk to myself."

"You know that's bullshit, and don't poke me in the snout. I'm getting sensitive."

Carol chuckled. "Right!"

"Gotta make believers of everyone," he sighed. "Okay, toots, watch this . . . and keep your paws to yourself." Plato shifted his eyes left, then right. "Wait! Here's the socko finish!" He slowly opened his mouth and closed it.

Carol doubled her fists and drew them under her chin. The smell of the hospital. His eyes moved. Stampler being solicitous. His eyes moved. ". . . man, woman, man, woman." He talks. The screaming at the Q Club. "Yes, babe, I'm talking to you."

"Yes, babe, I *am* talking to you," Plato repeated.

"You can't!" she exclaimed.

"Whadda I got to do? Sing?"

"It's a delusion, isn't it?"

"Oh man," Plato groaned. "Accept it. I'm trying to come through. I'm slowly crossing over. Accept it."

Carol covered her head with her hands. I'm going insane. That's what Diana wants . . . to drive me insane.

"But not me, babe," Plato whispered. Carol tightened the comforter around her. "Okay, play it your way. You pretend to talk to yourself . . . make believe you're crazy."

"I am," Carol replied.

"Fine, great," he answered. "Now can we get some cards on the table?"

"I won't listen," Carol muttered.

"Did m'peepers shift? And the jaw drop?" Plato asked. "Better believe it, sweet thing, 'cause you can't snuggle into them blankets much longer."

Carol didn't answer him.

"Carol, old Thornton's gonna stick you in the asylum unless we talk," he said coldly.

"He wouldn't," Carol answered.

"Well, you blew his mind with the Papa purple-eyes saga. It was a dumb play, babe."

"It was the truth," she replied.

"And the truth will put you away."

Carol uncovered her head. The mouth was moving, but it was impossible. His eyes shifted again. It couldn't happen, not to a rational person; to a psychotic, without doubt, but not to someone in control of herself.

"You're not flipping out," Plato explained. "I'm coming through . . . I'm trying to get into the physical, don't you understand? We're blending! You've given me a mind, and a personality. I want the whole thing, babe. I want a 'life.' Get it? You've got to go the extra mile . . . and give me an existence. Don't crap out now. You ain't bughouse!"

She reached up and touched his lips. Suddenly, Plato nipped the tips of her fingers, and Carol recoiled.

"Need more proof?" he sniped.

"No," she said hoarsely.

"It's simple, babe. An energy transfer. You to me. It's been building for years. First, old Bobby Backbite. That's m'pappy. You fed him some smart talk, but it was bits and pieces, and just enough to create yours truly."

"But you're the sixth, or seventh, Plato, and what about—"

"The head-smashing incident? That almost done me in. A close one, but you never let me die, didja? We were back in business, back at the club, giving the broads just what they wanted. It's thought converted to energy, babe."

"I must be crazy," Carol told herself.

"In your present condition . . . go to the head of the class. That's why you've got to tuck in, and I've got to take over . . . for a while . . . until you get your head together. Another 'appearance' as

'Carol' and you're away. Believe me, babe, I'm your only friend."

"Thornton!" Carol suggested.

"The cellar incident tore him up. He thinks he's helping you by calling the white-coat brigade."

"Papa Noir and the sisters are friends," Carol answered.

"Why didn't he nail Diana? Could've! He's not your pal, neither are the old biddies. Jeez, they're probably setting you up. Didja ever think of that? Where are they when you need them? Nowhere! Ain't it the truth?"

Carol stared at him blankly. He was right.

"I'm the only one who's stuck with you, babe. Didn't I pull you through Murray's schtick? Get you of the nuthouse? I'm you're main man. Who else can you trust, huh? The energy's seeping outta you. Kick back, babe. Take ten, huh?"

"Maybe that's best," she whispered.

"Yeah, lemme call the shots for a while? We'll swap roles until you pulled yourself out of the swamp. Who'll know the difference? They'll still think you're pulling my strings. Take a nap, babe. Let the only guy in the world who really cares for you do a number!"

"It's insane because *I'm insane!*" Carol replied.

"No way! It's smart," Plato answered. "I'll keep you out of the Resident Home . . . and I'll get rid of this tit freak that's aiming for you."

"How?" Carol demanded.

"Give me a week of freedom. I'll take over for seven days, and if you're not satified," he quipped, "double your personality back . . . and no questions asked."

Carol dug her nails into her palms. The fears returned: the letters, the accident, the cellar blended into the restraining jacket, and Diana maniacally hacking at the lock.

"How can I miss?" Plato asked. "Lemme pull the strings for a bit, huh? You need to get your batteries recharged, and old Mr. Plato wants to strut his stuff . . . until you wanna come back. You can't lose, babe, it's a dynamite act."

Chapter Twenty-one

It was as if the sisters were merely engrossed with personal projects, which wasn't the truth, and too preoccupied with details to acknowledge each other.

Agnes disguised her vexation by pretending to finish her needlepoint.

Josephine busied herself arranging and rearranging the silver in the side boy. An effort that certainly excluded Agnes.

Most often the reasons for their disharmony was banal, petty matters that were soon forgotten.

However, this time the matter of Carol's dress, and the type of ceremony, had caused a sharp disagreement. Agnes wanted Carol to be garbed in wine-colored velvet, Josephine thought it was "too formal." Josephine insisted on a simple burning, but Agnes felt it was "too common." On such remarks noses were turned-up, thus high tea wasn't served with its usual grace, and the sisters meticulously passed each other in the living room with great distain.

The color and texture of Carol's gown, and the manner of the rite created a major crisis in the Markham home.

The unfortunate third party during this, and most prior eruptions was, of course, Papa Noir. He would be the peacemaker, the arbiter, and healer, as he had been for decades. Papa disliked these "unnecessary dissensions" (so termed by sister Agnes in a moment of pique) but endured.

Beneath the squabbling lurked a darker concern; a concern triggered by Papa's recitation of the trunk room episode, of Diana slashing at Carol, of Diana's maniacal screaming.

"It was *too* close," Agnes muttered. "I told you we shouldn't have allowed it to go this far."

"You are blaming me, sister?" Jo had remarked.

"Papa could have stopped her."

Jo felt responsible. "I thought it could be handled this way. It was my idea and I'll accept the responsibility."

"Don't play the martyr, sister."

Papa didn't bother to intervene as the discussion brought a cutting edge to each sister's voice.

"What's done is past," he commented. "M'thinks missy is close to *fini.* We have need of the proper ceremony to sort *ces choses* out, *n'est-ce?*"

It shifted the conversation, but the bickering now centered on garb and rite. Velvet was out of the question. A burning was banal beyond words.

The sisters realized how close Diana had come, and how they could have prevented the incident.

The unspoken haunted each of them.

If we had kept Carol here.

If Papa had been with Carol from the outset.

If Plato had been in the cellar.

Finally Jo apologized. "I'm sorry, Aggie. I didn't mean to be discourteous."

"I understand," Aggie replied. "We've certainly made a botch of the situation. It's worse than before . . ."

"Indeed so," Jo said mournfully. "Poor, poor Carol . . . still entwined. He's a devil, that one!"

"She," Aggie corrected.

"I said 'she,' " Jo answered quickly.

"No, dear. You said 'he,' and Diana's a "she.' "

"I realize that!"

Aggie smiled, then patted Jo's hand. "Just a slip of tongue. No need to stir up your blood."

"I'm still out of sorts," Jo said wearily.

"All will turn out right. Always does!"

Jo nodded. "And I've made such a mess in the workroom. Her head's all smeared. The paint took forever to adhere to her lips. And I've been such a prig about her gown."

"We'll let Papa decide," Aggie replied.

"*Peut-étre,* it *would be* best," Papa suggested. "*Parce que le temps* is slipping *vite.*"

He followed the sisters into their workroom. Dolls of every description stood, sat, reclined. A wig was needed for the Armand Marsailles. The Bru was missing an arm. The two Jumeaus without gowns sat mute and naked next to a pile of designs covered with swatches of silk, linen, damask.

In the middle, supported by a clamp around its waist, a bisque-headed doll stood motionless. The perfectly molded hands dangled against the muslin body. The face, unpainted, except for blood-red lips, was lifeless. No eyes, no coloration. A platinum blonde wig was askew on the side of its head.

"It's her hair," Aggie remarked. "And the lips . . . just like Carol's shade. I don't think anything's wrong, dear."

"It's missy's color," Papa added. "Finish the face, *sœur* Jo," he begged.

Josephine was reluctant at first, then selected a narrow brush, dipped it in a splotch of rose-colored paint, and carefully worked on the doll's face. The coldness of the white bisque disappeared as the cheeks blushed, and took on a flesh tone. Subtle markings of the eyelids transformed the head into Carol Elliott's likeness. Papa Noir and Aggie smiled, and clucked, as Jo, quickly and skillfully, applied touches of color to the face. Finally, she inserted eyes into the skull.

"It's her! It's our Carol!" Aggie said excitedly. She laughed, then clapped her hands, as Jo reset the wig, gave it a slight touch-up with a miniature comb, and straightened the cloth body on the stand.

"*C'est le vrai!*" Papa exclaimed. "It's missy. *Sans* doubt, *mes sœurs,* it's her."

"Now you can dress her, Aggie . . . and I'll start on the little man," Josephine squealed delightedly.

"I'll use the silk. It's a little less formal," Aggie replied.

"Anything you want, dear, anything."

Papa smiled. He sat in a corner of the workroom as the two sisters happily occupied themselves. Agnes deftly sewed a ball gown for the doll. Yes, Chinese silk, she muttered. Jo placed another figure on a stand. Her fingers moved rapidly. The mouth and the lines leading under the chin were sharply outlined with black paint. The flick of a brush. His coloring. A wig. No, that one was too stiff; that one too dark. Finally, the right one. Plato was created in miniature. Plato stood mutely on the worktable; his arms limp, his mouth ajar. Plato reduced to a doll.

"I shudder just looking at him," Aggie said quietly. "He's a devil that one. A devil!"

"Dress him all *en noir,*" Papa suggested.

"Black?" Jo thought. "It seems too fearful. Especially with that reddish mouth. She closed the miniature's lips, and turned him toward the wall.

"I have something more appropriate in mind," Aggie chortled as she put the finishing touches on Carol's gown. "Yes, just the right costume . . . for that horror!" She cackled softly, and immersed herself in the last adjustment. "There it's done. *Fini, n'est-ce pas?*"

Papa Noir smiled as she fit the gown around the

miniature, picked a piece of thread off the bodice, and evened the hem.

"Très jolie, mes soeurs. C'est parfait. She will be a centerpiece of our rite," he whispered.

Aggie nodded, then rummaged through a pile of fabrics. Yellow satin. Red peau-de-soir. Pink silk. She worked quickly, cutting, selecting fabrics, sewing, piecing a swatch to another. Plato emerged as a harlequin. A gaudy, strutting figure swathed in outlandish colors. Pink britches. A purple vest. A mask.

Color was stitched to color. Aggie worked feverishly to create Plato the fop, the knave, the dissembler.

"He's perfect," Jo remarked.

"I know that," Papa agreed. "Yes, *mes sœurs,* it's all that the little man wishes to hide."

Plato's eyes gleamed from behind the red silk mask. Aggie placed the doll on a stand, then carefully adjusted the body. Hand on hip, legs crossed, the head turned in a cocky pose.

"*C'est parfait,*" Papa whispered.

"Now Diana," Aggie suggested.

Josephine smiled knowingly. She took a cardboard box from underneath the sewing table, and placed it on her lap. "I've been saving this for months," she replied.

Another bisque-headed doll was placed amongst a pile of fabrics. However, the cloth body was bloated, and a hairline crack etched down the center of the face.

"Oh, the head's imperfect," Jo remarked.

Aggie smiled brightly. "Just as we thought. And the neck, Jo, isn't the neck delightful?"

"Indeed. So shriveled."

"Almost pressed into the shoulders. Is Diana that stunted, Papa?" Aggie questioned.

"*D'accord,*" Papa answered gravely. "The shoulders, and head, seemed as one. The doll is *sans* change."

"Give it life," Aggie said gleefully.

However, Josephine hesitated. She reached for a paintbrush, then withdrew it.

"I don't see her," she replied. "The face is neither soft nor hard."

"Then create both," Aggie suggested.

"*Mais oui,*" Papa muttered. "*Parce que* in that cellar *je vois deux personnes.*"

Jo turned the doll toward her. Its neck hunched over the ceramic chest, ad the jaw was slightly turned to the right. Jo's fingers ran down the crack that split the face in two. "Ugly, evil," she muttered. "A grotesque being existing in an unwholesome body."

She eyed the doll carefully, then picked up a paintbrush, daubed it on her palette and began to work rapidly. Flesh tones covered the head and chest. Shading brought the cheeks to life. Coloring brought a depth to the eyelids, and mouth. Josephine worked meticulously to the left of the crack. Rose tones gave the cheek a softness, and delicate blues shaped a feminity to the eye.

"*L'autre,*" Papa said quickly.

"Yes, I understand," Jo answered as she applied the final strokes to the eyebrow.

Josephine turned the half-finished doll on the base, then brushed a shallow shade to the unpainted side. A rougher texture that contrasted with the other half emerged. A masculine feeling was stroked onto the eyelid, the brow became heavy and full, Jo painted a lifeless tone of gray over the entire section.

"It's finished," she announced.

The doll's face held two images, joined, yet separated by the narrow crack that traversed the head.

To the left, a delicate woman.

To the right, the ashen face of a man.

The sisters, and Papa Noir, stared at the creations. Plato, the mocking harelquin. Carol Elliott, a model of elegance. And Diana, imperfect, half man, half woman.

"A cloak," Aggie said quietly. "A black monk's cloak will suit her admirably."

Jo nodded, then wrapped the doll in black muslin. A cowl covered the head.

"*Les yeux?* What about the eyes?" Papa asked.

The sockets remained dark and empty.

"None," Jo replied. "She hasn't a soul."

"Eh, *bien,*" Papa answered.

"Or hair, Jo?" Aggie suggested.

"She's completed," Jo answered firmly. "They're *all* completed."

"Burn them!" Aggie said angrily. "Let the fire purify these creatures."

"Which ceremony?" Papa asked.

"No ceremony," Aggie replied quickly. "Just set a match to them, and rid the atmosphere of their poison."

"It's not enough," Jo answered thoughtfully. "We have to destroy their persona, and their auras. We can't allow them to infect others. No, we must perform a ritual and send these demons back to hell."

"Then we should have a *candomble,*" Papa said softly, "A celebration to purge *les diables.*"

"Yes," Aggie added," the *candomble* will serve this moment well."

"*Un feu au théâtre,*" Papa replied. "let *les trois* be consumed in the theater. Let lord Xango and mistress Yemanja grant our wishes."

"So be it," Jo answered.

"The basement," Aggie suggested. "We'll conduct the ritual there, then bury the ashes."

"No, dear," Jo insisted," we'll burn the ashes in the furnace."

"But they'll escape into the air, *dear!*"

"How true," Jo replied. "Then we'll bury them with the others just as you suggested."

Papa Noir felt a tinge of relief.

"*Je transporteraices poupées quand* you make the theater ready, *mes sœurs.*"

Both sisters smiled delightedly, then hurried through the kitchen, and down to the cellar.

"Doesn't Papa have marvelous ideas?" Aggie commented as she moved a small table to the middle of the basement."

"Indeed. He's so creative. Who else would think of a *candomble?*" Jo replied. She turned, then shoved a tailor's mannikin to the side. "I wished you'd put all the sewing equipment in one room, Aggie."

"When you decide to let me have more space in the attic," she countered.

The suggestion and riposte created a moment of tension, and both sisters worked diligently, but silently, to prepare for the ceremony. Jo reordered the stack of ceramic limbs waiting to be fired in the kiln near the furnace. Hundreds of doll parts were neatly placed on a row of tables. Eyeless heads, hands, legs, and shards of misfired, or chipped, appendages mounded on a workbench. Agnes inspected a line of steamer trunks carefully arranged at the far end of the room. Steamer trunks with fading stickers: THE CUNARD LINE, THE GRIPSHOLM, THE QUEEN MARY. The brass edges scrapped and pitted, but the black leather coverings remained unscratched, almost new.

In another corner were stacks of boxes marked: CHRISTMAS 1942; FORMAL SHOES, A.M.; FATHER'S CLOTHES; AUNT HARRIET'S BOOKS FROM THE COUNTRY.

Agnes moved certain cartons aside until she found the one she wanted.

"Could you give me a hand?" she asked semigraciously. However, the tone of her voice carried a sarcastic edge.

"Delighted!" Josephine replied. "Don't be snippy, dear."

The sisters gingerly moved the carton to the center of the room, opened it without speaking to each other, cautiously removed a balsa replica of a theater, then placed it on the table.

"Not a piece missing," Jo remarked.

"Mint condition. And *you* wanted to give this to a museum," Aggie remarked.

Josephine pursed her lips, but didn't reply. She inspected the model for chipped pieces, or broken detailing, but Aggie was right—it was in flawless condition. The stage, the apron, and the drop curtain were unmarked, or damaged. Even the miniature gilded sign L'ODÉON at the crown of the proscenium arch seemed freshly painted.

"A perfect setting in perfect scale," Jo said admiringly. "And I didn't want to donate it to that stuffy museum. I merely suggested we 'lend' it to them when they had that . . . oh, that theater exhibit, or some such nonsense. Besides," she added, "I was the one who wanted to use it for Carolotta's party."

"Oh yes," Aggie remarked pensively. "But it wasn't the right setting, was it? I know how you felt about her birthday, but you must admit the tea party was nicer?"

Jo nodded. "Let's not discuss it, sister, we have more important works at hand. You may tell Papa Noir that we're ready."

The haughtiness of Josephine's tone irritated Agnes. "Why don't you?" she retorted icily.

"This is *not* the moment to be piqued, Aggie!

Can't we have a ceremony without an undercurrent?"

Agnes shrugged. "Never mind. I'll get Papa, and advise him he can proceed."

Papa Noir, dressed in a floor-length black cape, appeared at the far end of the basement before Agnes had a chance to call him.

He cradled all three dolls in his arms as he slowly walked toward the miniature stage.

Mechanically, and without either looking or speaking to the sisters, he placed each doll on the stage. At first Plato stood behind Carol, then he moved Diana to Plato's right. Yet he wasn't satisfied.

"The positions are wrong," he whispered. He placed Plato between Diana and Carol. "Still *mal, mes sœurs. Je pense* . . . aha, *le petit* harlequin must stand nearer missy," he said. "I put him closer to her, and the evil one to her left, Eh, *bien,* they are staged. Now we are free to summon Lord Xango, and Lady Yemanja."

The sisters stepped back as Papa stood directly in front of the miniature stage.

He closed his eyes, and lowered his head.

Only Papa Noir's breathing echoed through the basement. His deep breaths became mixed with sighs, and sobs, as he drew himself into a trance.

Slowly, a murmur of singsong words came from his partially open mouth. The words were jumbled, muttered, incomprehensible until they blended with a lilting moan, which grew into a chant.

"Blessed Lord Xango . . . help me.
Dearest Lord Xango . . . help me.
Blessed Lord Xango, hear my prayers . . ."

The sisters watched Papa Noir with rapt fascination. The huge black man's eyes rolled; his body swayed as he became possessed by his spirits, and drawn deeper into his trance.

"Come forth Mistress Yemanja," he begged. "Come to this place and accept *ces mals*. Take these devils into your flames," he pleaded.

Papa's head moved side to side, his body became rigid, then limp, as the spirits seemed to jolt his frame. His words became slurred with a singsong of French and Spanish patois.

"Burn *ces diables. Au feu ces diables,*" he cried. "*Cette Diana . . . feu! Ce petit homme . . . au feu, Et mademoiselle . . . au le feu!*"

Perspiration streaked down Papa's cheeks as he struggled against violent, unseen forces. His body arched and shuddered as Lord Xango and Lady Yemanja were summoned forth. Finally, his body convulsed, then relaxed, and he knelt in front of the theater.

"The Gods will grant our wish," he said softly. "We can continue . . . we can burn *ces mals.*"

Aggie curled a piece of white paper into a funnel, opened the furnace door, and lit the end. A soft tongue of flame clung to the edge as she handed it to Josephine.

"Burn them, dear," she whispered.

Jo held the paper carefully. She smiled at Papa Noir and her sister as she daubed a flame on Plato's costume, then touched it against Diana's cloak.

"Carol . . . you burn our dearest Carol," she said to Agnes. "I want you to have the pleasure."

Agnes kissed Jo lightly on the cheek.

"You've always been too good to me," she answered, then took the paper and with a single stroke set Carol's figure, and the stage, on fire.

The miniature theater was engulfed in flames. Carol's dress smoldered then burst into a dancing orange shape. Diana's cloak was immediately consumed; fire bubbled the paint on her face, then shattered the bisque head. Plato was the last to be swallowed in the smoke and flames. His mouth fell open as flame inched up his face, then his head was a ball of fire.

The sisters and Papa Noir watched the dolls and their setting consume themselves until nothing but a pile of ashes and charred wood remained.

"Lord Xango and my Lady Yemanja have spoken," Papa said quietly. "We can proceed . . . *les temps est parfait.*"

"*Mais oui,*" Jo cackled. "It's time. Yes, dear Papa, it's time."

Chapter Twenty-two

Nick Anz turned the battered lock over, and examined the hack marks etched into its stem. The lab report proved inconclusive. Yes, minuscule shavings were present. No, the type of instrument couldn't be identified. Yes, the particles were "similar" to "physical properties extracted from the pubic bone of Arnold Cohen AKA "Latino" (deceased).

The yess's and no's of the two incidents annoyed Anz. The link between the murder, the threats, and the trunk room episode still eluded him.

He rubbed his forefinger across the grooves imbedded in the lock. Yes, we're dealing with a psychotic, but, on the other hand, someone rational enough to avoid detection. Sane, and insane, Anz thought. Inner Carol and outer Carol. The idea had appealed to him from the outset despite her "psychological profile."

Why couldn't she have sent the letters to herself, or the bra, and disguised her voice to the answering service? Yes, it was a distinct possibility to be negated only by the hard evidence. He toyed with the lock, then put it back in its plastic bag. Nothing fit into a pattern. Anz's men had questioned dozens of male performers. Some had received love letters, marriage proposals, but nothing from Diana, and most had been signed, sealed, mailed with a kiss, and included name, address, telephone numbers [office and home].

The lovely ladies certainly weren't shy.

The DIANA/ELLIOTT/COHEN file bulged with interviews, handwriting samples and analyses, letters, pictures of anxious ladies, and detective's reports. The manhours, and the results, were disproportionate. Diana evaded them, which drew Anz to refocus his investigation on Carol.

Wasn't she the center of attention?

Wasn't it possible she stabbed Latino in a moment of rage?

Weren't there two, maybe more personalities, running in that screwed-up mind?

What about the incident at Gristede's?

What about the latest story? A taxi driver named Papa Noir? In the trunk room?

What about the dummy talking to her? Moving its eyes?

Anz pushed the files to the end of his desk. Even her father admitted it was beyond reason. However, Carol Elliott—ventriloquist, and sicko—couldn't be matched with Carol Elliott—murderess, and psycho.

It didn't meld, he thought, and there wasn't any proof. No weapon. No witnesses. No motive.

The case stunk. If there was a Diana lurking in the wings, or in Carol's head, she would be virtually impossible to find *unless* provoked. Anz shook his head. It was illogical, irrational, and unfinished.

However, Anz and Thornton were caught off-guard by Carol's sudden change of attitude.

Yes, she wanted to seek help, but not the Resident Home. Anz was skeptical. Her decision came rapidly, and sounded too logical. He still hadn't placed all the pieces of the trunk room episode together. Oh, Papa Noir? Carol laughed. I just imagined him. Now, let's go over the description of Diana, he requested. It was dark, and I was scared. I really don't remember, Carol replied. Anz nodded, folded his notebook, and smiled.

When should I make an appointment for you? Thornton asked. In a couple of days. Let me get myself settled, Carol answered. Thornton didn't press the issue. Her concession to see a psychiatrist was, at least, "positive." Anz agreed outwardly, but wasn't convinced.

Yes, she would leave the apartment, but not move in with Thornton. At first Anz resisted the suggestion. We can maintain tighter surveillance, he remarked. Isn't there somewhere else? Carol asked. I'd feel like a sitting duck. Well, there's hotel on the East Side we use as a temporary safehouse for witnesses under protective custody. Carol liked the idea, and Anz conceded.

It's all too nice, he thought. I'm gonna watch you like a hawk, sister, 'cause I don't trust you.

Carol's rational facade chipped away some of Thornton's fears, and Anz's suspicions. She consistently agreed with both men, and accepted their advice.

Thornton was positive "the worst was over." "I haven't seen her this relaxed in years," he confided to Anz. "Maybe she doesn't really need—" Anz punctured the illusion. "All right, but I know my daughter!"

Sure you do! Anz thought. Keep it light, and simple, he told himself. Just listen, and she'll make a mistake.

Carol played her role beautifully, and Plato chortled. We got 'em conned, babe. Whadda I tell ya? Look at that frigging cop go for the bait. He's a schmuck, babe. Carol silently agreed. I told ya to tuck in, let old Plato handle the thinking. It's aces high.

Yes, Carol thought. Everything seems clearer, uncomplicated.

Play it my way, he reminded her, and we'll be out of New York before Anz can reload his mind.

We're going to split? Carol asked.

The only course of action, Plato remarked.

You've got six days left, she answered.

No sweat. It's a piece of cake. Watch this one! Keep a smile on your face, and repeat after me. . . .

"Thornton, I'd like to make Plato some new clothes, would you help me take down the sewing machine?" He did. "I haven't the right fabrics, could we go to the Cloth Shop on Broadway?" He was hesitant, telephoned Anz, who gave his permission only if "my man goes along, and he takes a squad car." The shopping jaunt, interrupted by a quick stop at a deli, concluded without incident.

"What happened, Carl?" Anz asked over the phone.

"Nothing, Nick. Absolutely zero."

"Any perfume stunts? Or faggots attacked?"

"She prowled through piles of cloth. I was with her. The old man was with her. Nobody even said hello to us. We went to a deli, got bread, and meat, then came back here."

"Where is she?"

"Inside, with her father, they're making a couple of suits, and junk, for the dummy."

"Any letters today?"

"She got some bills, that's it. Nobody called either, and Frank checked the basement . . . twice! It's quiet," the detective replied.

"Too quiet," Anz answered. "Time to move them over to the hotel."

"Today?" he asked.

"In the morning," Anz replied. "Have her pack

enough for a week." Anz hesitated. "On second thought let me handle it . . . I'll be over tonight."

"Good, I wanna get outta here. She's driving me batty with that Mr. Plato. Every time I ask her something she makes the frigging dummy talk. She's a case, Nicky, a real looney. And the way she treats that thing . . . ya would believe it's alive. Jeez, can ya get here sooner?"

"Have a sandwich, it'll calm your nerves," Anz scoffed, and hung up.

Plato enjoyed the charade. "Didja see that cop squirm, babe? He can't handle me," he laughed.

Carol bent over the sewing machine stitching his new jacket together.

"You shouldn't tease him," she whispered.

"Aw g'wan," Plato answered.

"Suppose he realizes . . . well, could he?"

"Naw," Plato replied. "They still think you're on top of it. Even Thornton's suckered in. We're on our way, babe. Make them new duds special. I wanna look my best when we hit Vegas."

Carol smiled. "Right!"

She emersed herself in his wardrobe. *Chic-chic-chic-chic*. The needle stamped a line of thread into a piece of blue serge.

"Sew on, and sew forth," Plato quipped.

Suddenly Carol felt overheated.

"Thornton," she called, "would you turn the thermostat down. It's too hot in here."

He did, but Carol still felt uncomfortable. Her face was flushed, and her eyes ached.

"Turn it off," she said curtly.

Thornton started to hover. Virus? Probably the flu. Aspirin? Hot tea? Why don't you—

"I'm all right," Carol answered. "Don't hover. Please stop acting like a mother hen."

Yes, of course. Sorry. Thornton smiled to cover his bruised feelings.

"I'm going to lie down."

"Good idea."

Carol was drenched in perspiration as she lay on her bed. Her head throbbed, and her hands pulsated. She reached across the bed to move Plato off a pillow. His clothes were warm. His cheeks were boiling.

"What's going on?" he demanded. "I'm burning up. It's like being in an oven."

"I'm sick," she replied.

"Great!" he sneered. "Just starting to roll and you pull this! I'm telling you, Carol, I don't like it."

"I didn't plan it!" she replied.

"Bullshit!" Plato snarled. "This wasn't part of the deal. When I said I'd take over . . . it meant without any of your crappy hang-ups."

"I don't want to be sick!"

"And I want to keep on schedule," Plato insisted. "Don't mess me up, lady. We're getting outta this apartment, into Anz's fleabag for a few days, then Vegas, Reno, and L.A."

"Yes!" Carol replied. "I agree."

"Why are ya creating problems? Since I took you by the head it's been gravy."

"I'm not complaining."

"You're making aggravation. You're trying to weasel into control. Don't do it! Not yet, babe. Lemme make the moves. Don'tcha trust me?"

"Yes," Carol replied softly.

"I'm not convinced. Face me," Plato ordered. "Look at me, and say it."

"I trust you," Carol answered.

Plato's eyes shifted. "You should, m'gal, but from now on I better go along in . . . the physical."

"I can't carry you everywhere."

"Why not? What's so unusual?"

Carol frowned. "It's stupid."

"Then I'm gonna throw you to wolves," he shot

back. "You'll handle the whole number, and remember what a frigging mess you made of that. In two days old Thornton'll have you at the nuthouse."

"I won't go back there," she replied.

"You won't have a choice," he sneered. "The screwed-up Carol Elliott, the paranoid, the psycho, will emerge, *again,* and her whole bags of tricks. 'Oh no, the perfume.' 'Help me, Papa purple-peepers—"

"*All right!*" Carol growled. "Enough! I'll carry you."

"You betcha, babe," Plato crooned. "Hey, it won't be that rough. We're going to a hotel . . . room service ain't too difficult to take. I didn't ask ya to take me shopping. And in Vegas . . . anything goes. Tuck in, we're doing real fine."

Carol turned away from him. He was right. The incident in the trunk room seemed but a fleeting nightmare. Maybe she had imagined the violence. Maybe 'Diana' was an illusion as were Papa Noir and the sisters. It's possible, she thought. A fantasy, a delusion, that made her act irrationally. Didn't Stampler suggest it? Didn't the group at the Resident Home suggest it? The episode in the supermarket wasn't terribly sane, was it? Carol smiled. That poor old faggot; he must still be afraid to go shopping. Plato was right! Everything was calmer since he . . . he? me? whomever? she reflected changed the patterns. Carol brushed a hair off of her face. The temperature was gone. Her head was cool. She turned around and felt Plato's cheek. Cool.

His eyes shifted toward her. "See, babe, it's all gone! Just in your head. Trust me, babe, trust me!"

Anz's hotel for protected witnesses and other assorted guests of the state wasn't as he had painted it. It wasn't on the East Side, but on the Lower

East Side off Houston Street. It was a dilapidated tenement no different from the surrounding buildings. Naturally, there wasn't room service except for a rotating shift of detectives that went out for a rotating menu of either "chinks," pizza, or hero sandwiches.

"Well," Thornton remarked, "this has all the comforts of a slum."

"Sorry about that, Mr. T. It'll only be for two days, then we can move her to another hotel."

"Where?" he demanded. "This is disgraceful."

"Listen, the city's broke. We're lucky to have this. It's only for a week, and you don't have to stay here. Hey, we can look after Miss Elliott."

"*A week?* But you said—"

"Somebody messed up at Departmental. Sorry about that. What would youse like tonight? With anchovies, or egg foo young?"

"I want to speak with Anz."

"He's on a job in the Bronx. Triple homicide. Didn'tcha read it in the paper? Musta been drugs, huh?"

Thornton tried to conceal the latest news from Carol, but in his rage he blurted it out.

"Another week?" Carol exclaimed. "We're supposed to be out of here tomorrow." Thornton shook his head.

Carol paced the dingy living room. The idea of spending another night in the apartment galled her. She had forced herself to accept the neighbor's screaming, the sounds of toilets flushing in the middle of the night, and the merry-go-round of seedy detectives bearing disgusting food, but "another week" was unbearable.

"Shit on 'em!" Plato snarled.

"I can't take another day here," Carol replied.

"It's Thornton's fault. He wasn't firm enough with Anz. Goddamnit, this throws the timing off."

"I'll tell Thornton we've got to get to Vegas by tomorrow."

"No way, babe, it's too sudden. You can't spring that number on him from left field."

"Then we'll go back to the apartment!"

"*No!*" Plato replied. "That's no good."

"It's better than this dump."

"We can't go back!" Plato insisted.

"Why not? Carol demanded.

"First, they'd never let ya," Plato replied. "Second, it sounds confused . . . and babe, you show them any signs of reverting and it's nuthouse time. Go back? I ain't never stepping back, again. Plato's onward and upward . . . with you, of course. Sure, you an' me . . . we can't go back."

"Why don't we walk out?"

"That's brilliant! They'd think you went off the deep end . . . running away . . . That's a sure-fire trip to the nuthouse. You want that, or a clean slate?"

"And Diana? You haven't told me how you plan to solve that number, Sherlock!"

"I been thinking about it," Plato replied.

"Really?" Carol questioned. "I don't believe you. Why wouldn't she find me in Vegas? Or anywhere else? Anz said she would. Anz said she hasn't finished her behavior pattern. Anz says—"

"*Screw Anz!*" Plato interrupted. "He's wrong! Once you're out of town Diana won't bother you!"

"I didn't 'bother' her in the first place! She selected me. I'm deep in her freaky thoughts, m'boy. She's killed a fruit because 'I dirtied' him. She went after me with a knife . . . when I was surrounded by police. Now, tell me how wonderful life will be in Vegas! Or how safe I am in Reno! She's got me ticketed for a coffin . . . here, or on the Coast."

"I'm telling ya different," Plato smirked.

"And 'I'm telling you' I'm just as screwed up as before, m'boy. You're calling the shots? Your eyes move? Hey, if I thought some jerk in the market was a woman, I can certainly pretend to talk to you, and see your peepers shift."

"Ya ain't pretending. I'm real. I'm coming through, and you know it. I ain't the back half of your head, sweetie. I'm old Plato, right?" he said convincingly, and winked. "Now tell me about 'pretend'!"

"Walk!" Carol commanded. "If you're real get up and walk. One step, that's not too much to ask."

"You got it, toots. Prop me against the bed, and I'll show you!" he sneered.

Carol picked him off the bed, and placed him on the floor; his back leaned against the boxspring.

"Make me a believer, Plato," Carol said coldly. "Show me how you're 'coming through' . . . how independent you are. C'mon, walk!"

The dummy's eyes shifted wildly. His jaw hung slack as he panted, and gasped. "I'm trying, you bitch!" he snarled. "I'll show you! You'll see!"

"You ain't going nowhere, fella."

"Yeah! Just watch!"

Carol waited, but Plato never moved.

"Time's up, m'boy, and you lost. And I lost, right? 'Cause I'm sitting here waiting for you to walk, and pretending you can talk."

"*I can!*" he seethed.

"No way, babe. I talk to myself. You're me, and that's all she wrote. Y'know I wish that frigging accident was the exit line."

She placed him on a chair, tugged at his collar, and straightened his jacket. "You look pretty good in the new clothes, babe. Too bad no one will see them."

Plato didn't answer her. His eyes stared straight ahead.

"Figured as much," Carol muttered. "Well, it was a nice game while it lasted. We went from Riverside Drive to a sleaze-bag hole-in-the-wall. I sure know how to screw myself up, huh? The best place for me is the nuthouse. We'll play mommy-and-sonny okay? And Plato, old scout, it won't make a frigging bit of difference 'cause all the rest of them are crazy too."

"Don't get desperate," he said quietly.

Carol smiled, and patted his face.

"I can get you outta here. Anz is wrong. Give it another chance."

"I'm always giving myself a second shot."

"So what's one more? And if you're right," he asked, "we're in the clear."

Carol leaned her head against her arm. The neighbors started throwing dishes at each other. Screams and curses echoed up the courtyard. Punk rock blared across the roof. The smell of uncollected garbage lingered in the hall. Poor Thornton, Carol thought, how he must hate this scene.

"He does," Plato replied. "It ain't his style, or yours either. Gimme another shot, babe.

"At the nuthouse . . . or Diana?" Carol said to herself. "It's been downhill all the way."

The angry voices subsided, and the music faded into the night. Terrific, Carol thought. End of round one. Carol watched a roach crawl along the edge of her blanket. It stopped, the antennae probing for enemies, then continued until its front legs perched on Plato's shoulder.

"Feel that?" she asked.

"No," he replied. "You sticking pins in my feet?" She smiled at him. "Listen, we stick together and by spring I'm dancing." Carol chuckled. "No stuff, babe, if'n I can talk, I'm sure as hell gonna walk . . . despite what you think."

"And I'm not crazy?"

Plato snapped his mouth several times, and rolled his eyes. "Was that a trick? In your head? Or the real McCoy, McCoy," he quipped.

"It *was* in my head," Carol replied.

"Shit!" Plato hissed. "*It wasn't!*"

"Then walk, babe," she answered softly.

"I can't. It's too early," he growled.

Carol laughed softly. "If Thornton, or Anz, or Stampler, could see me now. Oh babe, old nursie would really clamp me on that rack."

"Okay, have it your way!" Plato replied angrily. "Pretend you're crazy!"

"I am," Carol answered.

The cockroach crawled down Plato's arm, then to the boxspring, and disappeared under the bed.

"Super," he muttered. "You'll love it in the bughouse. Is that what you want? Chained like a freak? Looking at the blank wall for a hundred years?"

"No," Carol replied softly. "I couldn't stand to be locked up."

"So play it my way, which, if you want, is *your way*. It don't matter who's on first. The only number that counts is being free . . . from this pigsty, your frogged-up life, from Anz, *from Diana!* You gotta give me a break too, babe. You owe it to me. You gotta let me come out, and we'll swing. Listen to me," he insisted, "take another chance . . . you can prove they're wrong."

"How?" Carol said dreamily. "How can I get rid of Diana, or the mess I've made . . ."

"Gimme control once more," Plato asked.

"To do what?"

"To clean house," he replied. "And prove I'm more than just another pretty paint-and-plaster face."

"Why not?" Carol answered. "You! Me! Us! It doesn't make any difference anymore. I'm too tired to fight."

"*Good,*" Plato answered. "Get Thornton in here, but lemme do the talking. I'm gonna make you sound cool, calm, and *very* collected. We're gonna sell 'em a lovely bill of goodies."

Chapter Twenty-three

Anz was furious. "Forget it! There's no way you're leaving this place without police protection."

"I can't stay here another week," Carol replied. "The noise and filth are unbearable."

"This is only temporary," Anz insisted. "We've got another place in Queens."

"Equally as dirty?" Thornton remarked.

"Don't give me a hard time, Mr. Evans," he replied. "At least she's safe."

"And I'll be *safe* at Thornton's apartment," Carol answered. Anz shook his head.

"We'll be there two nights!" Carol argued.

"Oh, that's nice," Anz shot back. "Where you going after that? Back to your apartment? Or should I save this magnificent suite for you? Or if you're unfortunate, perhaps the morgue!" he said sarcastically.

"I'm leaving New York," she answered calmly. "Thornton and I have talked it over, and feel it's the best thing . . . no, the *only thing* to do!"

"Un-uh," Anz growled, "thanks for discussing it with me."

"We're going to Reno," Thornton replied. "I've made arrangements for Carol to work with Jack Lanzetta."

"Great! Super!" Anz said angrily. "It's like advertising: 'Come get me.' This Diana business isn't finished!"

"I'm not planning to go on stage . . . yet," Carol told him. "Jack's going to let me work with him. I'll book the comedians, and some of the variety acts. It's off stage, behind-the-scenes. And Thornton will be there."

"*And* it sounds so logical," Anz snapped.

"It's a damn sight better than sitting in New York . . . waiting for her to attack!" Thornton interjected.

"Jeez," Anz replied, "you're making *me* look like the heavy. All we want to do is make sure this freak's run her course, or we nail her!"

"I'm not hanging around for either," Carol answered softly. "I can't take another night in this disgusting tenement. And I want to clear out of this rotten city."

"Talk some sense to her," Anz pleaded.

"No! She's right," Thornton answered. "Besides, the private security people are always at hand."

"All right," Anz said wearily. "We can't hold you. All I ask is one favor . . . a detective stays with you until that plane takes off."

Carol smiled. "How about fat Carl? He's like one of the family."

Anz laughed. "Sure. Carl will love it."

Thornton was pleased. Carol was delighted, and Plato laughed gleefully. We're on our way, babe, he echoed. Stick with me and you'll wear diamonds.

"And Carl . . . don't let her out of your sight until she's on the frigging plane and the door's are locked."

"Why didn't you pick someone else, Nick?"

" 'Cause the dummy loves you," he joked.

"Thanks for nothing!" Carol griped.

"What's the big deal? In two days she's gone. Check your watch, buddy, her time's running out."

"Do I get a week of authorized leave for this, Nick? I hate that goddamn puppet, and she drives me bananas. That woman's a psycho!"

Anz patted him on the cheek. "Get her on the plane safely, and you can name your next assignment."

Anz's promise rang in his ears throughout the following day, and night. Carol Elliott was a flake, the detective thought, and her father is a pain in the ass. Aw, what the hell! I'll watch the tube, and keep my mouth shut.

Neither Carol nor Thornton appreciated Carl's presence. He wasn't messy, or unpleasant. He was just in their way. The details multiplied. Get rid of her apartment. Ship her clothes. What about the lawyers? And Murray? And their case? Thornton would stay through the weekend, then join Carol in Reno. Thornton bought her plane ticket, and another day passed.

"Twenty-four small ones," Plato whispered. "Yeah, babe, one more day, and we're free. Take a good look 'cause it's adios-time."

Carol sat him on top of Thornton's dresser while she wrote out another extensive list: insurance (car) to be canceled; Call Mike Rosenwasser at Chemical Bank about my loan; traveler's checks, etc.

She put the pad down, and stared out the window. What about Papa Noir? Or the sisters?

"Forget 'em!" Plato cracked." That's ancient history! You're washing yourself of all this garbage."

"Perhaps," Carol reflected.

"Definitely!" he shot back. "Old daddy dark-one, or the midget, weren't your buddies."

Carol didn't answer him.

"Cheer up," Plato said casually. "Everything's on schedule. Trust me. It's clear sailing."

"Yeah, sure," Carol muttered.

"Hey, look, I can move m'mouth." Carol smiled,

and stared at him vaguely. "Still gotta make a believer of you, huh?"

"Right," she answered.

"Too bad, but I'll hang in there. Hey, what about a farewell blast? The last look at this creepy town! How's that sound! You, me, Thornton, and the gorilla. We'll check out the Q Club for old times' sake! For kicks!"

"It'll never happen. Anz put the clamps on us," She replied. "We're under house arrest."

"C'mon!" he begged. "We'll use the old charm. Give the ape some schmooz, and we'll swing."

"He'll never buy it."

"Stick me in your ever-loving arms, babe. I'll do the talking, you do the eye-batting, and give you ten-to-one we'll be stepping out," he replied.

Carol smiled, tucked him in the crook of her right arm, and marched into the living room.

"Hey, Carl baby," Plato cooed. "Wanna see how the other half lives? Ever catch the mud wrestlers at the Q Club? Oh, by the way, they're lady mudders . . . half-naked! Interested?"

He wasn't, but Plato persisted.

"You, me, Thornton, and the babe!"

He had to check with Anz.

"Carl," Plato crooned, "don't you ever make your own decisions."

That stung him.

"Carl, we're leaving tomorrow. It's the last tango in Manhattan. What's to worry? A couple of hours out? C'mon, Carl, be a sport."

He relented. "You won't tell Anz?"

"Who's to know?" Plato snickered. "Wait till you see the lovely Candy. Oh man, she's got a bod."

Carl laughed. "Yer pretty good, Miss Elliott, I coulda sworn he said it by himself."

"He did," Carol replied.

* * *

The tempo at the Q Club never faltered. Male go-go dancers pranced over Latino's ghost. The spinning mirrored ball flicked patches endlessly.

Chick-a-boom. Grind it to me, Billy baby. Stuff a ten in there, honey, and I'm yours. He extends his hips, and thrusts his groin toward a pasty-faced brunette.

The sweat inched down Mr. Sleek's chest.

Take me home, honey, he mocked. He moves to the rock beat and edges closer to the audience.

Wah-wah-wah.

Pelvis in-your-face, sweet thing.

Look at his thighs, Selma.

Oh jeez, he's hung, Shirley. Jeez, you can see it right through his pants. Oh jeez!

Chick-a-boom. Move and thrust. Mr. Sleek always gives 'em what they want, and can't have. Oh yeah, honey, look but don't tear, fold, or mutilate.

Rim shot, and pose. The lovely ladies ooze with delight. Take me, big guy, take me!

The lights pulsate with the pounding of the music. It's business as usual. Big Billy, Mr. Sleek, and Harlem Harry grind out the fantasies.

Chick-a boom. Rim shot.

It's heaven for the libido. A middle-aged ugly fondles her drink, and wishes. The unattractive steno sucks on her straw, and wishes. The flashes of light splatters through the audience, but the darkness hides their thoughts.

Carol and entourage watch from the wings. Thornton excuses himself to make small talk with the owners, while the detective drinks in the frenzy.

"Jeez, this is wild! Those women are going bananas." *Wah-wah-wah.* Pose time, and cheers.

"That's nothing," Carol replied. "Sometimes they get on the stage."

"And go for the goodies," Plato quipped.

"Bet they do," Carol said blankly.

"Want a drink?" Carol asked.

"Naw," Carl answered. "I got stomach problems."

". . . and now," the emcee croons from the stage, "the moment we've been waiting for."

Cheers, and *drum roll.*

Carol tugs at Plato's collar. "This is new," she remarked.

"Yeah, lucky fuck night."

The detective winced.

". . . okay, m'lovelies, it's time for our nightly drawing. Get out your stubs . . . and the boys will get out theirs . . ." *Cheers,* and *Chick-a-boom.*

The women react. Purses are defiled. Wallets ransacked. Where the hell's my ticket? Oh shit, Selma, I lost the frigging ticket. Naw! It's in your coat . . . look again, dummy!

Carol watched with amusement.

"They got quick fingers, huh?" Plato quips. "Whadda ya think, Carl baby?" He shrugs.

The dancers stand impatiently waiting for the punch line. Big Billy winks at a plump redhead. Harlem Harry wipes the sweat off his face, and rubs it on his shorts. Mr. Sleek, hands-on-hips, arches his back.

". . . all right, girls, this is it. The chance of a lifetime. The chance to amuse, and abuse, your favorite hunk. It's time to pick the beefcake of your choice. . . ."

The emcee's spiel whets their appetites. Yes, the lucky lady will be able to . . . yes, tonight you'll have it all . . . yes, on this very stage . . .

Diana clenches her sweating hands as she sits at the bar. She looks at her ticket, then Mr. Sleek. She fantasizes licking his chest. She wipes her face. Finish, finish! she screams. Call the number! she begs. The emcee prolongs the agony by introducing each dancer, giving specific measurements. The sighs and cheers anger Diana. Get on with it! She sees her hands caressing Sleek's thighs. She stares at her ticket. Call me! Call me! she pleads. I want you, she whispers to Sleek. You'll always be mine. Nothing will destroy our love. Nothing will spoil you. I want you, she begs. Call me! Call me!

Her eyes dance wildly as the emcee jives through Mr. Sleek's proportions.

". . . look at those shoulders, girls. Izzat beefcake, or issat chicken shit . . . ?"

Diana stands at the back of the main room. She can barely restrain herself. More fantasies. He's rubbing himself against me.

". . . *Now!* The moment you've been waiting for. . . ."

Cheers. Drum roll.

" . . . I'm going to draw the lucky, lucky number!" *Rim shot, and cheers.* The emcee spots Carol, and changes his patter. Let 'em hang a bit longer. "Hold on, I've got a guest here tonight! A charming, talented lady, who's no stranger to the Q Club. *Miss Carol Lane with Plato!* Step out here, m'lady, and take a bow."

Carol hesitated, but the emcee, led her by the hand to center stage.

"Ya look great!" he crooned.

"And you look like shit!" Plato shot back.

A few laughs. "Haven't lost your touch, eh, Mr. Plato?"

"And I'm known to touch," he answered. "Why I've had my finger in almost everyone . . . I mean, -thing!"

Diana felt the blood surge to her cheeks as Carol appeared. Her lust turned to hate. She steadied herself against a pillar. Bitch! Slut! Whore!

Plato's wisecrack titilated the ladies, and he kept up a continuous patter with the emcee, then turned to Mr. Sleek.

"You're a big one," Plato quipped. "Bet he's as big on the bottom as he is on the top. Right, girls!"

Cheers, and *rim shot.*

Diana was furious. You're dirtying him! You're spoiling my love!

Carol knew Plato was out of her control, but couldn't stop a steady barrage of filth that poured out of his mouth.

"Shut up!" he whispered. "I'm getting it on with big boy here!"

She was floating again. She was the dummy, and Plato the ventriloquist. Finally, the emcee cut off the banter.

"Okay, here's the lucky moment. The lovely and talented Carol-l-l Lane will draw the ticket for tonight, then the crude and rude Mr. Plato-o-o will read, *aloud,* the winn-ah!"

Diana dug her hands into her dress as the announcement was made. You've spoiled everything, she muttered.

"Wazzat, lady?" a woman asked.

Diana glared at her, and the woman moved away. I should have killed you! Diana thought.

Carol glanced furtively at Thornton and the detective as the emcee mixed a bowl of tickets.

"All right, Carol-l-l. Pick a good one."

Her hand paused as he tipped the bowl toward her. Carol stared at him vacantly.

"Pick one!" Plato muttered.

Anticipation hushed the audience as Carol selected a ticket.

"I got the lucky number!" Plato announced. "Will the lady . . . or maybe the gent, with num-bah N-6-3-9-5 step right up and claim your rub!"

"*It's Shirl!* Shirley's won it." A table of ladies exploded with delight. Yes, frumpy Shirl, file clerk, going nowhere, had won "the thrill of a lifetime."

Her friends pushed her on stage. I bet she'll wet her pants, Selma joked.

Diana seethed. She dug her nails into the back of an empty chair. Don't touch my man, she warned. Don't put your hands on him! She gritted her teeth as the emcee guided "the winn-ah" to the front of the stage.

"Okay, big Shirl . . ." She tittered, and hunched her shoulders. ". . . the rules are sim-ple. You select any one of the big beef on this stage . . . and he'll, in front of all the world, give you everything . . . within good taste . . ." Diana rubbed her knuckles against her cheek. Don't touch him! she muttered. ". . . that you've dreamt about. One rule, you gotta keep your arms at your sides . . . and no biting!"

Shirl covered her face.

"G'wan," Selma yelled. "*Do it!*"

Carol stepped into the wings, and stood beside Thornton. "This is a new game," she remarked.

"Indeed, and rather crude," Thornton answered.

"What's gonna happen?" the detective asked.

"He's gonna dry hump her," Plato cackled.

"Nice. Real class," Thornton replied sharply. "Why did you have to say that? Just stop it, Carol!"

"Screw you!" Plato replied.

"Thank you," he replied. "I see nothing's really changed." Thornton glared at her, and walked away.

"You shouldn't have said that," Carol whispered.

"The hell with him," Plato answered. "He's nothing but dead weight. And I ain't dragging him around anymore."

Drun roll.

"Jeez! Holy shit! Yer right, Miss Elliott, the dancer's . . . jeez, the guy's all over her . . ." Carl exclaimed.

Chick-a-boom. Rat-ta-ta-tat!

Mr. Sleek danced closer, and closer to frumpy Shirl. His sweaty chest rubbed against her blouse.

Scream and scream again, gals!

The lovely ladies cheered wildly as he pushed his torso against her.

". . . it's a dream come true," the emcee crooned, "and he's all yours, Shirl . . . the man you've dreamt of . . . he's moving closer, his bod touching yours . . ."

Diana pressed her hands against her ears. Slut! You defiled him. You soiled his pure body.

Rim shot, and *drum roll.* Oh yeah, troops, he's moving in for the kill, and Shirl's in heaven.

Diana pushed her way through the club, and ran into the street. The screams, and cheers, buried themselves in street noises. Carol Elliott! *Carol Elliott!*

Subliminal flashes. Latino posing. Carol Elliott. Latino moving slowly to the music. Plato.

Diana tugged at her wig, then threw it into the gutter as she crossed Third Avenue, and hurried down a side street. She leaned against a building trying to catch her breathe.

"I'll teach you! I'll teach you!" she panted.

Diana lurched away from the wall, and walked rapidly to her car.

Step, heel, *click.* Step, step, step.

Latino danced in front of her. The tape recorder spun a moody, pelvis-grinding song. She watched him glide, and pose; glide, and pose.

Step, heel, *click.*

Why did you betray me? Why did you touch her? *Why? Why? Why?* kept pulsating as he posed, and played to the empty club. Her fingers curled around the bayonet. I wanted a pure love. Why did you let them touch you?

Step, step, stop. Diana steadied herself against the car door.

Echoes, and *flashes.*

Latino snapped off the tape.

"Sorry, lady, the club's closed."

I love you.

"You'll have to leave."

I'm Diana. I love you.

"I don't know how you got in but—"

The bayonet flashed.

I love you.

His stomach opened. *I love you,* Latino watched his intestines fall out. *I love you.* He stared at her wildly, then collapsed.

"You were always mine," Diana moaned as she unlocked the door, and slid into the passenger seat.

Diana glared at her image in the rearview mirror, then wiped the rouge and lipstick from her face. Her features, freed of cosmetics, were sallow, and lined. The face of an embittered, older man emerged as he ground tissues against his cheeks. His mouth turned down, and the lips were tight, and narrow. He worked quickly trying to remove any traces of femininity.

Latino's body welled up in his memory as he pulled off the satin blouse, and ripped away a bra. A thick mat of black hair covered his chest. He reached in the backseat for a turtle-neck sweater, and pulled it over his head. Latino's blood seeping onto the stage. He paused, the thought made him shudder, and he leaned back.

I love you.

He was wiping the bayonet with a cloth.

She did this! She defiled our love.

He shook himself from the incident, pulled the skirt down his legs, and kicked his legs free. The track of chest hairs curved over his stomach ending in a masculine bulge beneath satin underpants. He worked his way into his gray flannel trousers, adjusted the sweater, then pulled on a pair of loafers.

He stared into the mirror.

Chick-a-boom. Mr. Sleek was rubbing against her! *Against her! His* Mr. Sleek!"

The man's nostrils dilated, and his jaw tightened. He closed his eyes trying to squeeze out the scene.

Ching, ching, ching! He was hacking at the lock, then slashing at the wire bin with the bayonet. Subliminal pictures volleyed through his mind: Carol huddling in fear, the bayonet slamming against the lock, a shadowy figure standing at the end of the row. The pictures flickered and vanished.

"It's time, Carol, it's time." He reached underneath the front seat, placed the bayonet on his lap. He fondled the weapon, and carefully draped a sports jacket around it, then stepped onto the sidewalk.

Chapter Twenty-four

Rim shot, and cheers!

"Howzabout a big hand for old Shirl, huh, gang?" the emcee pleaded. "Wuzzat a real thrill for ya, big Shirl?"

She buries her head and stumbles off the stage.

"Ya loved it, didn'tcha?"

Oh yeah, good buddy, this is it! Out of sight! I mean, man, this is radical . . . *radical!*

Mr. Sleek grinds his pelvis "one more time" then prances off.

Drum roll.

"Settle back, machos and machettes 'cause it's only half-time. Next up, our lovely ladies of ooze! So cool it, gang, and keep your hands above the tables. *Ha!* Drink a lot. Eyeball a lot. Have a blast and we'll turn you on with big Cindy . . . the hot one, big Alice and all the other foxy foxes of mud wrestling!"

The mirrored ball on the ceiling spun wildly to the pounding rock beat. The noise level rose. Drinks were sold. Shirl and the girls tittered and giggled. "Oh, how did he feel?" Blush, and modesty. "C'mon, Shirl, was it . . . you know?"

Carol smiled at the detective. "Hang in there, Carl, the best is yet to come."

"It's unreal," he answered hoarsely. "I never

saw nothing so . . . so gross. I'd murder my daughter, or old lady, if they *ever* stepped in here."

"So ya don't want to stick around for the mudders, huh, flatfoot?" Plato cracked.

"I didn't say that," he replied.

"Sure thing, big guy!" Plato quipped. "Well, hang in there 'cause Miss Carol and I are mixing with the troops. Just a last look at this dump, and a few final words for the crew."

"Don't go too far," he said seriously.

Carol smiled. "We'll be backstage."

"Sure," he said absently while staring at a chesty redhead in a bikini.

"Look, but don't touch," Plato remarked. "Big Cindy's old man will cut your dork off."

Carol turned around quickly, embarrassed by Plato's remark. The noise and confusion behind-the scenes hadn't changed. The male dancers' high-pitched laughter mixed with the stage manager's curses. The mud was too thick! Where the hell is Barbara? Carol enjoyed the sounds, and smells.

"I ain't gonna miss this shit," Plato sneered.

". . . but I will," Carol said wistfully.

Thornton waved at her from across the stage, then continued an animated conversation with two of his cronies. Poor Thornton, he always loses, Carol thought.

"Miss Elliott . . . I can't believe it!" Harold Farrar called out. "Never imagined you'd come here again."

Carol smiled warmly. "How are you, Harold?"

"Same as ever," he replied. "And so's this club."

"Never miss a beat, do they?"

"No, ma'am. Nothing stops these owners. Well, we know all about that. I don't understand 'em. 'Nough o' that 'cause you're a sight for sore eyes. How you doin'?"

"Great," Plato interjected. "We're going to Vegas! To Reno, and never coming back!"

Harold laughed. "Good for you. This club's going nowhere, believe me. We get the strangest here. By the by, someone's been asking for you . . . seems he comes by here almost every night . . ."

Carol stiffened.

"A big colored fella—"

"With violet eyes?" Carol interrupted.

"Yeah, the very one. He's always asking after you, but I didn't tell him nothing."

"Did you see him tonight?" she asked.

"Naw! Maybe it was . .. two, three nights ago I knew he wasn't anyone you'd cotton to . . . I didn't tell him nothing, Miss Elliott, nothing!"

"Did he leave a message?" Harold shook his head. "You're positive?"

"I didn't tell him nothing," Harold repeated. "Listen, I gotta finish some chores. Nice seeing you again, and good luck. I mean it, 'cause you're one nice lady."

"Thank you," Carol answered.

"See ya around, Miss Elliott," he replied, then walked away.

"That sucks!" Plato seethed. "I didn't figure old daddy dark-one to show up! That really sucks, babe."

Carol didn't respond. She ambled to her dressing room, and sat down. Nothing had been moved. The jars of rouge and cold cream were in place. Carol sat Plato on the makeup table, while she combed her hair.

"*Didja hear me!*" he snarled.

"Yes, I did."

"We're going back to the apartment. Get the gorilla and Thornton." Carol looked at herself in the mirror but didn't reply. "*I said we're heading home!*" Plato shouted.

"Not yet, babe, not yet."

"*Now!*" he demanded.

"No."

Plato's eyes shifted wildly. "Don't screw this up, Carol!" he warned.

The *thump-thump* of the rock band floated through the room. The excited voice of the stage manager pleaded for everyone's attention.

Carol sat in front of the mirror.

"Take me home, bitch!" Plato ordered.

"I'm going to wait," she replied calmly. "He'll be back. Papa's coming back for me."

The man stood in the shadows behind the Q Club watching the kitchen help toss bags of garbage into a dumpster. He waited impatiently as they sat on the stairs leading to the club, and shared a joint. He gripped and regripped the handle of the bayonet. The blade of the weapon, hidden in his left trouser leg, felt cold against his thigh. The music and laughter floating from the club heightened his anger. Finally, the two men finished the cigarette, and went inside.

The man quickly stepped across the alley, and caught the steel door before it closed. He walked casually through the rear of the kitchen then into the backstage area.

Drum roll, and cheers!

"It's showtime, guys and gals!" the emcee shouted. *Way to go! Mud! Mud! Mud!*

". . . yes, friends, it's skin-time!"

All right! Far out! Get on with it!

A thin bead of perspiration curled down the man's cheek as he walked past Thornton.

"And here's the love-ly Can-dy!"

Chick-a-Boom.

The door to the male dancer's dressing room was open. Harlem Harry sucked on a beer, while

Big Billy toweled himself off. The man stared at them.

"What are you ogling at, creep?" Mr. Sleek asked. The man was stunned, and didn't reply. "Get the fuck out of here," he shouted, then slammed the door in the man's face. A surge of anger coursed through his body. You little bitch, he cursed.

". . . here's the rest of the beauties . . ." echoed in the darkened hallway.

Sleek's rebuff infuriated him. He wrenched the bayonet from beneath his jacket, and pointed it at the door. You're *all* the same, he seethed. You're all faithless whores.

"*. . . Now for your first match!*"

He lowered the weapon, and began slapping it against his side.

". . . in this corner from Butte, Montana!"

Subliminal flashes of Mr. Sleek, Latino, and Plato darted in and out of his mind as he walked slowly toward Carol's dressing room.

". . . weighing one-ten. Her measurements are forty-two . . ." *Rim shot,* and *cheers.*

Carol saw his reflection in the mirror as he stood in the doorway. His eyes were cold, and unforgiving.

". . . twenty-three and thirty-six," the emcee oozed.

She stood up quickly and pushed the chair toward him. He kept slapping the blade into his hand as he moved forward.

The chant of *Mud! Mud! Mud!* pounded through the club.

"Now you'll redeem your sins," he whispered. "I promised you . . . I would," he said maniacally.

Carol grabbed Plato and pressed him against her chest.

"He won't protect you, Carol." Suddenly, the man reached forward and yanked Plato away from her.

"Whadda ya doing, fella?" he shouted.

The man held him by the neck. "This is for my beautiful Latino," he said, then jabbed the bayonet into Plato's right eye.

The dummy shrieked in pain.

"And this is for my darling," he said crazily as he pushed the tip of the weapon through Plato's left eye.

"Caro-l-l-l . . ." Plato howled.

"And now *I'm* going to kill something *you* love," he told her. The bayonet sliced through the air and shattered Plato's head. Another slash into the dummy's groin sliced him in half. The man pulled at the shreds of clothing impaled on the bayonet.

"*Dirty! Dirty!*" he shrieked wildly.

Carol's scream resounded through the backstage area as the man frantically tore Plato's costume from the weapon. "*Dirty! Dirty!*" he whined.

Suddenly, the detective and Thornton were in the dressing room. The man lunged at them, but Carl grabbed his arm, and slammed him against the dressing table. The bayonet exploded into the mirror sending splinters of glass through the room.

Carol fought her way past Thornton, and ran under the corridor. She shoved through the crowd hurrying to see the chaos. The emcee's ooze-by-ooze description wafted above the frantic screaming, and curses echoing from her room. She pushed Mr. Sleek aside, then clawed herself out of the knotting circle that swarmed toward the scene.

Suddenly, a hand reached out, and pulled her under the stairwell. She tried to scream, but Papa Noir placed a forefinger against her mouth.

"No, missy," he ordered. "No shout."

Carol pulled away from him.

"Don't be afraid. All over," he said quietly.

She was frightened, her body shook, and her

hands trembled. A high-pitched screaming underscored her fear.

"Everything est *fini,*" Papa told her.

Carol backed against the wall, and shook her head wildly. Papa reached for her hand, but she drew her arms tightly against her body.

"Please, missy, have no fear. *Toutes les choses* are complete. No more Diana, huh? You understand?"

"No," Carol replied. Her voice was vacant, emotionless.

"Come," Papa answered. He held out his hand. "Time to leave, missy. *Les sœurs* say it time to come home."

Chapter Twenty-five

Thornton knew Papa Noir was watching him in the rearview mirror each time the cab stopped for a red light. Several times they exchanged glances, Thornton would force a smile, then look away.

"*Ne Pas* de concern," Papa remarked as he turned down Central Park West. "Missy is safe. The sisters have taken good . . . very good care of her. Don't worry, Mr. Evans, don't worry."

Papa's words echoed in Thornton's mind as they were frozen in another howling traffic jam.

" 'Don't worry' ?" he muttered.

"Don't worry" she had told him. "I'm with friends." (Where?) "Don't worry, Thornton, I'm safe. "(But Carol, Anz wants to ask you—) "I'll call you in a week—"

The line went dead, and he was left to face Anz's questions with ridiculous answers: I don't know where she is. I'm not lying. I don't know. . . . I don't know anything.

Thornton leaned his head back, and tried to shove the scene at the Q Club out of his foreconscious.

Crash. The fragments of mirror exploding in the air. The darts and slivers pincushioning into the detective's face, and the lines of blood dripping on his collar. The screaming. The man flailing and writhing on the floor, his clothes spotted with blood, and pieces of Plato's head. The dust, the moaning, the sobbing. A maniac in a madroom. The man weeping and asking for vengeance, begging to die, pleading to be with his "love." And all the while hugging the shattered side of Plato's head.

Thornton relived the smells of vomit welling in his throat, and his body flushed with sweat. The press of curious faces jamming the doorway. The ghouls, fighting each other for a glimpse.

"Horrible, horrible," he muttered.

"To be certain," Papa replied. "The traffic is very poor . . . very poor."

Thornton stifled a laugh. Perfect misunderstanding, he thought. The irony was marvelous. The frantic mixed with the mundane.

Papa Noir edged his taxi to the left lane, then swung into the uptown side with a grinding U-turn.

"We go another way. Don't worry. *Arrivez* at the doll shop *très vite . . . mais oui, très vite.*"

"Don't worry?"

Anz's anger. What the hell did she mean?

Where is she?

If you're hiding her. . . ?

Anz's anger turned into threats: "Thornton, I'm warning you . . . Thornton, get her into this office by tomorrow or else . . . Thornton, I want to talk to her!

"*Why?*" Thornton shot back. "You don't need her . . . you've got your Diana or whoever the hell he is. Put that freak in the deepest, darkest institution you can find!"

The streets sped past. The noise of the traffic became yelps and blips. Papa Noir guided the taxi down a side street, up Broadway, then quickly into another tenement-lined street. Thornton closed his eyes, trying to squeeze out a sallow little man handcuffed to a detective. A nondescript; a nobody; another faceless nothing that rode the subway, occupied a gun-metal desk, then retreated into a gray, dull world of cagelike apartments.

"He's nobody," Anz had told him.

"I don't want to hear," Thornton had replied.

But Anz insisted, and Howard Fletcher's squalid life unraveled. His frustrations, his pent-up anger, his obsession. Howard Fletcher, "no previous arrests," no previous life. Howard Fletcher, AKA Diana the Chaste, AKA invisible, uncared for, unloved. Anz was right: "he was nobody" and nobody cared about him. He lived in his fantasies; he loved in his illusions; he killed in his madness.

Finally, almost happily, Fletcher had confessed.

Yes, he killed "his love."

Yes, he would have murdered Carol.

Yes, he was glad he killed her dummy.

Thornton sighed. Perhaps it was better that Carol had disappeared. The taxi lurched to the right, then Papa accelerated, beating a red light as they crossed West End Avenue.

The madness of the last few months seemed to slip away as Thornton felt the cab dart through the streets.

"A few more minutes," Papa announced.

"There's no one following us," Thornton replied. "I didn't call the police."

Papa flashed a smile. "Oh maybe, but we can take no chances," he said in a singsong voice. "The sisters say not to risk being followed. So Papa give them a merry chase if'n they tag a long."

Thornton settled back as the cab plunged up Columbus Avenue. "The sisters." "Papa Noir will come for you." Carol's second call, brief, to the point, abrupt. Then the "don't worry" again. Did it matter? He felt indifferent. What did anything matter now? Diana was in custody, under observation, being interviewed by "the team." . . . It didn't matter, Thornton reflected.

Anz's words kept pounding in his mind.

"Y'know, Thornton . . . I never had it figured for a guy. Y'know, Thornton, she's lucky to be alive. Y'know, Thornton, we had the case ass-backwards . . ."

Papa Noir brought the taxi to halt.

"*Nous sommes ici, monsieur,*" he said. "Missy inside . . . Don't fret she's safe."

Thornton hesitated.

"Got to go in," Papa told him. "Got to see missy and the sisters."

Chapter Twenty-six

Josephine moved the drapery aside and peered through an almost imperceptible slit. The street was quiet; only two boys playing catch occupied the sidewalk in front of the doll shop.

"Where are they?" she muttered.

"At the next corner," Agnes replied. "Don't be so unsettled, dear. It's going to be a perfect afternoon. Have you finished the dusting?"

"I don't care for the tone of your voice, dear. You needn't be snippy. Yes, all the chores are finished, and have *you* brewed the tea?"

"They're down the block," Agnes countered. "And not only have I prepared our tea, but I've placed the doilies under the petit fours . . . which someone forgot."

Josephine stiffened. Agnes could be quite irritating at times, especially the wrong times.

"He's here," Josephine announced as Papa Noir's taxi stopped in front of the shop. "Take him through the front door, not the shop." Agnes hesitated. "Agnes, would you let our guest in, please!"

The little woman squealed with delight, rushed down the hall, and opened the door as Thornton was puzzling which entrance to use.

"Do come in, Mr. Evans," Agnes told him.

Thornton, startled by her size, stood dumbfounded. He forced a smile, nodded, then managed to take off his hat, and mumble, "Yes, of course."

"I'm Agnes . . . Agnes Markham," she said as they walked into the front parlor, "and this is— Oh, she's disappeared. Oh my,, I thought—" Agnes spied the drapery move, and one of Josephine's shoes protruding from the bottom edge. "Oh, do come and meet him," she begged. The drapery remained stiff, and still. Thornton flashed a quick but nervous smile, then Agnes walked over to the window, uncurled Jo from her hiding spot, and introduced her. "This is my sister, Josephine Markham."

"My pleasure," Thornton stammered and bowed slightly.

Jo covered her mouth, giggled, ran down the entry hall, then disappeared into the pantry.

"She's like that . . . at times. Get's so high-strung. I guess it's your presence, Mr. Evans. Your aura must be very strong. Do come this way."

Thornton, completely at a loss for words, and in jeopardy of losing his composure, mumbled a yes and dutifully followed Agnes toward the living room. He tried not to stare at her back, or think about her size as they walked through the hall.

"Our father brought us that watercolor from Paris in 1921," she told him and pointed to a landscape hanging on the wall. "And this has been our home . . . oh goodness, it's seems forever. Come this way, Mr. Evans, or may we call you Thornton?"

"Thornton would be fine."

"I'm so glad," Agnes replied. "Jo!" she called. "We're in the living room. Do bring the tea."

Thornton forced a smile. Agnes motioned him to sit down on the red velvet settee, which he did, while she struggled to seat herself in the wing chair opposite him.

"You must be so curious about us, about Carol,"

Agnes remarked once she was settled. "And of course, our dear Papa Noir. So much for you to comprehend, *n'est-ce pas?*"

"Yes . . . yes, indeed," Thornton replied.

"And all shall be answered in due time. Oh, where is sister? Always was quite shy," Agnes whispered. "I was the brazen one," she confided.

"You were nothing of the sort," Josephine retorted as she appeared in the archway carrying a silver tea service on a large enscrolled silver tray.

"Let me help you," Thornton volunteered.

Jo swept past him, and placed the tray on the side boy before he could get up.

"Guests are never allowed to help," she said brusquely. "Despite contemporary manners," she added haughtily.

Josephine giggled as she handed Thornton a cup of black coffee, which he took, stared at, and smiled.

"Tea is coffee," Jo told him. "Cream? Sugar? or black? Quite delicious au naturel. French roast and a pinch of arabica. It's heavenly, and expensive too."

"Cream will be fine," Thornton answered.

"Sister always has a little stage fright when she meets new people," Agnes explained as she poured.

"Must we—?" Jo asked.

"It's not every day we have such a distinguished-looking gentleman in our home."

"How true," Jo replied. "Last time was 1931. The Harrison twins called on us."

Thornton tried to maintain his aplomb. "1931?" he questioned. He sipped the coffee to his further astonishment.

"We've had others since," Agnes answered. "Don't imagine that we're hermits, or reclusive. Not at all, Thornton, we're always interacting . . . not with our peers, but with special people."

"And your Carol . . . oh my, she's very special,"

Josephine interjected. "A marvelous gift of the higher sense. She's an exceptional child."

"Yes, she was always quite gifted," Thornton answered. "We never had to teach her . . . she seemed born to the theater. Always mimicking, or doing impressions."

The sisters smiled, sighed deeply, then looked at each other knowingly.

"We know," Agnes said dreamily.

"Yes, I'm certain you do," Thornton replied. He was about to take another sip, when an unexplained chill made him shudder, then he stiffened as he saw Carol standing at the foot of the staircase. She was dressed in a floor-length chocolate-brown Victorian dress. Her hair, no longer brassy blonde, with its natural shade of auburn, and streamed down her shoulders. A slight tough of rouge replaced her usually accentuated makeup. Her eyes sparkled with clarity. Carol appeared younger, prettier. The unexpected change stunned Thornton. He remained motionless, staring at her, almost disbelieving that this was really Carol.

The Markham sisters beamed with delight, then discreetly left Thornton and Carol alone.

"It's quite a shock," he mumbled, then he lurched across the room and hugged her.

"Don't cry," Carol begged.

Thornton stepped back, wiped his eyes.

"I didn't know what to expect," he muttered.

"Isn't it for the better?" Carol asked.

He nodded, sniffed back some more tears, then patted his nose with a handkerchief.

"Sit down, Thornton. Everything's going to be fine. All of it's behind me. I'm renewed."

"Yes," he said hoarsely, then sat next to her on the settee. "You . . . you look marvelous."

"And I feel 'marvelous,'" she replied. "The transformation has washed everything away. The sisters have energized what I was, what I should have been."

"I don't remember the last time I saw you look so natural . . . well, perhaps when you were teaching school."

Carol was delighted. "That's what Aggie told me, and Jo said it was bound to happen after Plato was destroyed. I feel different, Thornton. You can't imagine how that little monster infected me."

"We don't have to talk about him. It's over and finished."

"But I want to," Carol answered. "He'll never return. The sisters wouldn't permit it."

"Yes, of course," he replied wryly.

"Do you realize Plato was planning to assume my personality? He had such an ugly persona, and it became worse after the accident. Jo feels he would emerge despite the wreck. I think she's correct."

Thornton smiled, and nodded.

"Aggie told me he was one of the worst eidolons they've encountered. I was very lucky. In another few weeks, maybe days, he would have dominated me completely."

"Yes, I guess so," Thornton agreed. He smiled at Carol to hide a growing sense of uneasiness.

"Plato was so terribly cunning. He sounded sensible, but he was really malevolent. Always hooking me; playing games, then disappearing with a smart remark, or a crude joke." Carol shuddered. "I'm glad he was crushed. He would have assumed my form, did you know that?"

"No, I didn't," Thornton whispered.

"And much more if he had been allowed to exist. He's the one that really attracted Diana." Thornton felt uncomfortable. The violent scene at the club welled in his memory. "Plato was a very negative catalyst. Yes, he brought Diana to me."

She smiled, then laughed easily. "However . . . that's all in the past. His arrogance is destroyed. I'm safe, and I'm happy. Don't I look happy, Thornton?"

He patted her hand. "Yes, you do."

"I shouldn't tell this, but—" Carol's voice became a whisper. "Well, I imagine it's all right. The sisters are starting my lessons next week," she said confidentially.

"Lessons? How nice. Which instrument are you learning?" Thornton asked.

Carol stifled a laugh. "Not music lessons. They're teaching me about my inner powers . . . and the other forces. Even Papa Noir will help me. I want to know all about the energies."

"Oh?" he answered dumbly. "Yes— The powers, of course."

"They're such wonderful people," Carol whispered. "They've had many, many lives. Agnes wants to share all the secrets with me, just as she did with Carlotta . . . and Josephine said I looked exactly like her."

"Carlotta?" Thornton asked. "A dau—a relative?"

"I really don't know," Carol whispered. "I wanted to ask, but I was embarrassed."

"It doesn't matter, does it?"

Carol smiled. "Not really."

Thornton was quite uneasy. Carol's smile was too glowing, her mannerisms a bit too animated. She seemed almost girlish. No, that's not it, he thought. Reborn! Yes, she appeared to be reborn. The clothes, the lack of makeup, even her hair gave Carol a fresh, almost virginal appearance. Plato, Murray, Vegas were washed away. It was as if the hard years, no less the recent terror, never existed, and the Markham's front door sealed her from the harshness of reality. He sipped his coffee, and tried to understand what had happened to her, and what she had become.

"Do you remember Alpha Betty?" Carol asked.

"Yes," he replied.

Carol nodded. "Yesterday Josephine gave me a bisque-headed doll that looks exactly like her. It was uncanny, Thornton. Every feature was almost identical. Even the wig was the same color. I just held . . . and held her. And I cried. It was like finding a lost child," Carol said sadly. "A lost, lost little girl."

"She sounds quite beautiful."

"It's her soul that's beautiful . . . *and* I started to practice with her."

"Practice? Throw your voice?"

Carol nodded, and beamed. "My lips move slightly, but in time I'll be true to form."

"I thought— Well, I didn't imagine you'd want to go back on stage."

"Not at all, Thornton. I'd never do that, again," Carol answered. Her voice had a hollow, brittle tone. "Never something so artificial . . . the sisters have other plans . . . they want me to develop my powers and channel them into Betty . . . they want to make Betty come alive . . . yes, come alive."

Thornton stared at her in amazement.

Carol looked straight ahead; her gaze was fixed on everything, yet nothing. "Oh, Thornton, Betty's so beautiful. Her eyes are dark and lustrous. Her face seems soft and warm . . . and her lips glisten. I love to hold her . . . to make her talk. I wish you could see her, but she's sleeping right now."